FRIENDLY FIRE

CARI Z

RIPTIDE
PUBLISHING

Riptide Publishing
PO Box 1537
Burnsville, NC 28714
www.riptidepublishing.com

Friendly Fire

Cover art: L.C. Chase, lcchase.com/design.htm
Editor: Carole-ann Galloway
Layout: L.C. Chase, lcchase.com/design.htm

ISBN: 978-1-62649-482-4

First edition
October, 2016

Also available in ebook:
ISBN: 978-1-62649-481-7

FRIENDLY FIRE

CARI Z

RIPTIDE
PUBLISHING

This is a book about being outside of your comfort zone, which makes perfect sense, because writing it took me outside of mine. I hope you enjoy the ride.

TABLE OF CONTENTS

CHAPTER ONE

Excerpt from *Shockwave* reporter Clarissa Hanes's article on Elliot McKenzie, founder of Charmed Life:

Conman.

Businessman.

Player.

Penitent.

Elliot McKenzie could, and sometimes does, lay claim to all of these labels, the contrasting pieces of his complicated public persona. He's one of the up-and-comers in the psychospeak community, a self-made self-help guru of the modern kind. His company, Charmed Life, has been called "Facebook for felons," and it's managed to turn a person's criminal history into an exclusive entrance pass to the hottest social media site in years. Applicants are admitted on a case-by-case basis, and while you won't necessarily be denied if you don't have a record, it does make it a lot harder to get access.

McKenzie runs his self-help business out of a communal office space in a converted firehouse in downtown Denver. The unalloyed brick interior gives the place a rustic feel overall, but there's nothing rustic about McKenzie's eclectic office. There are hints of the Victorian in the antique wooden desk that sits apart from the center of the room, kowtows to the East in the Hokusai prints on the walls, and elements of a frat house playboy in the beanbag chairs that sit next to demure black leather couches on the blue-tiled floor.

The air smells like expensive coffee and cologne, and along the far wall, on top of a cocktail table, is his fabled shrine to a silver-screen star from Hollywood's golden age, Wilhelmina VanAllen. I go to get a closer look, but before I can take two steps, he's here.

"**W**here the hell have you been?" Serena hissed at Elliot the moment he walked in the door, jumping to her feet and coming around her desk to yell at him with her hips. He didn't know how she did it, but his personal assistant's hips could speak more clearly than most people's mouths. Right now, with that slight cock to the left and her fingers tapping along the seams of her skirt, they were calling him a fuckup. Not that he didn't agree with them at the moment. He ran a hand over his navy silk tie, checking its line as he set his briefcase down on Serena's desk.

"My lunch meeting ran late! I texted you from the car."

"I got that, and *don't* text and drive. You don't need to be in an accident," she scolded him. "But you should have let me know sooner, so I could have had a plan in place for when Stuart showed up!"

Elliot groaned, internally at first and then externally when that just didn't cut it. "Stuart Reynolds?"

She rolled her eyes. "How many other Stuarts do you know? *Yes,* Mr. Reynolds. He brought you a cupcake." Sure enough, there was a red velvet cupcake in a silver foil wrapper, topped with a perfect swirl of cream cheese frosting, sitting on the edge of Serena's desk. Elliot frowned.

"I told him to stop doing that." Stuart Reynolds had a greater capacity to cling than dog hair on a wool suit. "How did you get rid of him?"

"I told him you were out for the rest of the day and that I'd let you know he stopped by. He and Ms. Hanes missed each other by a few seconds, thank God. I got her into your office the moment I saw him coming."

Elliot's greatest and most inconvenient admirer and a hard-nosed, unsympathetic reporter in the same room together? It would have ended in bloodshed. "You are the light of my life," he told Serena with complete seriousness as he buttoned his suit jacket. "Now tell me truly: am I hopelessly rumpled?"

"Hopelessly," she said with a little smirk, "but it's Zegna, so you get a pass." She adjusted the angle of his fedora, then nodded. "Go, impress, be charming like you always are."

"I'll do my best." He shut his eyes for a moment to get his mind back to where it needed to be, then picked up his briefcase and walked into his office. "Ms. Hanes!" He smiled brightly as she turned to him, ready to set her at ease.

It wasn't necessary. Clarissa Hanes was a dark-haired viper in crimson silk, snapping her fangs before Elliot could so much as apologize for being late. Her whiskey-colored eyes narrowed as she looked him over. "Mr. McKenzie. You move very fast for a man who's been shot twice."

Ah, so it was going to be one of *those* interviews. Elliot bought himself some time by unlocking his desk drawer to put his briefcase away. Interviews generally tended to come in three flavors, starting with vanilla, which were safe and dull and easy on everyone. Vanilla interviews were decent press but boring to do, and he preferred to avoid them unless he owed someone a favor.

Chocolate interviews were fun, full of oddball, zany questions that ran the gamut from fluffy (mostly about his dog) to semiserious (the transition from lawyer to self-help magnate) to truly bizarre (his favorite Disney princess, what he liked best in a cheese). Those ones could get him trending if he answered just right. BuzzFeed's piece on him three months ago had done more for his business than a dozen vanilla interviews could.

Then there were the chili interviews. They were the ones that made Elliot sweat, the ones that cheerfully raked him over the coals of his history, holding his feet to the flames of every poor decision he'd ever made and asking him, yet again, to justify himself. As far as he was concerned, doing these interviews was a form of penance. If there was a god, Elliot hoped he took note.

"I made a full recovery," Elliot said as he finally locked his desk up again, keeping his smile on but toning it back a bit. Charm wasn't going to help him here. "And neither of the bullets hit me in the legs. Would you care for something to drink? Serena can bring water, tea, coffee . . ."

Ms. Hanes *hmm*ed thoughtfully. "A martini, perhaps?"

He shook his head. "No drinking alcohol of any kind at work. It's a firm policy of mine."

"Because of your issues with addiction, Mr. McKenzie?"

Shots fired, shots fired. He changed tack. "Please have a seat." He pointed to the leather lounge chair. "And do call me Elliot, Ms. Hanes."

"Clarissa is fine." She sat down and crossed her legs with a raised eyebrow. "You're not going to offer me a beanbag chair?"

"I wouldn't want to insult your dress. It would clash so terribly with the paisley pattern." Elliot sat across from her. "Now. What would you like to talk about first, my being shot or my addictions?"

Clarissa tilted her head slightly, examining him. He bore the scrutiny without blushing. His life was an open book: all his triumphs, all his many, many mistakes out there for any interested party to know. Relentless personal honesty was his platform; it was what he'd built his new reputation on. He wasn't going to be intimidated by the past.

"Actually, I was wondering about the Gauloises." She nodded toward the little table in the back, one eyebrow arched as she took in the crumpled packet of cigarettes.

Elliot's smile fell away for a moment. "Those aren't my bad habit. I keep them around to remember another time."

"And another person?"

"Yes."

"Hmm." Clarissa took a recorder out of her purse, turned it on, and set it on the table between them. "Tell me about meeting Wilhelmina VanAllen in rehab."

Elliot had a spiel he liked to give whenever he talked about Willie, but Clarissa had already brought up the addictions angle. She wanted to play? They'd play. "She was a chain-smoker when I met her. Smoking was no match for the morphine addiction but by that point she was convinced she was dying anyway, so why should she give up one of her last pleasures in life? She used to smoke Picayunes, the brand that Audrey Hepburn's character smoked in *Breakfast at Tiffany's*. Once she couldn't get those anymore, she switched to Gauloises, which use the same sort of tobacco."

"You call her your inspiration for Charmed Life," Clarissa noted. "How is a former movie star turned chain-smoking morphine addict who, if I remember correctly, committed suicide not long after you met her, a logical choice as a muse for second chances?"

Ooh, the redirection game. Yes, let's. "Willie died at the age of eighty-eight, in the time and place of her choosing. Given some of the demons she fought against her whole life, that should be considered a triumph, not a tragedy." He could handle people coming at him for his mistakes—he did every day—but Willie's circumstances had been different. "She was born during an era when struggling with depression could get you institutionalized. It *did* get her institutionalized, several times, when she was a young woman. Her family actually tried to have her lobotomized at one point. The fastest way out of that bad situation was marriage. Her first of five, in fact."

"A serial bride," Clarissa noted. "Even after she found success in films with the help of her second husband, who was a director, if I remember correctly."

"Willie was someone who wasn't afraid to strive for what she really wanted out of life," he said. "Someone who wasn't afraid to fight for a second chance. And her success was entirely down to her own skills as an actress, not nepotism from her husband," he added. "They were divorced before she ever got a starring role in a film."

Clarissa glanced back at the table again, and Elliot followed her gaze. It had the cigarettes, a copy of her favorite poem, and a picture of Willie lying back against a couch wearing enormous white sunglasses on her gaunt face with her dog in her lap. "And did she achieve the life she wanted in the end?"

He shrugged. "I couldn't say. I can't speak for anyone but myself."

"And what would you say about yourself?"

Ah, back into familiar territory. "That's what starting up this company has been all about: living a better life than I had before, and helping other people to do the same. It's about being more genuine in everything you do, and letting your present actions speak louder than your past mistakes."

"Hmm." Clarissa wrote something down on her phone. "Do you think you're a more honest person now?"

"I think that honesty, especially with yourself, is a vital part of living a more genuine life. Honesty toward everyone else can be a little harder to follow through on, but if you want to make connections that will help you move forward in life, then you need to come to terms with being open about your life. At least professionally," he amended, because while his skeletons were all very much out of the closet, not all of his clients' were. And considering who some of his clients happened to be, ruthless honesty wouldn't always be in their best interests.

Clarissa smiled slightly. "What's the biggest lie you've ever told about yourself, Elliot?"

He smiled right back at her. "That I thought I could ever truly be anything other than an opportunist."

She arched her eyebrows. "You admit that you're exploiting people, then?"

"No more than they're exploiting me," he said. "Charmed Life is a company made to facilitate networking between like-minded individuals with similar, challenging histories. We don't only specialize in romance, work, or everyday life, though—we specialize in *betterment*, in helping our members climb up from the very bottom rung of the ladder. Charmed Life is about how to commit yourself to the path you've chosen, how to persevere where others would get knocked back. How to endure the slings and arrows of outrageous fortune and emerge stronger and more focused than ever. My company is about providing second chances, and our members share their success with the next generation of seekers."

"It sounds lofty and high-minded when you put it like that," Clarissa said. "But you rather pointedly market to celebrities, don't you? I don't see Charmed Life reaching out to halfway houses or prisons and working with the people there."

"Believe it or not, I have great compassion for that segment of the population. I almost ended up there myself, after all," he said candidly. "But you can't force someone to make a positive change in their life; they have to decide that for themselves. I'd like to offer classes and maybe mentorship in prisons, particularly for juvenile offenders, but currently I'm focusing on growing other parts of the business."

"The lucrative parts, you mean."

"The self-directed parts." Clarissa could dig at his business model all she wanted; Elliot could doublespeak with the best of them. Not that that was the purpose of his work, but it was definitely the way to survive a chili interview without getting bad publicity.

"I see." With a tiny toss of her hair, Clarissa changed the subject once again. "Let's talk about your sister."

Oh boy. He hardened his smile and straightened his spine. "What would you like to know?"

Seeing the red soles of Clarissa's Louboutin pumps vanishing two hours later gave Elliot a far greater sense of relief than her exodus really merited, but *damn*, that had been rough. He was an old hand at interviews at this point, but none of his experience had prepared him for anything quite as thorough, or as diverse, as Clarissa Hanes had managed. It would either be the greatest article he could ever ask for, or public perception of his company would tank the day after it was published next month.

It was after hours, but Serena was still there, parsing through the usual pile of snail mail that seemed to accumulate more quickly the closer they got to the Meetup. Elliot had embraced a paperless format for communicating with his clients, but some of them wouldn't be dragged into the future even if he tied their feet to the back of the Mars rover. He sat down on the edge of Serena's desk and sighed heavily. "Why did I ever let you convince me to do an interview with *Shockwave*?"

"I didn't convince you of anything—it was your idea," Serena said, wielding her letter opener like she was cutting throats. "I said to avoid Clarissa Hanes at all costs: look what she'd written about Zuckerberg, remember what she had to say about the guy who wants to make those mobile apartments. But you told me—"

"Hey, in her defense, mobile apartments really are a terrible idea," he said. "Why bother moving your tiny box of a home from New York to LA when you could put a down payment on a new tiny little box for less than the price of shipping? It doesn't make sense."

"See? You have being very opinionated in common, so the results might be better than you think. *I* can't believe that she convinced you to give her an invite to the Meetup. The way she snatched it out of your hands, I thought you might lose a few fingers."

"She said she'd persuade her editor to make it a feature."

"Maybe she will," Serena allowed. "But you're rolling the dice on whether it would be complimentary or not. You haven't even read what she's going to be writing about *you*, but you're willing to subject the company to that kind of exposure?"

Honestly, he had started having second thoughts about inviting Clarissa to the Meetup almost as soon as he'd invited her, but if there was one thing she was good for, it was press. She'd been an award-winning investigative journalist for twenty years before abruptly pivoting to specialize in writing about startups and tech companies a year ago, and she had a wide audience for her work.

He shrugged. "Too late to back out now. Is there anything interesting in the mail?"

"Let's find out." Serena sliced open a large black envelope and poured the contents onto her desk. "Ah, it's the vendor confirmations from the Studio Loft, excellent."

Charmed Life was about to have its first annual Executive Meetup for Elliot's top tier of clientele. He'd chosen a venue inside the Denver Performing Arts Complex, since there was nothing like combining dinner with a show, and the theater was less pretentious than shoving all his guests into a gallery and expecting them to make intelligent conversation about modern art. He repressed a shudder just thinking about the latter.

"Check and make sure their numbers are right," he said. "If I'm paying a premium for these services, then I want to make sure we don't leave people underfed and parched."

"With the amount of alcohol you're providing, no one is going to be left parched, but I'll check," Serena assured him as she moved on to the unmarked package on her desk. She cut through the plain brown butcher paper and pulled it back to reveal an equally nondescript cardboard box.

"If this is a covert attempt by Stuart to sneak you more baked goods, I'm going to laugh," she warned as she took the top off the box.

Inside weren't cupcakes. It was a pair of shoes cradled in tissue paper instead. Serena frowned as she lifted one out, examining the tag. "Did you order these? Why did you have them sent here?"

Elliot stared at the gray and black Nikes and a familiar, slithering unease wrapped around his lungs and started to squeeze. Another one, and this time at the office. *Fuck.* He'd been okay as long as it had

just been at home, when he'd been the only one to know . . . having
something like this show up at his office felt like a far worse violation.

"Elliot?" Serena's fingers on his hand snapped him out of his
unpleasant reverie. "What's wrong?"

He must be off his game. That was the only reason he answered
honestly: "I don't know who those are from." But he knew why they
were here. "I went jogging in City Park yesterday evening, and my
right shoe's sole came off. I had to walk over a mile back to my car,
half barefoot." He smiled, but his heart wasn't in it. "I was a bit of
a spectacle, I suppose. The plan was to buy another pair after work
today, but it seems like someone beat me to it."

Serena looked unimpressed with his candor. Worse, she looked
concerned. "Someone? Someone who's willing to spend around two
hundred dollars on a pair of sneakers?" She pulled the other shoe out
and compared their tags, and her concern darkened to actual worry.
"Someone who knows your right foot is a size smaller than your left?
How the hell did this mysterious someone figure that out?"

"I threw the shoes into a garbage can in the parking lot," Elliot
said easily, forcing himself to stay relaxed. "They must have retrieved
them."

Serena shook her head incredulously. "Are you honestly telling
me that someone went searching through the innumerable bags of
dog shit filling those cans to fish out your busted sneakers, just so they
could anonymously send you a new pair today? Is that what you're
telling me?"

He shrugged. "What can I say? I seem to have attracted a secret
admirer."

"No, no, no." And now Serena was standing and oh, there went
her hips, shimmying into disapproving overdrive. "A secret admirer
is someone who leaves you cute notes on Valentine's Day or the
occasional sinful, delicious cupcake."

"Which I notice is gone, by the way."

Serena *humph*ed. "Not the point. And please, Stuart couldn't be
more blatant if he stuck heart-shaped Post-it notes to his eyes—he's
not keeping anything a secret. And besides, you hate red velvet, so I
feel no guilt. No trying to distract me." She came around her desk and
stood in front of him, shoes in hand. "Expensive gifts in unmarked

packages indicating that someone is *watching* you without your knowledge? That's creepy. Not romantic, not admiring, nothing other than unsettlingly creepy."

"I never said it wasn't also creepy," he said defensively.

"I think there might be a *lot* you didn't say." She glared at him over the tops of the shoes. Elliot hadn't quailed this hard since the last time he'd seen his sister. "Is this the first present you've received?"

"I get a lot of fan mail."

"And you have it sent here because you're not stupid enough to give out your home address. Stop avoiding the point, Elliot. Just talk to me. Please."

Serena's *please* was a mortal blow, and she knew it. If there was one person in his life he had to come clean to—personally as well as professionally—Serena was it. "There have been a few other things."

"What kind of things?"

"Only pictures, before this."

"Pictures." Her voice was completely flat. "Pictures of you?"

He nodded. "And my house. My car. My dog."

"And how were you given these pictures?"

"My mailbox, mostly," he said. Serena shifted, her posture shouting obscenities at him as she waited. Elliot sighed. "And a few stuffed through the letter slot in my front door."

Serena's dark eyes went wide. "Elliot, this is stalking! You need to take it to the cops."

He was shaking his head before she'd finished her sentence. "Absolutely not. A few pictures and a pair of shoes don't constitute a threat to my safety."

"You have no idea what kind of person this is. And they know where you live; they followed you on your evening run—"

"It's not like I live in a gated community," Elliot reminded her. "Anyone can drive down the street there, even if we are a ways outside of town." Golden was growing in size fast, but Elliot's little subdivision still consisted of older houses with nice, private plots. "And City Park is open to the public. Whoever this is, they haven't trespassed."

"But the police—"

"I can't." Elliot shook his head. "You know I can't. Not right now." Not with the election for district attorney coming up. He wasn't going to sabotage things for his sister again.

Serena tossed the shoes onto her desk with a weary sigh. "You don't think she'd rather have you alive and well than win a damn election?"

"I don't like to postulate about what Vanessa wants for me," he said. "But I do know I'm not going to rock the boat unless absolutely necessary. I'm fine. I doubt I'm in any danger."

Serena opened her mouth, but Elliot was done arguing. "So! I'll take those—" he swiped the shoes from where she'd left them "—and go home."

"Tell me you're not going to wear them jogging."

"They're nice shoes," Elliot pointed out. "And just my size. Of course I'm going to wear them."

Serena scowled. "At least check the soles for razor blades, all right?" *Idiot*, her tone added, but Elliot was an expert at ignoring negative subtext.

"Should I check for bombs too?" he asked, then winced as Serena smacked his arm with her surprisingly hard hand. "I mean, yes, I'll check them. Promise."

"I guess that's the best I'm going to get."

"It's not your job to worry about me," he reminded her as he gathered the shoes under his arm and grabbed his briefcase with the other.

"No, it's my hobby." She crossed her arms. He could tell she was desperate to reach out, to grab hold and gather him in like she did with everyone in her life, it seemed. Serena excelled at making connections, like Elliot, but where his were all professional these days, most of hers were deeply personal, even if they didn't start off that way. She could coax a turtle out of its shell or a reluctant investor into exchanging life stories in under an hour, and Elliot appreciated that about her.

He appreciated her efforts to appropriate him into her family far less. Families were messy, and he'd already done enough damage to the one he'd been born into. He didn't need to tempt fate by getting entangled in someone else's.

"I'm fine. I'm going straight home," he assured her.

"Text me when you get there."

"Serena . . ."

"Please?"

Fucking pleases. "Fine. But just this once."

She looked relieved, which made giving up a little of his evening autonomy worth it. "Thank you."

"You only thank me when you get your way," he complained, and mentally punched the air in victory when he saw her smile. "Don't stay here working, all right? I'm tired of paying your overtime."

"You need to hire me an assistant," she said immediately. "Or at least an intern. Someone I can shove the paperwork onto while I manage your elaborate schmoozing schedule. And don't worry about your precious budget; there'll be no more overtime tonight. My sister's having a barbecue and I'm bringing the chips."

"The chips?"

Serena sighed. "She said to bring a side and I don't cook, you know that. This is why I have all my parties catered."

"Don't worry," he assured her with a wink. "I don't judge."

Elliot walked out of the office, calling a goodnight to the janitor who was already at work in the other half of the building. He headed down the street to the parking garage where his car, a sleek, modern Porsche Panamera, sat waiting for him.

Elliot stood at the driver's side door with his keys in his hand, wondering for a moment whether or not he really *should* check the car, at least, for bombs. After a second he shook his head at himself. He wouldn't even know what to search for, and they probably wouldn't try to kill him. Not like this.

"You're fine," he said quietly as he opened the door and got inside. "It's fine." He set his things in the passenger seat, resolutely not looking at the shoes that he was going to throw in the next dumpster he saw, then buckled up, and slowly put his key into the ignition and turned it.

The car started with a purr, and absolutely no explosions beyond its regular internal combustion. Elliot let out a breath he hadn't realized he'd been holding and pressed his forehead against the smooth leather of the steering wheel for a moment. His car acting normally felt like a stupid thing to be grateful for, but the rock lodged in his throat suddenly melted away.

Before he could second-guess himself, he pulled out his phone and brought up Vanessa's info. He dug his fingers into his palm as he resisted the urge to outright call her, just to hear her voice message—she wouldn't reply. She never did, but she'd never told him not to text her either, so he'd made it a ritual for whenever he was feeling overwhelmed. Elliot tapped out a message, *Thinking of you*, and hit Send fast.

Maybe his note would make her smile. Maybe it would inspire her to reach out to him once the election was over—it was so close now. And if she won, if he didn't ruin things for her again, if everything went perfectly, then maybe he could have the most important part of his old life again: his family.

Maybe. Elliot turned his phone off, set it aside, and backed out of his parking space. Until Vanessa made her move, he'd be fine. He *was* fine. He refused to let himself be any other way.

CHAPTER

TWO

Partial transcription of most recent appointment with West, Lennox, Staff Sergeant US Army Rangers (R), January 28, 3:03 p.m.:

JS: How did you sleep this past week, Lennox?

LW: Why, do I look tired?

JS: That's not what I was implying.

LW: Why else would you be asking?

JS: It's a starting point when it comes to talking about your overall health. We have to start somewhere, after all.

LW: Right. Listen, I'd rather you be upfront about what you're prying into instead of trying to coax it out of me. You want to ask about the nightmares, just ask.

JS: I do want to know about your nightmares if they're something that's bothering you. But they're not all I care about.

LW: Well, the answer is I slept like shit, and yes, the nightmares are happening on a regular basis, and no, I don't want a prescription for sleeping pills or Valium or anything else you're gonna offer me. Not interested, full stop.

JS: There's no shame in treating your health issues. It would be worse to leave them untreated and ignored.

LW: I'm not ignoring them. I'm here, talking to you about them now. But I don't want any drugs.

JS: If this is about the possible side effects, I can assure you—

LW: Change the subject, Doc, or we're done for the day.

There was a very particular sound a perfect hook to the heavy bag made. It was a sweet, cracking *smack* that reverberated through the room but not the hand, a smooth motion that made his body sing with how good it felt to sink power into the bag. Lennox worked the hooks into his combos, slinging them onto the end of simple one-twos and throwing them repeatedly in the middle of a flurry, imagining the bag was a body under his hands, not leather but flesh.

Smack—smack—smack-smack—

"Move your feet," Carl called out. Lennox wanted to snap at the guy for interrupting his flow, but since Carl was the resident coach, as well as the owner, it was easier just to do it. Lennox started working slips back into his rhythm, weaving down and across and throwing a tight left-hand hook while he was at it, searching for that sweet sound.

Smack. The scent of leather filled his nose—leather worn by years of use and hundreds of gloves, thousands of hits. Leather and his own sweat, and not the sharp, awful tang of blood and that was good. Maybe if he breathed it in deeper and sank it into his bones, he'd be able to carry the scent with him into sleep and stop dreaming of the other.

"You have to dance better than that if you wanna go into the ring with Marty."

Everybody wanted to go into the ring with Marty, a retired pro—even Lennox, whose only claim to fame here was maybe angriest newbie. He wasn't there yet, but if he had his way, he would be soon. Lennox came to the gym every evening he could, working the bag or pads or sparring in the ring, trying to exhaust himself so his night would go a little easier. Boxing wasn't the best solution for killing his nightmares, but it was the healthiest one available to him.

Smack—smack—smack. His last hit actually made his back twinge, and Lennox knew he'd had enough. He couldn't afford to go until it hurt tonight—he had a barbecue to get to.

A barbecue. In January.

In his ex's defense, it was an unusually warm sixty degrees out, but Lennox hadn't quite made the switch from a Washington winter to a Colorado winter. The first meant freezing temperatures and little to no snow; the second meant plenty of snow, but it was all gone in a day. Lennox was grateful that getting around on his Harley Deuce was easier, but still. It just didn't seem right.

He stepped away from the bag and pulled on the knot at the top of his right glove with his teeth.

"Oh, come here," Carl muttered, waving Lennox over to his bench next to the ring. Two of his other students were going at it inside, and Carl never let his eyes leave them while he got to work. "That's just unsanitary," he continued, taking Lennox's glove in hand and starting on the laces. "Don't be like those fucking kids from the university, treating your equipment like shit because your daddy can afford to buy you a new set of gloves every week."

Lennox suppressed a smile. "I'll try not to act like a trust-fund baby."

"Not that I can really knock 'em," Carl said, finishing with Lennox's left hand and picking up his right. "Those kids are what keep me in business. Fifty new clients each semester that sign up for cardio-boxing bullshit, and ten or so keepers twelve weeks later. Eh. It's a living."

"So it is," Lennox agreed, pulling his left hand free of the glove. He flexed his fingers in their tape. No spots of pain, nothing hot or sore—he'd pushed it to the edge, but not over.

"You're done early tonight."

"I've got a thing with the ex and her family."

Carl shook his head. "What part of *ex* don't you understand? You don't stay friends with 'em, Lennox; that's how you go crazy. You give 'em alimony and child support and take the kids over the summer. *That's* how you handle an ex."

Lennox shrugged. "I'm just lucky, I guess." And he was, he knew that, even if he really wasn't in the mood to spend time with Gaby and her extended family tonight. He'd be lucky if his daughter said two words together to him. Everyone told him it was because she was thirteen, but Lennox knew better. He'd fucked up royally with Lia, time and again, and if going to a January barbecue and listening to Gaby and her sisters bitch at each other was what he had to do to make amends, then he was doing it.

Besides, he'd already cooked.

"Lucky my ass," Carl grunted. "Go on, then, get out of here. Marshall! Did you hear a fuckin' bell, or is it your ears that are ringing? Ten more seconds, you lazy jackass!"

Lennox took a moment to rinse off in the locker room before packing his bag, grabbing his offering for the barbecue from Carl's fridge, and heading to his bike. The sky was starting to get dark, but it was still plenty warm out. He stuffed the gym equipment into the leather bag on the back, put his helmet on, and started the engine up. The bike growled to life underneath him, and Lennox's spine relaxed. Right now, post-workout and pre-family, was probably the most peaceful he was going to feel all day. He might as well enjoy it.

After the too-fast twenty-minute ride, Lennox pulled his Harley into the driveway and killed the engine. The neighbor watering a bunch of unseasonal potted mums across the street glared at him as he took his helmet off. Lennox waved, grabbed his obligatory side dish out of the saddlebag, and stowed his helmet back in its place, then headed for the front door, which had been propped open with a brick—an actual brick—that read *WELCOME* in black letters on top. Lennox briefly contemplated having a life that involved extraneous decorative bricks, shook his head, then walked inside.

He sidled into the kitchen quietly, hoping to put his mac and cheese on the counter and get out before Gaby or Serena noticed him. His odds were pretty good: at the moment they were arguing about . . . chips?

"I said bring a side dish, not grab the nearest bag of fat and carbohydrates on your way out of the 7-Eleven," Gaby snapped from where she was chopping tomatoes to put into a salad. She was using one of the knives Lennox had given her and Marcus last Christmas, handling it like a pro. He smiled a little even as he winced in anticipation of Serena's comeback. The older Rodriguez sisters were incapable of being in each other's company for more than a minute without an argument developing.

"Are you kidding me?" Serena grabbed a bag and shook it. "These are imported, organic potato chips made with cask-aged Italian vinegar and pink Himalayan rock salt! These came from *Boulder*; there's nothing healthier than a Boulder potato chip!"

"If I wanted you to bring potato chips, I would have asked for them! Just because they're organic doesn't mean they're healthy, and I'm trying to keep three kids junk food–free as long as they're eating at home."

"Lee is thirteen and the boys are *seven*. Do you really think they're going to be interested in salt and vinegar potato chips? It's a very adult flavor."

Gaby slammed her knife down and tossed the tomatoes in the salad bowl. "They might be!"

"You're crazy if you think this is the worst thing they'll be eating tonight. Like, here—Lennox!" Serena turned toward him like a human heat-seeking missile. "What did you bring for dinner?"

Lennox resisted the urge to back away. "Mac and cheese."

"Ha!" Serena glared at Gaby. "He brings noodles mixed with butter and cheese and gets nothing from you, and I bring one little bag of chips and get interrogated like it's the Inquisition!"

"Lennox knows the rules." Gaby pointed a finger at the covered casserole dish. "Are there any vegetables in there?"

He nodded. "Broccoli."

"There, you see? He brought broccoli."

"He wrapped it in *cheese*!"

Lennox made good on his chance for escape this time, almost jogging down the hall and out to the backyard where Marcus was at the grill. His twin boys were playing some combination game of tag and bouncing on a trampoline, Gaby's younger sister, Rommie, was stretched out on a lounge chair in front of the pool, and Lennox's daughter was nowhere to be seen. He sighed and headed for Marcus, who glanced up from turning the corn and bratwurst and gave him a welcoming smile. He was a big guy, taller than Lennox by a few inches, and wore an apron over his button-down and suit trousers that read *WOMEN WANT ME, COWS FEAR ME.*

"Hey, man, glad you could make it." He reached into the cooler next to him and passed Lennox a beer. It was cold, dark, and just what he needed at the moment.

"You're a saint," Lennox said, popping the cap off and taking a long drink.

"Is it still a free-for-all in there?"

"Eh." Lennox wobbled his free hand back and forth. "It could be worse. I think it's more habit for them than anything else these days."

"Maybe," Marcus said judiciously, a pensive frown on his broad face. "Serena looked ready to spit nails when she got here though. I think something bad went down at work, but you know how Gaby feels about her job."

"Like she drank the Kool-Aid." Yeah, Lennox had been in earshot of several arguments over Serena working for a famously bad man with equally famous powers of resurrection. Gaby thought Elliot McKenzie wasn't trustworthy; Serena told her sister she shouldn't condemn someone based on their past behaviors.

Personally, Lennox was inclined to trust Serena's judgment. When he'd first met her fifteen years ago, Serena had been falling from one bad relationship into another. She'd done three years in a state prison on drug charges when Lia was a baby, and from how Gaby had talked back then, her life might as well have been over. But Serena had turned things around, and since being hired by Elliot McKenzie, she was doing better than ever.

Not that that was enough to keep her sister off her back. A particularly pointed exclamation from Gaby drifted out into the yard, and Marcus winced. "Today's a little worse than usual."

"They'll get over it." They always did. "Where's Lia?"

Marcus smiled. "Up in her room with her headphones on listening to Fall Out Boy, probably."

"Not a fan of the samba music?"

"She's not a fan of anything much lately." Marcus shrugged the shrug of a parent, sort of a *not gonna get worked up if it's just a phase* shrug. "She'll be down for dinner. Which should be in a few more minutes, the way these things are coming along. You bring your mac and cheese?"

Lennox nodded. "With broccoli in it."

"Way to game the system." Marcus clinked Lennox's bottle with his own and went back to minding the grill. They watched the boys continue their game of full-contact trampoline bouncing and drank in companionable quiet for a while until the meat was done. Then Marcus passed Lennox a plate of hamburgers to take inside as Gaby called out that it was time to eat.

"Go and get Lee, will you?" she asked as he set the food down, then washed his hands in the kitchen sink.

"You think she'll open the door for me?"

Gaby looked unamused. "She's thirteen, not thirty. She'd better open the door when one of her parents tells her to." *Even if that parent is you* went unsaid, but Lennox heard it regardless. He didn't say anything, just dried his hands on an old dishtowel and went to retrieve his daughter.

Her door was liberally crisscrossed with yellow and black DO NOT ENTER tape. That was new since he'd last been here. Lennox took it at face value and knocked loudly on the door. "Hey, Lia? Dinner." There was a long silence, so he rapped again. "Lia!"

The door jerked out from under his knuckles. "I heard you the first time," his daughter informed him haughtily. "And it's *Lee*, Dad, not Lia."

Christ, two years ago this hadn't been so hard. Two years ago, right before Lennox's last deployment, he'd still known how to relate to his daughter. She'd gone by *Lia* then, sweet Lia who'd loved horses and Saturday morning cartoons and who'd decorated her room in purple and pink, not black and blue. He'd had her for almost a month that summer before shipping out, and she'd been his little girl.

After eleven months in Afghanistan, though, followed by another seven months working with Oliver as Lennox tried not to lose his mind, before finally giving in to Gaby's pleas and joining her family here in Colorado, well . . . Lennox didn't know how he and Lee fit now. He didn't know how to talk to her anymore, and the one time he'd tried to have her over at his new apartment, the night had gone, in a word, abysmally.

"Dad!"

"Sorry, sweetheart." Lennox shook his head and refocused on Lee, who had her arms folded in front of her chest, like she was trying to hug herself. She looked a weird combination of annoyed and worried, but there was something else about her that was niggling at his brain. It took him a moment but—

"You cut your hair." He blinked. "And dyed it purple." Actually she'd cut one side very close to her skin. The other side still touched her shoulder. Plus it was *purple*. Lennox opened his mouth, then took a deep breath and shut it again. If his goddamn therapy sessions had been useful for one thing, it was reminding him to stop and take a moment when he was surprised or upset before he let himself react to whatever was causing it.

"Nice color, Lee," he said at last, which seemed to shock her out of her funk. She smiled at him, and uncrossed her arms.

"Thanks. Aunt Rommie took me to get it done. Mom wasn't happy with us."

"Maybe it'll grow on her," Lennox offered as he moved back from the door. "You hungry, sweetheart?"

Lee shrugged. "Kind of."

"I brought mac and cheese."

"With cauliflower?"

"Broccoli."

"Ugh." She made a face. "Well, I guess I can pick it out."

"Cauliflower next time," he promised her. She shut her door, and they headed down the stairs together. "What made you decide to cut your hair?"

"I wanted a change." That seemed to be her final word on the subject, as Lee darted into the dining room faster than Lennox could follow.

Dinner for eight was a noisy affair in the Smith-Rodriguez household, with Gaby alternating between chatting with her sisters and keeping her stepsons still for long enough to eat. Lennox was seated between Lee and Serena, who did seem unusually subdued. When he had a moment as the conversations around them picked up, he murmured, "You need me to beat someone up or something? Because you look like somebody kicked your cat."

"No," she sighed. "It's just Elliot being stupid. He's gotten into a situation—*not* an illegal one," she added with a mild glare at Gaby, who glared right back, "and I'm worried about it, but he refuses to get help. I understand his reasons, but I don't agree with them."

"What kind of situation?"

"The kind that— Well, it's really not my place to talk about it." Lennox's eyebrows rose at that admission, but Serena ignored his surprise. "I feel like he should take some measures to be safer. And he doesn't feel the same."

"Safer." Lennox's brain went into professional mode. "Safer as in a personal carry, or safer as in a home security system?" The company he worked for, Castillion, had started as one man's knife-making endeavor and grown into a multimillion dollar personal-protection business. Rodney Castillion still made custom knives, but he sold far more weapons than just his Wharncliffe blades now. His company did security system installs, monitored hundreds of clients' homes and vehicles, and had a few specialists on site who consulted with insurance companies on high-tech crimes.

Castillion was a rapidly growing organization, and one that preferred to hire veterans. Gaby had gotten Lennox the job, and despite being forced to deal face-to-face with customers, he liked the work. It was by far the simplest thing in his new life, and the easiest to learn.

Serena laughed brightly. "Oh my God, I can't imagine Elliot carrying a gun! He'd say it ruined the line of his suit or something, and him with a weapon? He won't even use a pair of scissors if he can help it. No, no guns for him, although . . ." Her expression became thoughtful. "A home security system might be just the thing. The office building has a security system, but as far as I know his home has nothing like it. That's actually a *fantastic* idea. Oh, Lennox!" She twisted to put a hand on his arm. "You have to come and meet with him tomorrow! Talk him into this—it's exactly what he needs."

Talk him into it? Lennox was more the "I'll install it for you after you buy it, preferably when you're not around to bother me" type. "I'm not very good at being persuasive."

"He's much better at giving orders," Gaby added. Lee snorted quietly.

"Ganged up on by the women tonight, I see how it is," Lennox teased, and was gratified to see Lee smile at him. "Serena, really, he'd do better to talk to Kevin at the office—"

"But he won't!" Serena insisted, her voice tight with frustration. "He persists in thinking nothing is wrong and if someone isn't there to ride him on this, he'll just ignore the problem until something bad happens!"

Well, that sounded ominous. "Maybe you two should be going to the police with this."

"You'd think that," Serena said, her voice so saccharine sweet Lennox could almost taste it in the air. "But no, apparently not. Lennox, please, will you come by the office tomorrow?" She whipped out her phone and pulled up a calendar. "Around . . . four? He's got a break at four, and I can make it last as long as you need." There was genuine eagerness in her voice, backed by clear worry.

Fuck it. "Yeah, I can do that."

"Amazing! You are amazing." Serena reached around his shoulder for a one-armed hug. "You might be a *literal* lifesaver, Lennox. Has anyone ever told you that?"

The faint satisfaction of a job well done evaporated in an instant, leaving Lennox cold and breathless. His heartbeat sounded louder in his ears already, and he knew he had to get space, fast. He gently detached Serena's arm and pushed away from the table. "No. They haven't. I need some air, excuse me."

He walked out to the back deck and shut the kitchen door behind him, then sat down on the edge of the steps and put his head in his hands. He breathed, in and out, slowly and steadily. He could handle this. He could. It was only because it was a therapy day; those sessions brought all this shit to the foreground, all the things he worked so hard to forget in his day-to-day life.

Lennox wasn't a lifesaver. He was a murderer, even if it hadn't been his hand on the trigger, even if he'd technically been exonerated. Heat of battle, malfunctioning equipment, bad weather—none of it mattered to the two men who hadn't come away from the fight.

Lennox wasn't sure how much time he spent there, breathing and trying not to think, before a soft, familiar voice said, "Hey there. You doing okay?"

Gaby. He rolled his shoulders and opened his eyes, surprised to see that it had gone dark outside. "Yeah, I'm fine." For a given value of *fine.* "How long have I been out here?"

"Fifteen minutes, maybe. Lee and Serena were worried, but I told them to give you some space."

He smiled crookedly at his ex-wife as she sat next to him. When they'd been together they'd been terrible to each other, their marriage a mistake from the very beginning, born of nervousness and homesickness when both their units had been posted overseas. But after an amicable divorce and doing their best to raise Lee together despite numerous deployments, they'd become better friends post-breakup than they'd ever been while married. "Thanks for that."

"Serena had to leave, but Lee is hanging out downstairs. She's still worried."

And here it came. "Gaby . . ."

She didn't wait long enough to let Lennox defend himself, not that he quite knew what to say. "She was so excited when you told us you were moving here, you know? She couldn't wait to spend time with her dad. She idolizes you; all she wants is to be with you. But that sentiment's not going to last much longer, Lennox, especially not if you keep pushing her away."

"I can't have her at the apartment yet," he said. Gaby snorted, but he cut her off before she could speak. "I can't, Gaby. Not overnight, not until I'm a little better. I'm working on it—you know I am."

"Rodney's still paying for your counseling?" Gaby had known Rodney a lot longer than Lennox; she and his daughter Becky had gone through basic together.

"Perk of the job," Lennox huffed. "Also the worst part of my week, but I'm going, babe. Every week, I'm going."

"Maybe it would be more effective if you stopped dreading it so much," Gaby suggested, but there was no real hope in her voice. "I understand. I'm glad you're going, I just . . . She's your kid. You need to do right by her. You need to spend some goddamn *time* with her, while she's around for you to spend time with."

"I'll take her out on Friday," Lennox said impulsively. "Dinner and a movie. It's not an overnight, but it's the best I can do for now."

"Better than nothing," Gaby said, but it was light enough out that Lennox could see the little smile on her face. "Thanks."

"Fuck, don't thank me for doing the bare minimum." Hearing it made him feel exhausted.

She knocked her shoulder against his. "Oh, c'mon, West. Take it like a man."

"I'm shit at gratitude, you know that."

"Yeah, I know." She pressed a brief but firm kiss to his cheek, then levered herself to her feet. "That's another thing for you to work on, mister. Now get up, there's Rommie's homemade apple pie for dessert. Lee saved you a slice."

"Our kid is wise beyond her years." Lennox took Gaby's hand so she could help lift him to his feet. It hadn't been bad, as panic attacks went. He didn't even have a headache to show for it now.

Lee was hovering by the back door, and handed Lennox a piece of pie and a fork as soon as he was inside. Once he took it, she folded her arms up immediately, a little frown on her face that reminded Lennox uncomfortably of himself. He put the pie down on the counter.

"The twins will get that if you don't eat fast," Lee warned him, but she didn't pull away as he carefully drew her into a hug.

"Thanks for saving it for me, sweetheart." Lennox gave her a squeeze. "Listen, I was wondering . . . you wanna go out this Friday? Dinner and a movie or something?"

Lee hummed thoughtfully but didn't lift her head from his chest. "Maybe. Can I pick the restaurant?"

"You can even pick the movie, as long as it doesn't have Ryan Whatshisname in it."

"Oh my God, Dad, I'm so over him. Why would you bring him up?" Lee moaned, but she sounded more happy than annoyed. "When will you be here?"

"It'll take me a bit to clean up after work, so maybe . . . six?"

"Not earlier?"

Lennox cringed inside. "If I can, Lee." Fridays tended to be install days at Castillion, and those could run long. "I'll let you know."

"Okay."

"It's a date, then." Lennox kissed the top of Lee's purple head and closed his eyes for a second to savor the closeness that had been missing from his life for what felt like an eternity now.

A second was all it took for Khalil to sidle up and try to swipe the pie. His giggle gave him away though, and Lee practically forced the pie plate into Lennox's hands before she took off after her little brother, who screamed with glee.

Lennox did as he'd been told and ate the pie.

CHAPTER THREE

Excerpt from *Shockwave's* article:

There's a certain Machiavellian charisma to McKenzie, a primped and polished demeanor at odds with his exhortations to live genuinely and be true to yourself. Then again, this is not a man accustomed to privation. A cursory investigation into his background reveals an emotionally damaging but materially comfortable childhood, making him come across a little like a lesser Bruce Wayne.

If there's a crusader for justice in the McKenzie family, though, it isn't the prodigal son. Or at least, it wasn't before he became famous for all the wrong reasons. His sister, Vanessa Travers, is a prosecutor for the Denver DA's office with an impressive number of successful cases under her belt.

She's also currently running for the position of Denver's district attorney. I wonder if these siblings will dare to exchange holiday cards this year.

"**A**aand . . . action."

Elliot smiled for the camera, careful not to let his eyes track away to either side of it. He'd done close to a hundred of these videos now, and was pretty much an expert. He didn't really need to read from the cue cards anymore, although he had Ted make them up for him just in case. "Hey, guys! It's Elliot at Charmed Life, here with your weekly insight." He clasped his hands in front of his chest for a moment before tapping them to his chin. Body language spoke as loud as words, and Elliot liked to set the stage for his subscribers, even if it made him feel like he was in an amateur acting class.

"Before yesterday," he began, "I had a clear-cut idea for what I was going to talk about in this video. But after yesterday, well, it seems that my priorities have changed." Elliot shrugged and grinned. "They do that sometimes—I've learned to roll with it. So today I want to talk with you about . . . preconceptions. Specifically, about other people's preconceptions of you, and a few strategies for dealing with them.

"I was thinking about this because I did an interview yesterday, and let's just say things started off with a bang and never quite slowed down." He shook his head slightly, his smile turning rueful. "I get where they're coming from. It has to be hard to meet your subject for the first time and try to get any depth out of them. Reporters are trained to ask the tough questions, and I respect that. Conversely, though, it's hard on me to sit across from someone and listen to them recite my history like they're reading it off a wanted poster, and then ask me how I feel about it. How would anybody feel about that?

"Defensive." Elliot let his smile wash out now. "Frustrated. Like there's nothing you can do to keep people from bringing up the same old stories, over and over. It's a painful loop to be caught in, and if it happens often enough, it can be destructive to the progress you've made so far. You don't have to forget the lessons of the past to want to move beyond it, and get to the second chance you deserve.

"But how do we handle this kind of presence in our lives? Yesterday for me it was easy: I just had to wait for the interview to end. Other times though, there is no end. We might be living with someone who won't let us move on, or we might be missing someone who refuses to move on with us." Elliot sighed and closed his eyes for a moment, expressing some of the fatigue he felt every time he thought about the people who had left him behind. His lover, Willie, Vanessa . . . He looked out at the camera again.

"Sometimes you can talk to them about it. Set clear boundaries, come to an agreement about what is and isn't fair to bring up. Sometimes," and he held up a hand, as if forestalling an argument, "and I hate to say it but it really is true, folks: avoidance is the only way. That doesn't mean you'll never be able to talk to them about it, but it does acknowledge that some people need time to learn to deal with a new reality. Just because you're ready to move on doesn't mean your support network is.

"And lastly? Guys . . ." Elliot shook his head. "Sometimes you have to be willing to leave them behind. If someone in your life can't let go of their preconceptions of you, if someone in your life can't accept the changes within you and support you in maintaining them, then it might be time to step away and find some new friends. We all need a community to lend a hand when it comes to staying on a new path, and as wonderful as I think my subscribers are," he smiled again, "I'll be the first to admit we're just one piece of the puzzle. We can be there for each other, but we can only do so much in forums online. The physical component is as important as the emotional one. Which isn't to say I'm not trying to solve that problem too, but one thing at a time.

"So, preconceptions!" Elliot rubbed his hands together. "Think about how they affect you, both your own and other people's. Think about the ideas you may be holding on to about other people in your life, maybe even about yourself, and consider how you can better come to terms with them. Share your ideas on the forum, so our friends can see they're not the only ones going through this. Next week, we'll go over some coping strategies that do *not* involve marijuana, so stop asking—I know it's legal here but, c'mon, don't get me into more trouble, okay? Thanks for listening."

"Aaand . . . cut." Ted poked his head out from behind the camera and gave Elliot a thumbs-up. "Nice. We can use this; it'll hardly need any editing at all."

"Are you sure? I think I stumbled a bit at the end there," Elliot said, stroking the sides of his head below the edges of his fedora. "And am I frizzy? This feels a little frizzy."

Ted sighed the sigh of the immensely put-upon. "You're not frizzy. And if there was a stumble, I'll edit it out. Give me a day to get the final version to you and then you can post it." He was already packing up his equipment, all of it fitting into a guitar-sized case.

Ted might be bit impatient with Elliot sometimes, but he did good work. If he said it was fine . . . "Thanks, Ted."

"No problem."

Elliot left him to deal with the lights, and headed back upstairs for his next big thing. Which was . . . actually, he didn't know. He headed for his office, but Serena met him in the common room before he got as far as his door.

"Hi! Filming go okay?"

"It went fine, like every other week," Elliot said, a little taken aback. All day, Serena had been . . . not manic, exactly, maybe excited? And anxious? It was a nerve-racking combination coming from a woman who generally seemed unperturbable. "Why?"

"Just making sure you don't have anything else to do down there." She checked her phone. "Your timing is perfect. He should be here any minute."

Elliot frowned. "Who should be here?"

Serena beamed. "Your four o'clock! I set up a meeting with a representative for a personal and home security company, who—"

"Serenaaa." Elliot drew her name out with a groan. "I told you, I don't need extra security!"

"*Who*," she persevered, "also happens to be my ex-brother-in-law, but he's still a friend of the family, so before you get started with him, let me tell you something." Her expression went deadly serious. "You be nice to Lennox, or as God is my witness I will make you suffer as only a personal assistant can. You don't have to use his services if you really don't want to, but you should give this a chance, Elliot, and that starts with behaving yourself now."

Elliot was intrigued despite himself. Serena never got this defensive over people who weren't, well . . . him, mostly. "He's your ex-brother-in-law? And he's still friends with your sister?" Elliot hadn't met Gaby, but she sounded like more the "burn the bridges and set fire to the town along with them" rather than the forgiving type.

"They're very good friends, and have been ever since their divorce. He got here three months ago and is working hard to settle in. He can be a little *touchy*, but he's great and I don't want you to be rude to him."

Elliot snorted. "Why, will he cry?"

"No. But he might leave *you* crying, and I don't want to have to deal with that today. Oh!" Her face lit up. "He's here!" She left Elliot and practically ran across the carpeted floor and greeted the man coming inside. Elliot got a vague impression of someone in worn jeans and a dark Henley as Serena smothered him in a hug. As soon as he moved back and Elliot could take in the entire view, however . . .

Damn. *Damn*, get him a martini and a recliner, because he could watch this guy for hours. He was about Elliot's height, maybe slightly less broad across the shoulders, but his bare forearms were whipcord lean, and darkly tanned. He had golden-brown eyes under low brows, a sharp jaw covered by a closely trimmed beard, and thick, dark hair just long enough on top to be stylish, which was probably accidental given the worn state of the man's clothes. His face was a little hollow to be strictly handsome; it made him look too intense for a simple *handsome*. The lines of his muscles under his shirt were cut, compact. All in all, he was about the last person Elliot had expected after being warned so vehemently not to be rude. If Elliot *was* rude, this guy would likely bend him in half and tie his limbs in knots. Which might be fun . . .

If he weren't the ex-husband of Elliot's best friend's sister, that was. He couldn't be more off-limits if he were *Serena's* ex. The two finished their greeting, and Elliot straightened up and smiled winningly as they came over.

"Good afternoon." He extended his hand. "I'm Elliot McKenzie. Thank you for meeting me on such short notice."

"Lennox West." He had a low, easy voice with a touch of a Southern drawl to it—Georgia, perhaps? "And I should probably be thanking you for making the time, since I know this wasn't your idea."

Elliot smiled more broadly. "Well, if we're being completely honest, then I'll confess that I didn't actually know I was meeting with you until about a minute ago. Not that I'm in any way disappointed now you're here." Was he . . . *flirting* with Mr. Unavailable? Maybe he was going crazy.

"Neither am I."

Wait, was—was Lennox West flirting *back*? He couldn't be. Elliot should ignore it, chock it up to Southern gentility, and keep things in a purely professional realm.

Except he wouldn't be himself if he did that.

"Let's hope you stay that way," Elliot said. "Are you thirsty? Hungry? I'm not sure if you know this, but within these four walls I'm *allowed* to ask Serena to bring me things. Every day at work feels like being in the eye of a hurricane: as exciting as it is dangerous."

"Oh, stop." Serena whacked him on the arm, and then smacked Lennox as well when she caught him grinning. "And you, what is this? You two aren't allowed to gang up on me!"

"We're just trying to get along," Lennox said, as innocently as a child with his fingers crossed behind his back. "I thought you wanted me to be friendly to your boss."

"You practically demanded that I be nice," Elliot added. "How much nicer can I be? Actually," and he knew it was a bad idea but he went ahead with it anyway, batting his eyelashes at Lennox, "I could be a hell of a lot nicer to you, but that sort of thing has no place in an office where other people are in earshot."

"That's a shame," Lennox said, and Elliot probably looked like an idiot, he was grinning so hard, but he didn't care.

"Oh my god." Serena looked between the two of them like she'd just realized she'd left her curling iron plugged in, and whether or not the house would still be standing by the time she got back was clearly up in the air. "You're getting along. I thought I'd have to stand by with a cattle prod to keep things civil, but you're even . . . You *can't* be serious."

"I try never to be serious, but we do have business to discuss thanks to you, so." Elliot shrugged and opened his office door for Lennox. "Come on in. Pick anywhere you like to sit, and we can talk. Serena, if I could have a bottle of water, that would be wonderful; I'm still hot and bothered from being under those lights."

If there was a prize for obviousness, Elliot would have won it right then. Judging from Serena's glare, she agreed, but her ex-brother-in-law steadfastly refused to show any hint of offense as he stepped inside. "I'd like one too, if you don't mind."

She nodded warily. "I'll get them. Just . . . give me a minute."

"Thank you." Elliot shut the door and looked over at Lennox, who, after a moment of debating between the leather couch and the beanbag chair, flopped down in the chair. His legs splayed as he got comfortable, and it took more willpower than Elliot was comfortable with to force himself to sit down on the couch across from Lennox.

"You're allowed to decorate with beanbag chairs in a place like this?" Lennox asked bemusedly.

"It's my place, I can decorate it however I want to," Elliot said. "And for certain people there's nothing better than a beanbag chair. Take you, for example. You opted for it."

"True," Lennox said, smiling as he ran his hand over the fabric. He seemed different when he smiled: softer and, dare Elliot think it, slightly sweet.

Elliot had seen pictures of Serena's niece, Lia, numerous times. While before he'd thought her looks came from Serena's side, now he could recognize hints of this man in the sharpness of Lia's jaw and the length of her coltish limbs.

"I had one as a kid," Lennox said. "It was just blue vinyl, not nice fabric like this, but I loved that thing."

"Did you keep it until it was all worn out?"

"Ah, no." Lennox was too tanned for Elliot to see if he was blushing, but the way he averted his eyes for a moment spoke volumes. "Once I was too big for it, I ended up using it for target practice."

Elliot tsked and shook his head. "You shot your favorite chair? Such a fickle lover."

"Actually, I used throwing knives." Lennox shrugged. "I went through a ninja phase when I was in my teens."

The thought of Lennox flinging knives into cheap vinyl should absolutely not be hot. Elliot cleared his throat. "I hope you'll be kinder to my chair. Please don't stab it in a fit of nostalgia."

"I promise not to take a knife to any of your pretty things," Lennox said mock-seriously. "Cross my heart." He did so, and then seemed mildly surprised by his own actions.

"Well, that's a relief." The man was carrying a knife too; Elliot saw the clip holding it in his right pocket. Of course he was. Elliot considered asking Lennox to whip it out so he could see it, but then Serena came in with water. He took advantage of the break to get control of his rogue brain. *You cannot hit any harder on this guy. He is off-limits until you have clear proof otherwise.* Like Lennox pushing Elliot up against the wall and sticking his hand down his pants. That would be nice proof.

"Thanks, I really need this," he said to Serena when she handed him an icy bottle. He drained half of it in one go, refreshingly chilled by the end of it. Yes, he could handle this.

"No problem," she said, not sounding like she was brimming with belief, but Elliot took what he could get. "Can I bring you anything else? Do you need someone to take notes?"

"It's a security system, not rocket science. Right?" He looked expectantly at Lennox.

"If it was rocket science, I wouldn't be doing it," Lennox said easily. "The really high-tech stuff I leave to the MIT grads. These kinds of systems are easy. You can even get one that you install yourself, if you want. Motion detectors, alarms on the doors and windows, cameras . . . it's all wireless now."

"Keep in mind that *I'm* not a rocket scientist either," Elliot warned him.

"Stop being modest," Serena chided him, then turned to Lennox. "He's so good with his hands, you wouldn't believe it. He can fix cars, appliances—he fixed my washing machine last week, took the whole thing apart and put it back together and voilà! It works better than when I bought it. You should have been an engineer, not a lawyer, Elliot."

Lennox's eyebrows lifted. "I didn't know you were a lawyer."

He could have heard a drop of water hit the floor, it was so still for a moment.

"All fine? Nothing needed? Lovely! I'll just go, then!" Serena pivoted on her very high heel and walked out, quietly shutting the door behind her.

Elliot raised one eyebrow. "Really? I thought everyone knew that. Past tense, of course; I was disbarred, but I used to be a patent lawyer."

"Why were you disbarred?"

"Why don't you know already?" Elliot said. "I may be wrong, but I was under the impression that the reason I've never met any of Serena's family is because they're quite aware of my past, and unanimously disapproving."

"I haven't been here very long yet," Lennox said as he twisted the cap off his water bottle. "And I've found it's always better to get information straight from the source." He took a sip, and Elliot tracked the motion for a moment before getting his mind back in the game.

"That's true." Fine. He would lay it all out there; he hated to rehash his past, generally, but something about Lennox made the prospect less aggravating. "Five years ago, the law firm I worked for was hired to represent a company called Redback Industries. They were in a dispute over the rights to a new technology developed by a former biomedical engineer of theirs named Frank Gunderson. Frank had left the company several years previously, formed his own corporation and proceeded to pioneer a method of 3D-printing cell scaffolds for seeding transplant organs."

Lennox frowned. "Can't we do something like that already? I thought I saw an article on organ manufacturing not too long ago . . ."

"We can *now*," Elliot emphasized, "but five years ago the technology was very much in its infancy, and the man on the cutting edge was Dr. Gunderson. A lot of the research and development that went into his product had been done while he was still an employee of Redback Industries, however, so they claimed intellectual property rights over his work. They had a device of their own in development to do the same thing, although it was nowhere near as far along, and they didn't want the competition. He disputed their claim, so it went to mediation."

One man and his lawyer against a multibillion dollar corporation and an entire law firm. Elliot hadn't envied Frank Gunderson, who'd been hemorrhaging money trying to continue his research and marketing efforts all while fighting off the sharks.

"Frank publically stated that he would rather go bankrupt than settle and see his hard work thrown away," Elliot went on. "It was kept quiet then, but his wife was on dialysis for kidney failure. She was on the list for a transplant organ, but her time was running out. Kidneys are incredibly complex compared to something like the liver, which is far easier to propagate, but Frank was convinced that he could use his technology to save her. He kept stalling the mediation and pushing hard at his own research. Finally, Redback Industries decided they needed to step up their game. They hired a fixer."

Lennox's eyes narrowed. "A fixer?"

And so it begins. "Someone who uses underhanded or illegal means to turn the tide of a conflict of interest in their employer's favor," Elliot clarified, working hard to keep his voice cool and even. Of all the black marks in his past, none of them still gnawed at his soul the way this one did. "In this case, the fixer was a man named Jonathan Lehrer, who was meant to intimidate Mrs. Gunderson and, through her, her husband. Supposedly he was good at his job; he should have had Frank on his knees in a matter of weeks. Unfortunately he went too far and forced Mrs. Gunderson's car off the road one day. She died in the resulting crash."

Rachel Gunderson had been forty-four. The only picture Elliot had ever seen of her had been a photograph next to her obituary in the newspaper, a round-faced woman with dark, curly hair and a smile on her lips. Elliot had kept it—it was tucked away in a folder at the back of his filing cabinet, beside a few other things he didn't deserve to have but couldn't bear to forget about. He cleared his throat. "Things were falling apart for everyone. Frank was bankrupt. He couldn't even afford to bury his wife, and Lehrer was being investigated after what happened to her. The police were closing in on Redback, but the CEO, Mr. Pullman, wouldn't stop pushing. He was obsessed with owning Gunderson's work. He kept forcing the mediation."

Elliot found himself rolling his right shoulder unconsciously. It still ached, constantly echoing the pain of a fresh bullet wound. "Frank got a call during a meeting with us two days after his wife's death. It was the police, although the rest of us didn't know it at the time, telling him that Lehrer had implicated Redback as his employer. Apparently that was all he needed to hear."

"Frank came back into the room and shot Pullman and me, then turned the gun on himself. I was hit twice, Pullman once. We were taken to the hospital, and during my stay there the investigation found definitive evidence linking Lehrer to Redback, and from there, to the law firm. More specifically, to me." Elliot chuckled, but not because it was funny. "Later, I found out he'd only bought the gun after his wife's death. Frank was basically intimidated into getting a gun by the same people he almost killed with it."

Lennox looked at him steadily. "But you weren't the one who hired him."

"But I knew about it." Of course he had. Not *explicitly*, per se. He hadn't known Jonathan Lehrer's name until after the fact, but he'd known there was someone taking care of things for the company. He'd known enough to assure Mischa, his boss at the law firm and his lover in the privacy of their own home, that the case was as good as settled in their favor. He'd been stupid, and careless, and complicit in a crime he'd never meant to turn into a murder. But then it had, and all his intentions hadn't counted for shit once people had ended up dead. Elliot would never forget the expression on Frank's face just before he'd pulled the trigger. He'd never seen a man so heartbroken. It had almost felt good to get shot, after seeing that.

"I offered to testify against Redback in exchange for immunity. I barely avoided going to jail, lost my license to practice law, and was fired by my firm." And had been kicked out of the house he and Mischa had shared, but it had been no less than he'd deserved. "I got addicted to painkillers during my recovery, and was sent to rehab by my family. They haven't spoken to me since, but I got the inspiration to start Charmed Life there, so." He spread his hands. "I can't say it was all bad."

The silence drew out for a long moment. Elliot took a deep breath to clear his head, then smiled his most practiced smile. "And so, you know. That's the short version; the long version only comes out after copious application of alcohol."

"Amen," Lennox muttered, so quietly that Elliot wasn't sure he was meant to hear it. Then Lennox went on in a more normal tone, "Thanks for telling me. Which part of that history is making you worry about your safety here and now?"

Well, there's an assumption. "What makes you think it is? Maybe I'm a very safety-conscious person."

"That's not what Serena says."

"Serena doesn't know everything," Elliot snapped.

"Don't let her hear you say that," Lennox said with a smirk, and Elliot's chilly defensiveness melted away before he could shore it up. "I'm not asking for the sake of asking. What you're worried about factors into the kind of system you buy, like whether or not you go for twenty-four-hour monitoring or just link your sensors to a loud-ass alarm in the middle of your house."

"Oh." That made a certain amount of sense. "There have been a few notes left in my mailbox. A picture or two. It's nothing serious," he emphasized, not bothering to bring up the shoes. "Stupid stuff, but I wouldn't mind the extra monitoring. I don't have a lot of close neighbors, so an alarm that just makes noise wouldn't do much good."

"Do you have many ground-level windows?"

"Yes." Elliot didn't know exactly how many, but one of the things that had drawn him to the house was how sunny it was.

Lennox had his phone out and was tapping information into it. "How many entrances?"

The phone's case had a familiar face on it. Elliot leaned closer to get a better look as he answered, "Two doors. Do you actually have a picture of Lennox Lewis on your phone?"

"Yep. My kid got it for me last Christmas." Lennox glanced up at Elliot and smiled. "I like to box, and he and I have the same first name. Lia—*Lee*, damn it, pays attention."

It was fun to see Lennox lose some of his composure. "Which is it, Lia or Lee?"

"Depends on her mood." He immediately shook his head. "No, that's not fair. Lee, these days. It used to be Lia, back before I left on my final tour. She changed it while I was gone."

"Time waits for no man, I suppose."

"No, it doesn't." Lennox put his phone away and folded his hands. "When do you want a system installed by? Because I can have parts shipped to you and you can do it yourself next week, or I can get it installed as early as tomorrow if you decide what you want and can be at home for an hour or so."

Elliot's reticence had evaporated, replaced by a strange urge to see this man, hardly more than a stranger, in his home. Preferably climbing high things or bending over, but a view of him sitting at the kitchen bar drinking a cup of coffee would be acceptable if that was all he could get.

Goddamn chemistry. It always struck when he least expected it, and certainly Lennox wasn't Elliot's usual type. Maybe he'd finally grown tired of going after people like himself; it was like fucking in front of a mirror sometimes, except less fun. "If you're the one doing the install, I can make tomorrow work," he said. "Send me some examples and quotes tonight. I'll make a decision on what to go with in the morning and let you know first thing."

Lennox tilted his head slightly. "And if I can't do the install, you'll do it yourself? Or let someone come by next week?"

"Maybe. Or maybe I'll pass for the time being."

Lennox frowned. "Mr. McKenzie, try to take this seriously."

"I *do* take this seriously, Mr. West," Elliot said calmly. "I'm very careful about who I let into my home. I'm willing to let you in because Serena vouched for you," *and I'm having visions of you pressing me up against a wall that are neither here nor there right now,* "but some random person who says he's affiliated with your company wanting to get in? Not likely."

They stared at each other for a long moment before Lennox nodded. "Fair enough."

Elliot smiled victoriously. He was good at reading people, good at presenting information in a way that made sense to them. Understanding what made them tick was the key to changing their minds, and while getting Lennox to agree to do his installation was a minor win, it was intensely satisfying despite that. "Perfect. Four o'clock again?"

Lennox seemed to be doing mental math. "Four should work if you don't live in Fort Collins or the Springs."

Elliot shook his head. "Too far a drive for one, too much crazy for the other. I'm just a few miles outside of Golden. When I reply to your quote, I'll include the address."

"Good." Lennox stood up and Elliot copied him, taking the hand that came his way and holding it for a tad longer than he might under normal circumstances. Interestingly, Lennox didn't make any move to pull away.

"I'll see you tomorrow, then, Mr. McKenzie."

"Elliot."

"Right." When Elliot eventually let go of his hand, it was like stretching taffy, a long, slow glide as their skin gradually separated. "Elliot. Thanks, Castillion appreciates your business." He turned to go.

"Don't I get first-name privileges with you?" Elliot asked, surprising himself with how much he wanted them.

Lennox shook his head. "It wouldn't be professional. Only family and friends call me by my first name, anyway."

"I bet we could be friends." Elliot could almost guarantee it, in fact.

Lennox appeared to be sizing him up. Elliot had to resist the urge to square his shoulders. "Maybe we could be," he said at last. "We'll find out tomorrow. Good night, Mr. McKenzie."

He left, leaving the door open. Elliot listened to him say good-bye to Serena, heard the warmth in their mutual farewells, and wondered if he was reading too much into what amounted to a ten-minute meeting. Maybe Mr. West—Lennox to him by tomorrow, if he had anything to say about it—was a cautious flirt with everyone.

Serena came into the room a moment later, her eyes wide. "Are you magic? Because I haven't seen him that friendly with anyone he isn't related to since Lee's best friend came to dinner a month ago."

Or maybe I really am special. He winked at Serena and stuffed his hands in his pockets. "I'm secretly magic. Don't tell anyone or Hogwarts won't let me back in."

Serena laughed. "You're a little old for wizarding school, don't you think?"

"I'm not a student; I'm a teacher. Transfiguration, naturally."

"Naturally." They shared a grin.

"Can you clear my schedule from three thirty on tomorrow?" he asked. "He's coming over to do the install at four."

Serena thought about it for a moment. "The only thing you've got that isn't flexible is that check-in with Stuart at four fifteen."

Oh, that was nothing. "Tell him we need to reschedule. Give him a half hour sometime next week to make up for it." Stuart wanted a hand-holder more than anything. A little push out of the nest would be good for him.

"I'll make the change."

"Good." If all went well tomorrow, then by the time Elliot was done with Lennox West, he'd get to call the man by something other than his first name.

CHAPTER
FOUR

Partial transcription of most recent appointment with West, Lennox, Staff Sergeant US Army Rangers (R), January 28, 3:06 p.m.:

JS: You haven't actually said anything to me about your nightmares, you know.

LW: Sure I have.

JS: You've told me you have them, but none of the details.

LW: Look, you've read my file. You can guess what's stuck with me.

JS: This file only pertains to your military service, which is far from all of your life. And I'd rather you tell me about your nightmares yourself.

LW: Of course you would, Jesus Christ. (Patient shifts in chair, stares out the window for almost a minute before speaking.) It's the last firefight, usually. The dark, the cold. The blue force tracker going down. Menendez and Phillips, dead. Mostly that.

JS: What else?

LW: That isn't enough?

JS: It's enough if that's all there is.

LW: You're out for blood today, Doc.

JS: And you're avoiding the subject, Lennox.

Gaby had mentioned to Lennox more than once that it was easy to tell when he was getting pissed off. "You get this kind of murderous gleam in your eyes," she'd said, only half teasing. "Like if you had a knife in your hand you'd be drawing it across the person's throat just to stop them from being stupid at you." She'd seemed to appreciate it, personally—Gaby said he'd be better than half a dozen dads boasting about shotguns when Lee started dating.

Which would be when she was twenty-one or Lennox was cold in his grave, whichever came first.

Class after class of Army Rangers had learned the perils of annoying their staff sergeant, and the ones who hadn't been observant enough, he'd been able to render teachable through the simple expedient of making them run obstacle courses with full packs on at oh four hundred. Given plenty of time and constructive profanity, anybody could learn.

The biggest problem with working in retail? Being confronted by idiot customers and having no mandate to tell them how fucking stupid they were sometimes. If it was simply ignorance, he could deal with it. A person had to acknowledge that they needed to learn before they ever would. He didn't have a problem with neophytes. It was the swaggering idiots who walked in like their dick was so big they kicked it with every step, talking about what badasses they were and being complete morons at the same time.

Case in point: the genius pressing his sweaty forearms against the glass counter, right next to the sign that said *DO NOT LEAN ON GLASS*, trying to impress Lennox with how much he knew about nothing useful.

"Hey, I told my brother, I said to him, 'Listen, Dougie, the thing you need for home defense is a goddamn shotgun, not a baseball bat. Like the tripped-out meth head in the apartment next to you is gonna be scared of a baseball bat, am I right? You gotta have that sweet sound, the *ka-chink* that puts the fear of God into 'em, ya know? Plus, hell, you don't barely hafta aim with a shotgun!' Which is good, 'cause my brother's blind in his left eye and he can't see well at night in the right one these days. A shotgun's what he needs. I'm thinking a semiautomatic, but—"

Lennox couldn't take it. Fuck it; Rodney shouldn't have left him on counter duty anyway. "You've still got to aim a shotgun, you know."

Mr. Moron squinted, like he might somehow process sound with his eyeballs if he stared hard enough. "Huh?"

"The spread for buckshot isn't that big, not if you're talking home defense. With a standard twelve gauge, at fifteen feet you might get a hole as big as a tennis ball. Aiming is still a requirement."

"Huh. But what about—"

Lennox pressed on. "And if your brother lives in an apartment, he's going to have to worry about hitting his neighbors even if he's using birdshot. A slug would definitely go through walls. Does your brother have any pets, any family in the apartment? He'll have to worry about hitting them too."

"Well, he—"

"And I know that slide-racking sound is nice, but a semiauto's not going to give you that sound." *Hence the* auto *part of the name.* "Not to mention, if the person breaking in is a tripped-out meth head, they might be too gone to hear it anyway. Frankly, it seems to me like a baseball bat is exactly what your brother needs, and lucky for him, he's already got one!" Lennox spread his hands. "Problem solved."

Mr. Moron squinted at Lennox again. "Are you sassing me, son?"

Lennox shook his head. "I do not sass grown men, sir. I'm not above fucking with them," he added, "but that's not what I'm doing here either." He saw Rodney come in from the back, do a double take, then sigh and head their way. He had his placating face on, but Lennox wasn't ready to hand over the reins of the conversation quite yet. "I'm just offering up some friendly advice. If your half-blind, apartment-dwelling, untrained brother really wants a shotgun, he should come in here and buy it himself. Which, incidentally, is also the law."

"What my associate means to say," Rodney broke in, his round, mustachioed face still genial probably by dint of sheer will, "is that we're happy to help first-time buyers learn the ins and outs of their weapon. We have a range right here on site, and we'll go through everything with them, from assembly to loading to safely unloading, until they feel completely comfortable handling their firearm responsibly." His faint German accent tinged his *w*'s with a *v* sound, but his enunciation was better than Lennox's.

"Huh." Mr. Moron scowled suspiciously. "That's not what it seemed like to me."

"Lennox was just leaving; he's running late for a security system install."

Actually Lennox had an hour before he needed to be in Golden, but he took the out and headed into the back room. It had been a quiet day in the shop, for the most part: David, Rebecca, and Francis were all on installs, and Kevin was manning the phones. Really, he was probably playing Candy Crush, but he was still there in case a call came through.

Lennox went ahead and checked his kit. Might as well make sure he had everything he'd need for Elliot's house. Elliot McKenzie wasn't at all what Lennox had been expecting. He'd radiated charisma like some people radiated dominance.

Lennox didn't have a temperament that necessitated he be in control of every situation. He could take charge with ease—the Army had taught him how—but he'd never sought the spotlight. Hell, he could all but disappear into a crowd if he needed to, a skill that had made both of his exes jealous more than once. He liked being able to step back and observe, to watch the flow of people around him and see where tension built. But someone like Elliot? He was never going to escape anyone's gaze.

He clearly didn't want to, either. Lennox didn't think he'd ever seen a prettier man, and knowing Oliver the way he did, that was saying something.

The suit, the shoes, the sleek chestnut hair under the ridiculous hat he'd made work, and the square jaw that should have made his face seem blocky but somehow made it chiseled instead. Then there were his *eyes*. Lennox couldn't quite get over those eyes: one brown, one green, both completely devilish. He didn't make a habit of checking men out, but honestly, almost anybody would have spared the time to check out Elliot McKenzie.

His story had been rather revealing. Incomplete, but Lennox would be a hypocrite if he complained about that, given how little he'd shared about himself. Elliot hadn't pried, though, so Lennox would work with what he'd been given. A disbarred lawyer turned self-help star with enough dirt in his past to worry him in the present? Maybe there had been other clients Elliot had screwed over before one of them finally turned on him. He wondered where Elliot'd been shot. It was likely that if he asked nicely, Elliot would be more than happy to strip for him.

Fuck it, he was *not* gonna get hard at work. Lennox repacked his kit and resolutely pushed Elliot from his mind, just in time to get a face full of disappointed Rodney when he turned around.

"Jesus," he breathed after jumping a little. "You startled me."

Rodney didn't give him long to find his feet. "Why were you so rude to that man, Lennox?"

"Because he didn't know what the hell he was talking about."

"The key to helping such customers is *educating* them, not tearing them apart." Rodney shook his head. "Dealing with people is difficult sometimes, I know. But it is absolutely essential to this job."

"I do fine on installs," Lennox protested.

"Yes, but I've had three customer complaints about your work in the shop in the past two weeks. You are not patient enough, Lennox. We are not here to judge their reasons for purchasing from us; we're here to sell them what they're looking for."

Lennox set his jaw. "He wanted something inappropriate."

"That isn't our decision. Although in this case, I agreed with you. The gentleman left without buying anything, but I managed to mollify him first, I think. However, now he will likely go to Walmart and buy a poorly made shotgun off the rack, and give it to a man who will never learn to properly use it. Then we will all be grateful if we never hear about such a man having an accident with his weapon."

Lennox frowned. "If we're not allowed to judge their purchases, then we can't take responsibility for what happens after the purchase is made, either. That sort of thing isn't healthy, or so my therapist says."

"Ah yes, Janet!" Rodney's somberness fell away almost instantly. "You and she are getting along, then? She helped my Rebecca very much."

"We . . . making progress."

Fortunately for Lennox, that seemed to be all the detail Rodney needed. "Good, good. That's the most anyone can hope for. I'm pleased you're seeing some benefit from the sessions."

"Me too." *Benefit* was maybe a generous word for it, but if having a therapist made Gaby happy and kept Rodney off his back, then it was worth it. "I do actually have to leave for an install now, so . . ."

"Of course." Rodney nodded easily. "You can take Number Three." There were five company cars, enough for everyone to be out in one if needed, but Lennox shook his head.

"I'll take my truck. I've got a place to be right after, and I don't want to come back here first." He'd brought his truck today so he wouldn't have to return to his apartment and swap vehicles, which would save him some time getting to Lee, and he knew she'd appreciate that.

"Boxing today?"

"Nah, taking my kid out."

Rodney beamed. "Little Lia. I gave her her first tactical folding knife, you know. Two and a half inches, with a pretty pink handle."

Lennox sighed. "She's Lee now, and she covered the pink with black electrical tape, but she still carries it when she's not going to school."

"Ah, children, they change so quickly." Rodney tugged on one side of his moustache. "Perhaps I'll make her a new one with a black handle, hmm?"

"Maybe for a special occasion," Lennox said. "I don't want to spoil her."

Spoil her with knives, honestly. He could almost hear his mother's voice in his head as he grabbed the kit and headed out to his rattletrap 1984 Nissan pickup, its body more rust than metal at this point. It started reluctantly, and Lennox frowned. He'd have to make an appointment with a mechanic soon; that guttural sound couldn't be good.

Finding 217 Cody Lane was pretty easy. Believing that it belonged to Elliot McKenzie? That strained Lennox's belief. The house wasn't a mansion like so many of its neighbors: it was a modest two-story Victorian painted white and trimmed in lilac, which matched the enormous bushes that obscured much of its front fence. There was an ash tree in the yard with a swing hanging down from one of its long, low branches, and a porch with flower boxes—empty for now, but they were still vivid spots of color against the white of the house.

The house didn't appear slick or grandiose or particularly fancy, and if Elliot himself hadn't been standing on the porch waiting, his hands in his pockets, hat and tie discarded in favor of a close-fitting blue sweater, Lennox would have thought he'd gotten the address wrong. And even with Elliot standing there, the tableau still strained Lennox's credulity since Elliot carried what looked like a struggling orange puffball under one arm.

Lennox turned off the truck, which coughed distressingly before it went silent, and got out with his case. "I see you found me," Elliot said brightly. "Although I didn't intend for you to sacrifice your vehicle to the road gods in order to make it here," he added with a little frown. "That sounds bad."

"I know, I need to get it checked out," Lennox said. "But it only has to last me through tonight."

"Oh yeah?" Elliot lifted his eyebrows and smirked. "Hot date?"

"Only if you're a pervert." Which, damn, had that come off rude? He hadn't intended it to be rude, but apparently he was shit at interacting like a normal person today. Elliot just grinned, though.

"Well sometimes, yes, I certainly am. Perhaps not in this particular case, but I can't know without more details, so . . ." He left his sentence hanging, and Lennox was happy to disabuse him of any kinky notions. This time, at least.

"I mean, I'm taking my daughter out tonight." He was trying to look forward to it, but it was shamefully hard. Lee would probably subject him to sushi, and then he'd spend a few hours fumbling his way through the minefield that was conversation with her these days, before they took refuge in a movie theater. "Her mom won't let her ride on the motorcycle with me in the winter, so I'm using the truck."

"Ah." Elliot glanced from Lennox to his truck and back again. "To be honest, normally I'd say something slightly deprecating here about the state of your vehicle, but you manage to make it look good."

It was an odd compliment, but Lennox would take it. Or, better yet, he'd ignore it and get to work. He stepped up onto the porch and the puffball started to wiggle insanely, until Elliot put it down. It ran over to Lennox's feet, barking excitedly, and he smiled despite himself.

"What kind of dog is this?" he asked as he bent over and scratched it behind its tiny ears. The dog bounced up and down with the force of its enthusiastic welcome.

"A Pomeranian. Her name is Holly."

"Hey, Holly," Lennox said gently, and got a lick for his trouble before he straightened up. "I have to say, I didn't see you as a dog person. Too much . . ." He waved a hand at Elliot's still-dapper outfit. "Shedding."

"Eh, she came with the house," Elliot said nonchalantly, but he gave the little dog a pat of his own before he led the way into his home. "The place was left to me by a friend, and even though it's been almost five years, there are some things I just can't bring myself to change. Including Holly."

Lennox looked around with an eye toward the job, but he couldn't help appreciating the vintage movie posters and black-and-white photographs of golden-age Hollywood stars that decorated the walls. The one of Humphrey Bogart was actually signed. "It must have been a good friend," he said as Elliot led him through the foyer and into the living room. The furniture here was more in line with what he'd expected of Elliot: plenty of leather and steel, fewer doilies and floral imprints, and the hardwood floors were unsoftened by accent rugs or any of the other accessories that Gaby insisted a house needed.

"The best," Elliot said. "She helped me pick myself back up after everything that happened with Redback, and she was wonderfully nonjudgmental." From Elliot's slightly awed tone, the novelty of that still hadn't worn off.

"*She*, huh?" Lennox prompted as he set his case down on the coffee table. "She who?"

"*She* who was about sixty years older than me, and the wrong gender for anything other than a purely platonic love," Elliot said, but his grin showed that he hadn't taken offense. "Willie and I, we . . ." He shrugged. "Had an immediate connection. It's hard to explain."

Lennox was no good at pushing, even when he was curious, so he changed the subject. "Clearly you haven't had Serena in here yet," he said as he opened his case on the dining room table.

Elliot cocked his head. "What makes you say that?"

"No throw pillows."

He chuckled. "You know the family so well. How is that possible, by the way, given that you and your ex have been divorced for so long?"

"Just because we were a bad idea as a couple didn't mean we couldn't raise our kid together." And now things were getting a little too personal for comfort. *Time to move on.* Lennox pulled out the central station of the security unit.

"This is your system's brain. It communicates with the entry sensors and motion detectors and sounds a physical alarm while sending a distress signal to Castillion. It's best set in a central location where it can be plugged in, but it's got batteries as a backup in case you lose power." He held it up. "Where would you like it?"

Elliot turned and surveyed his living room. "How about right under Cary Grant?" He chuckled. "Which is where we'd all like to be, honestly."

Lennox did his best to keep his voice even as he set up the small black tower. "Does your boyfriend know you're side-eyeing Cary Grant when he's not around?"

"If I had a boyfriend, he would certainly be made to understand that in the pantheon of history's fascinating men, Cary Grant is nearly impossible to surpass. He was a stilt walker in his teens, you know. He ran away from Jolly Old England to Hollywood and never looked back."

Elliot sounded faintly jealous. It was none of Lennox's business, but . . . "Are you thinking of taking a second career as a stilt walker?"

"Oh, hell no. I'm not crazy about heights, although," he added slyly, "I do happen to be a big fan of exposure. But no, no stilts for me. I'm already on my second career; I think one successful reinvention per lifetime is about all most of us can hope for."

He seemed a little embarrassed. Lennox could relate. In the months between his discharge from the Army and finding work with Castillion, he'd struggled to make sense out of his life. Honestly, he hadn't been able to understand why he still deserved one. Oliver had done his best to help, but Lennox hadn't been able to hear him. The only good thing to come out of that period was the realization he truly wanted to live, even if it meant bearing so much guilt it nearly debilitated him at times. Lennox still wasn't sure if what he was doing with himself was the best thing, but it was enough to keep a roof over his head and let him help support his daughter. That was all he could ask.

"Mr. West?"

"Hmm?" Lennox was jerked out of his introspection by Elliot's question. "Yeah?"

"Are you waiting for something else to happen here? Because the light is green, and the machine isn't buzzing or telling us 'I'm sorry, Dave, I'm afraid I can't do that.'"

Lennox shook his head. "Sorry, I got distracted. Let's do the doors next, I'll show you how." He stood up, and Elliot nodded as they walked back to the table. "And you should call me Lennox, I think." He barely remembered to respond to his last name without *Sergeant* attached to it.

Elliot's face brightened. "I thought that was solely for family and friends!"

"What can I say?" Lennox gestured at Holly, who had calmed down enough to stop barking but was still standing right beside his feet, gazing up with an expression of canine wonderment on her little face. "Your dog makes a convincing argument for trusting you."

"Holly would have been a great dog for me when I was a lawyer. Cuteness is a sound strategy at the negotiating table," Elliot teased. "I wish she worked this magic on everyone I met. My business would be twice as big."

"You'd have to get Serena her own personal assistant." Lennox handed Elliot a sensor. "I'll show you how to do this on the front door and then you can do the back."

"No need, it seems pretty self-explanatory to me." Elliot looked over the two-part sensor. "They can be, what, as much as an inch apart without triggering the alarm?"

"Two inches."

"And the backs are self-adhesive. No drills required? I'm feeling a bit let down." He pouted. "How can I impress you with my DIY skills if I don't get to pull out my drill? I have a versatile drill."

Lennox stared at Elliot for a moment, trying to wrap his head around the man's latest declaration. "I can't tell if that's innuendo or serious."

"I never joke about my power tools," Elliot said soberly. He held on to his laughter for a few more seconds before saying, "Although there's a first time for everything. My drill may be off-limits, but I'm happy to tell you about my hammer. And in this metaphor," he leaned in and murmured, "the hammer is my penis." He waited for a moment while Lennox stared at him. "No? Not a fan of *Dr. Horrible's Sing-Along Blog*? Or maybe you're just very straight and very polite simultaneously. That's a shame."

Lennox couldn't help himself. He started to laugh. He actually had to shut his eyes for a moment; it felt so wonderfully ridiculous. He probably should be self-conscious about it, or at least apologize for laughing at Elliot, but the man was laughing along with him.

"I don't understand more than every other word out of your mouth," Lennox said once he'd gotten a handle on himself. "But no, I'm not usually very polite, and sorry, no power tools needed." He gently pushed Elliot's shoulder, mindful to only touch the left one, the one Elliot hadn't been favoring the other day. "Get to sticking."

"I notice you didn't have anything to add about the straight part," Elliot said as he walked backward toward the kitchen door, keeping his gaze on Lennox.

"Maybe I'm still reeling from your use of metaphor," Lennox suggested as he headed to the front. How long had it been since he'd felt this comfortable with another person? Not just like they could talk together, but like they were someone he could actually have fun with, banter with, without fear of judgment? Not at work, where he was friendly but not close with his colleagues. Not with Gaby and her family, whom he loved but couldn't afford to be himself around. Could it have been before Oliver, when he had been too numb to care what anyone said about him? Maybe even longer, not since he'd had a whole and healthy squad in Kabul.

"Let me know if you're going to faint, and I'll try to catch you," Elliot called out. "Okay, it's on. What next?"

"Same thing, only on the windows," Lennox said.

Between the two of them, it took less than an hour to get the entire house hooked up with entry sensors, motion detectors, and a few extra perks that Lennox threw in for free. Elliot had a quip every time they passed each other, and skillfully sidetracked Lennox's inquiries about how many notes had been left, how often, and when it had all started. In turn Lennox managed to keep most of his personal life to himself, although Elliot was able to tease a few details out of him that he'd had no intention of revealing. Like the fact that he was a cat person.

"How is that possible?" Elliot demanded. "Cats are cruel, vicious killing machines with no remorse and a finely honed ability to bullshit you into doing whatever they want. My sister has cats, and they're the devil. Dogs are affectionate, interactive, cuddly—how can you not be a dog person?"

"Too high maintenance." Though Lennox had to admit that Holly was about as sweet as a dog could be. She was sitting on his lap right now, while Lennox and Elliot were sitting together at the dining room table going over the user agreement. "And my mom was allergic, so I never had them growing up."

"Was your mom a do-the-housework-in-her-pearls kind of lady?" Elliot asked as he signed the last page of the contract.

Lennox shook his head. "Wrong decade. And pearls were never her thing anyway. Try flower crowns and Mardi Gras beads."

Elliot stared at him for a moment before firmly shaking his head. "No. No way."

Lennox was probably more gleeful than he should be. "Yep."

"Your mother was *not* a hippie."

"She was, and is, an antiwar, free-loving, pot-smoking, artist hippie. We lived in a commune in California for most of my childhood." That had lasted for a decade, until his grandmother got sick. At that point they'd moved in with her in New Orleans, and his mother had gotten a job as an elementary school art teacher.

Elliot cradled his chin on one hand. "I don't quite get how *you* emerged from that background, Mr. Army-Ranger-Security-Man-Who-Carries-a-Knife-at-All-Times."

And a gun too, but Lennox thought better of adding that if Elliot hadn't noticed it. "What can I say? I'm an enigma." He glanced at his watch and stifled a curse. He'd spent almost as much time talking as he had installing the damn alarm system. If he wasn't careful, he'd be late picking up Lee. "I've got to get going."

"If you must." Elliot smiled his bright smile. "Unless there's something I can do to tempt you into staying?"

Shit, just *being* with him was more temptation than Lennox had counted on. Maybe if Elliot wasn't Serena's boss, maybe if he knew him better, maybe if he didn't have a date with Lee . . . but none of those things were true. "I can't."

"Then I'll see you off." Elliot stood up and shook Lennox's hand. "Thanks for fixing me up with this. I'm sure it will do a world of good for Serena's peace of mind."

"I hope it does that for you too." Lennox barely managed to stifle the protective urge that rose in him to push a little harder, to find out what Elliot was worried about. He handed over his card. "Call me if there are any problems with the system."

Elliot's eyes sparkled. "Oh, I certainly will."

Lennox would bet money that by the end of the weekend one of the sensors would be malfunctioning. He couldn't quite bring himself to mind. "Good."

His last word to Elliot would have made for a decent exit, if his truck had bothered to start. Lennox got it going, but almost instantly the engine stopped again, the rough grind of it giving way to a choked mechanical cough before it died altogether.

"Shit," he muttered, staring blankly at the dash. His clock read five thirty. He tried the engine again. Same thing. "Fucking *shit*."

By now Elliot had left his place on the porch and sauntered over to Lennox's door, a little frown on his face. "That doesn't sound good," he said.

"No kidding."

"Open up the hood."

Lennox grimaced, his knuckles going white as he tightened his grip on the wheel cover. "I don't have time for this right now."

"You have plenty of time, since you're not going anywhere in a car that won't start," Elliot said. "Let me take a look."

Lennox popped the hood and got out of the car, feeling more than a little useless as Elliot propped it up and started checking various parts of the engine. "It's dying when you try to start it?" Elliot asked as he inspected the spark plugs.

"It wasn't before now," Lennox said, then felt like an idiot for it. This wasn't Elliot's fault. "It was rough, but still worked. It hasn't been smooth at any speed for a while, though."

"Hmm. You could have a fuel pump problem."

That couldn't be good. "Fuck."

"Try it again?"

Lennox got back in and turned the key. The car started, but died before ten seconds had passed. A third try yielded the same result.

"Probably the pump, but that's not a quick fix," Elliot said at last, letting the hood slam back into place. "Should we call you a tow truck?"

Lennox checked his watch, then pressed his fingers into his eyes hard enough to send sparks flaring across the black of his lids. "I don't have time for a fucking tow; I'm going to be late as it is. I'm sorry," he added, because he really was. "I don't mean to be an asshole about this, but things are a little unsteady with me and Lee, and the last thing I need is to run late on her."

"Better late than not at all," Elliot pointed out.

"Yeah, but I've got no option other than a cab since I can't use the motorcycle," Lennox said. "Gaby would let me borrow her car, but she'll already be at her kickboxing class, and Lee's stepfather is traveling." A cab would be expensive, especially since he now had car repairs coming on top of everything else, but . . . "Shit. All right." He took out his phone and started searching for cab companies. "I'm sorry to have to ask, but can I leave this here for a while?" He glanced up. "I swear I'll come back tonight and get it towed away."

Elliot frowned. Why the hell didn't that expression make him any less attractive? "No, this is silly."

Lennox resisted the urge to start shouting. "Look, I apologize for the inconvenience, but—"

"No, I mean that you're actually considering getting a cab for your evening out with your daughter is silly. I've got a car—let me drive you."

Lennox wasn't quite sure he was hearing this right. "Excuse me?"

"Let me drive you," Elliot repeated calmly. "The Porsche seems small inside but it seats four. I can take you to pick her up, drop you at a restaurant, and you can call me when you need to move on to the next stop."

It was too much. "Elliot, I'm not going to ask you to be my chauffeur for the night."

He shrugged. "You're not asking; I'm offering. And there's plenty that I can get done downtown while you and Lee enjoy yourselves. I'd let you take the car if you promised to return it with a full tank, but—"

"No, Jesus no," Lennox broke in. Elliot looked a little offended, and he raced to explain himself. "I mean no, you can't just let me take your Porsche. You don't even know me—of course you can't do that."

"I know you enough." Elliot's smile was back now. "And we both know Serena. I think she's as good an insurance policy as anyone could ever ask."

It was a bad idea. It was a ridiculous idea, letting someone Lennox barely knew drive him to pick up his kid and haul them around, but he was already going to be late. He'd just have to accept being an inconvenience and hope that Lee was okay with the slight change in plans. And that her mother never found out.

"Okay."

Excerpt from *Shockwave*'s article:

If there's one thing I can tell you about McKenzie, it's that the closest he gets to true genuineness in our interview is when he's talking about the woman who supposedly set him on his path, Wilhelmina VanAllen. Mentioning her name brings an animation to everything he does, and when he dubs her his muse, I have to believe him.

It probably helps that he lives in the home she left to him, along with the dog she used to own. They knew each other for two weeks, just fourteen days. In that short time she changed his entire future, and he endeared himself enough to her to inherit her personal home ahead of her family members. Was it love at first sight? A closeness born of shared circumstances and life experience? Or is Elliot McKenzie really that good at convincing people to follow his lead?

Five minutes into the drive it became clear that the only person Elliot was going to have to worry about having a good time was himself, because Lennox was completely enthralled—as he should be—with the Porsche. That he wasn't a car person was obvious, since he'd been ready to throw in the towel instantly when his truck failed to start, but he could evidently appreciate something beautiful. Elliot watched Lennox's long fingers run over the creamy leather of the seat and the sleek dash, then swallowed and dragged his eyes back front and center. He had a place to be, and an opportunity along with it.

He'd been curious about Lee ever since Serena's extended family had moved here. Serena had done an actual dance of glee when she found out they were coming, bouncing in place so hard that Elliot had wondered if she was going to fall out of her heels. Lee was Serena's only niece, and as a consequence, she was a frequent topic of conversation during the slow times at work.

All of that meant Elliot had a better than normal chance to make a good first impression with this kid, and he really wanted to pull it off. It would make Serena happy, and it might lift him a little higher in Lennox's esteem, which would be . . . nice. Very nice.

Elliot was sure at this point that Lennox batted for both teams. No completely straight guy would have let him get away with flirting like that. He had been prepared to reel it in as soon as Lennox told him to back off, or even looked vaguely uncomfortable, but he'd kept playing along. Hell, Lennox hadn't objected to the most ridiculous and blatant pop-culture references Elliot had been able to muster on short notice. You didn't have to know anything about *Dr. Horrible's Sing-Along Blog* to understand the line about penises—the innuendo spoke for itself. That was part of its allure.

Did he want to start something with Lennox West? Elliot didn't know. He certainly wouldn't say no to a very athletic night in bed together, but beyond that . . . well, Elliot didn't deal in anything more permanent than a single tryst nowadays.

So why was he *really* playing chauffeur now? Elliot brushed the question off and focused on the present. Namely, making sure he was still heading in the right direction. "It's the next turn?"

"Yeah, and then the first left after that," Lennox said, leaning back against the headrest and flexing his fingers. "Third house on the left in the cul-de-sac. Look for the basketball hoop in the driveway."

Elliot turned smoothly, enjoying the feel of so much power under his hands. Serena might tease him about his love affair with his car, but Elliot thought it suited him. Slick, fast, and lovely: clearly the Porsche was his soul mate. "Where are you two doing dinner?"

"Wherever Lee picks out." Lennox's phone rang at that moment. "Speak of the devil . . ." He took the call. "Hey, sweetheart."

Her reply was faint but audible to Elliot. "You're fifteen minutes late, Dad!"

"I know, I had some car trouble, but I'm literally ten seconds from you now," Lennox said as Elliot made the second left and slowed down. "You see me?"

"No . . . Wait, are you in the Bond car?"

"Bond car, I like that," Elliot murmured, and Lennox cast him a little smile before answering Lee. That sly smile dug under Elliot's skin and lodged against his breastbone, just deep enough to get him revved up. Bastard. He had no fucking idea.

Lennox put his phone away and unbuckled as the car came to a stop in the driveway. A purple-haired kid wearing black tights and a blue sweatshirt walked off the porch, her eyes wide as she took in the car. When she hugged her father, Elliot caught sight of the stylized raven holding a wand in its beak on the back of the hoodie, and he grinned. It was the perfect icebreaker.

"What happened to your truck?" Lee asked as Elliot got out of the car.

"It broke down on my last call of the day. Mr. McKenzie offered to give me a ride to come get you."

Lee stared at her dad like he was terribly slow. "But Mom's not here. There's no other car for us to use."

"Elliot's going to drive us to dinner too."

"Elliot?" Lee turned to him, her expression changing to an odd blend of wariness and excitement. "Are you the Elliot who's my Aunt Serena's boss?"

"That's me," he affirmed, leaning on the hood of the car. "And I've got to say, I love your style, although I've always thought I'd be sorted into Slytherin."

Her eyes went wider. "You've seen the movies?"

"Oh yes. I've even read the books. Snape is my hero."

"Snape is my hero too!" Lee said enthusiastically.

Lennox looked between them like he had no idea what they were talking about, which, to be fair, was probably right on. "What's Slytherin?"

Lee sighed heavily. "Oh my God, Dad, you watched the first Harry Potter movie with me. How can you not remember?" She stuck her hands in her pockets and stepped a little closer to the car. "You're eating dinner with us, right?" she asked Elliot.

Now it was Lennox's turn to sigh. Elliot wondered if either of them realized how alike they were. "Manners, Lee. I know for a fact you weren't raised in a barn. You can't force the man to eat with us."

"I'm not *forcing* him. I'm *asking* if you asked him to dinner too."

"I don't want to interrupt your plans," Elliot broke in smoothly. "Just tell me where to drop you off and I'll be happy to oblige."

"You wouldn't be interrupting," Lee insisted. "It would be fun. I want to know more about Aunt Serena's job. It sounds so cool, but Mom doesn't like me to talk to her about it." She was clearly bursting at the seams to explain *why* her mother had forbidden Serena's work as a topic of conversation, but Elliot already knew. He was, after all, very aware of his own reputation.

"Lee—"

"Dad, come on!" They stared each other down silently, and Elliot held his breath. Finally Lennox turned to him.

"We'd love to have you join us for dinner," he said, the invitation flowing off his tongue like music to Elliot's ears, "but please don't feel obliged."

"I'd be happy to join you," Elliot replied. "As long as neither of you mind."

"I don't!" Lee chimed in victoriously.

"Not at all," Lennox said, shaking his head a little ruefully. "The least I can do is feed you after hijacking your car for the night."

"I completely agree," Elliot said airily. "It'll be nothing but steak au poivre and champagne for me this evening."

"What's steak au poivre?" Lee asked.

"Oh, it's delicious," Elliot promised her. "You'll love it."

Apparently his recommendation was enough to sway her to his side, and ten minutes later they were sitting in a booth at a steak house. Lee and Lennox took up one half, leaving Elliot on his own. That was fine. He could fill any space he found himself in.

They ordered dinner and got their drinks—iced tea instead of champagne, sadly, since he was driving and Lennox seemed like the type to be anal about combining cars and even a small amount of alcohol—and then Elliot made the first move. "It's nice to finally put a face to a name, Lee. Your Aunt Serena talks about you all the time."

Lee brightened. "Really?"

"Oh, absolutely. She always talks about how wonderful you are at everything you set your mind to. It's enough to make a person worry for their own ego."

"Surely not you," Lennox said, before taking a drink of his own iced tea. Elliot refused to let himself get distracted by how the man's lips wrapped around a straw.

"My ego is very healthy," Elliot agreed instead, "but I can't put things together the way Lee can, apparently. Serena says you're great at puzzles."

"And word games," she said. No false modesty there. "And chess."

Lennox seemed a little stunned as he turned to her. "Since when do you play chess?"

"Since Marcus taught me when I was eight? And I've been kicking his ass at it ever since I was nine. You *know* this, Dad. I've told you, like, twenty times."

Hmm, a brewing argument. Elliot wondered if he should intervene, but Lennox beat him to the mark. "I've been hit in the head too often to keep it in there, I guess. And watch your language, kid."

"Learn to duck, old man," she teased him, and just like that they were back on an even keel. Elliot was impressed. He'd done his best as a child, first with his parents and then with his siblings, to keep the infighting between them all to an absolute minimum. He'd failed more often than not.

"A boxing dad, a kickboxing mom . . . Lee, are you secretly a ninja?" *Like your dad was at your age*, he wanted to add but didn't. It wasn't his story to tell if she didn't know.

"I wish," Lee almost moaned. "A ninja would almost be as good as a wizard, but Mom still wants me to go back to ballet."

Lennox frowned. "You hated ballet."

"I *know*! It hurt my feet and the only show I ever got to be in was the stupid *Nutcracker*. Every year, the *Nutcracker*." She leaned her cheek on her fist and sighed gustily. "Mom wants me to try out for the Colorado Ballet, and she won't take no for an answer. She says I need extracurriculars." The sheer disgust on her face spoke volumes about what she thought of that. "I asked if I could do circus arts instead and she said no."

"What, like a clown?"

Lee wrinkled her nose. "No, like trapeze, Dad."

Lennox frowned. "Your mom might have a point. I'm not sure how I feel about you going up on a trapeze."

"It's only a low trapeze to start with, though!"

"I dated a clown once," Elliot broke in. Both of the Wests stared at him, and he grinned. "He was a busker on the Sixteenth Street Mall who could juggle knives and clubs and flaming torches all while balanced on an eight-foot-tall unicycle. The guy wasn't much of a conversationalist, but—" Elliot cut off his normal digression into *boy was he good at multitasking, if you know what I mean* and finished with, "but I learned a few fun things."

"Really?" Lee seemed intrigued. "Did he teach you how to juggle?"

"Only balls," Elliot said, because there was a genuine limit to how innuendo-free he could be in one evening, and he'd apparently hit it. He managed an innocent look for Lennox when the man raised an eyebrow. "You know, the soft ones. Like hacky sacks."

It all went right over Lee's head, thank god. "I tried to learn to do that, but I wasn't very good at it. There's a boy at my school who can juggle knives! He goes to the circus-arts place too, only once he was juggling barefoot out in front of school and he missed one of the knives and it went straight down into his foot. He wouldn't let us call the nurse for him. He just walked himself to her office and left bloody footprints all over the place. It was gross," she said admiringly.

"Jesus Christ." Lennox rubbed his forehead. "Promise me you won't start trying to juggle knives without me there to help you out, okay?"

Lee looked skeptically at him. "How would you help, Dad?"

"I'd stand off to the side and tell you not to do it, that's how."

"Dad!" She punched him in the shoulder; maybe it was a familial trait, this affectionate violence.

Lennox laughed and lifted his hands in surrender. "I'm kidding! I'd show you how to do other, much cooler things with knives."

"Like what, throwing them?" Elliot asked.

"Exactly."

That was *not* the answer he'd been expecting, given they were talking about what was and wasn't appropriate to teach a thirteen-year-old. "What, really?" he asked once he'd picked up his jaw.

"Well, not pocket knives, but throwing knives, yeah." Lennox shrugged. "That's what they're for."

"Dad knows all sorts of cool things," Lee said, not a minute after she'd appeared convinced that her father could do nothing cool. "I think he'd probably be a Gryffindor, since he was in the Army and now he's kind of like an Auror. He'd totally ace Defense Against the Dark Arts."

"I could see that," Elliot agreed. "Although I think there's maybe some Hufflepuff in him too."

"Seriously, what are you two talking about?" Lennox half demanded, half pleaded. Lee took pity on her father and started to explain the many twists and turns of the Harry Potter series to him, a conversation that lasted through the bread and salad courses.

"And then there's the new movie, which is so, so good." Lee looked at Elliot expectantly, and he winced.

"I'm afraid I haven't caught up on the new stuff," he said apologetically. "I just don't have time for it the way I did for the first series."

"But it's all about the fantastic beasts! It's so good!" Lee seemed boggled at this breakdown in Elliot's Potter cred.

"I know, I'm missing out," Elliot said with a sigh. "But I've been a lot busier lately." *Much busier than when I was in rehab and the Harry Potter series was the only set of DVDs in the place.* "I'll have to catch up on it."

"You should make Dad watch the original films with you, and then we can catch up on the new stuff together," she advised.

"Ah." Elliot's usually quick tongue stumbled over nothing. Apparently they'd jumped from "friendly dinner out" to "Netflix and chill" in the blink of an eye. "Um."

Lennox gently tugged on her longer hair. "What's next here, huh? Red? Pink? Polka dots?"

Lee rolled her eyes but let her father get away with changing the subject. "Polka dots would be awesome, but I like the purple for now."

Dinner took long enough that in the end, Lennox vetoed the idea of a movie even though it wasn't a school night because "Elliot's already gone out of his way for us, sweetheart, I don't want to keep him up until midnight."

"Because then my car turns into a pumpkin," Elliot added, and Lee laughed. The more engaged she'd become, the more relaxed her father had been. It had been nice to see the lines of tension in Lennox's angular face lighten when his daughter laughed. He liked being the one to make him relax. Elliot's college pranks had proven to be a gold mine of dubious life choices with hilarious results, and he was always ready to sacrifice his dignity on the altar of self-interest if it meant those dark eyes following his every move like they couldn't bear to look away.

"Fine," Lee capitulated at last. "But next time we're gonna watch *Hamlet*. The *good* version, and you don't get to say anything or make any comments about it, okay?"

"*Hamlet*?" That seemed a strange choice for a thirteen-year-old. "You're a Shakespeare fan?"

Lee nodded enthusiastically. "I'm named for Shakespeare!"

"Oh really? Is Lee somehow short for William?"

"Oh my God." She clunked her head down on her dad's shoulder. "It's short for *Ophelia*, Elliot. *Obviously*."

Lennox held his hands up when Elliot turned a questioning look on him. "Hey, it was her mom's choice, not mine. I voted for Jenny."

Lee rolled her eyes. "Jenny is so boring, Dad."

"Jenny is a cute name."

"I want to be memorable, not cute," she protested, and just about won Elliot's heart right there.

"Good idea," he agreed. "Although I recommend you avoid Danish princes if you can help it."

"I don't need a prince," Lee informed him loftily, making Lennox laugh again. "And Dad got to pick my middle name, so it all turned out fair."

"Ophelia Jenny, huh?"

"Nope." She held on to her answer for a moment, like she was savoring it. "It's . . . Ophelia Sky!"

Now he was even more surprised. "Your middle name is Sky?"

"Uh-huh," she said smugly. "Just like my dad."

Lennox was blushing. He was actually blushing. Elliot loved it. "Your mom really is a hippie, isn't she?"

"I told you that."

"Yes, but I didn't know you were Lennox *Sky* West. That's hard evidence, my friend."

"It's Dad's secret from his Army friends," Lee said. "He tells them all that the *S* stands for Sam."

"You should own it," Elliot advised. "It breaks down stereotypes, knowing that a guy like you is named Sky and isn't ashamed. You can be a badass and a hippie child at the same time."

Lee stared at him with a broad smile on her heart-shaped face. "You totally remind me of Uncle Oliver." Lennox stiffened, but his daughter charged on obliviously. "He calls dad Sky sometimes, when he's trying to be cutesy. It's kind of adorable."

"I didn't know Serena had a brother in addition to her sisters."

"Oh, he's not an uncle like that. He's Dad's best friend. They've known each other *forever*, but he travels a lot so we don't get to see him very much."

Elliot managed to keep any sign of his intense surge of discomfort down to a single blink. "A best friend, huh?" *Is that what kids are calling it these days?*

"Aaand I think we're done here," Lennox said as he stood up. He had already handled the bill, insisting it was the least he could do when he'd basically dragged Elliot out with them. "Text your mom and let her know we're on our way."

It was a good thing the drive back wasn't long, because Elliot wasn't feeling loquacious anymore and Lee spent all her time texting. He pulled to a stop outside the house and saw a familiar woman exit the front door. *Oh please, don't let her come down here to talk.* The last thing he wanted to do tonight was be introduced to Serena's perennially disapproving sister. Fortunately she just gave Lennox a quick hug, then escorted her daughter into the house.

The ride back to his own house was unfortunately longer, but neither of them seemed inclined to tackle the silence, although Lennox kept glancing over like he was trying to read Elliot's mind. Well, too bad. Lennox could figure it out by extrapolation, which was apparently what he expected everyone else to do when it came to him.

Anyway, it wasn't like Elliot had already asked Lennox out. They'd flirted a bit. That was the sum total of their interaction. And Elliot didn't want anything more. He wasn't really interested in taking Lennox to bed. He could handle a bit of disappointment. He could.

So the man was spoken for, so he flirted like a cheeky fucker, who cared? *I don't need to be around another person I can't trust.*

Getting back to his place was a relief. Elliot shut off the engine and got out of the car. Lennox followed. "I know it's late but I'm pretty sure there are still some tow places that—"

"I'm not dating Oliver." The words sounded like they'd been forced out of Lennox's mouth, but he was staring straight at Elliot, serious and earnest all at once. "Not anymore."

Ah-hah. "But you used to?"

"Until recently, yeah."

Elliot was more than a little shocked. "Are you saying you had a boyfriend while you were in the Army?"

Lennox winced slightly. "Not so much a boyfriend as a . . . friend with benefits? That's not why Lee calls him her uncle, though. Oliver and I have known each other since high school. He's always been part of her life."

"That's much more cosmopolitan of you than I was expecting," Elliot admitted. It was heartening too—the flirting hadn't been a rude move on either of their parts. And now that he had confirmation that Lennox was as open to being with a man as Elliot had hoped he was . . . "You know, you could hold off on calling a tow, if you'd like." He smiled slowly: it was his bedroom smile, calculated for maximum effectiveness.

It was too dark to see if Lennox's eyes dilated, but Elliot heard him swallow. "Are you sure about that?" Lennox's voice was still composed, but huskier than it had been a second ago. "I don't want to impose."

"I wouldn't ask you to stay if I wasn't sure I wanted you here."

Lennox paused for a moment, and then said, "Fuck, I'm so out of practice at this. Just to be clear: you're not talking about putting me on a couch, right?"

Elliot laughed. It broke the tension he'd been trying to build, but he had to. "No, no couches, unless," he added slyly, "you really like the thought of bending over one. I'd much rather do you in a bed, though."

"Mm-hmm." Now Lennox's voice had gone gravel-deep, and when he took Elliot's hand it was all Elliot could do not to shiver. It had been a long time since a hookup had affected him like this before they'd even gotten undressed, and Elliot was enjoying every moment of it. He let Lennox tug him a bit closer as the man said, "And what makes you think you're gonna be doing *me* in that bed, huh?"

"Just throwing it out there." Elliot resisted the urge to clear his throat. Lennox pulled a little harder, until their bodies bumped softly together. It might be dark, but there was no hiding Elliot's arousal when they were this close. He didn't want to hide it, not when it meant he got to hear that sudden, gratifying inhale from Lennox. "We can do whatever you want," he murmured, bringing his free hand up to Lennox's neck. They were so near to the same height that it was easy to brush their lips in a kiss as he guided Lennox's hand to rest on his lower back in a not-so-subtle hint. Lennox obliged and drew Elliot in tighter.

"Whatever I want?" Lennox almost purred, and Elliot was glad Lennox was holding on to him because he wouldn't bet on his own legs doing a good job of keeping him up right now. "You sure about that?"

That was promising. "Why, what did you have in mind?"

"I'm thinking . . . I'd like to suck you until you scream," Lennox said, and yeah, that was it for the knees. Elliot leaned harder against Lennox, sliding one hand up into his hair as he held on tight. "And then, if you manage to keep from coming for long enough, I might let you fuck me in your bed."

Holy shit. Elliot had to shut his eyes and bite his own lip for a second, just to regain a sense of control. "Sounds like a plan," he said at last, and his voice barely wavered. Barely, but it still did, and Lennox clearly heard it. He leaned in close and pressed his nose against Elliot's cheek. It was cold, but it wasn't the temperature that made Elliot shiver suddenly.

"Lead the way, then."

Elliot pulled back far enough to turn away, but kept a grip on Lennox's hand, dragging him impatiently up the porch stairs. He unlocked the front door and stepped inside, then punched the code into his keypad before his new alarm system dubbed him an intruder. Holly was at his feet in a flash, bouncing urgently back and forth, and he cursed under his breath. "I have to take her for a quick walk," he said. "Otherwise she might explode."

"That wouldn't be a good thing," Lennox agreed. "I can wait here for you."

"No, no, go on upstairs." He couldn't quite believe he was sending Lennox into his bedroom alone, but balked at the thought of leaving him standing in the foyer or making him go back out into the cold. "It's the second door on the right. There's an en suite bathroom as well, if you need it."

"I'll try not to get lost." Lennox laid his hand on Elliot's chest, fingers slipping possessively into his shirt pocket and giving it a little tug. The heat was a brand even through his clothes. "Go, before she really does explode."

"Yes. Right." He headed for the back door.

It was a quiet night, the stillness broken only once by the hum of a passing car. It sounded like it was going slowly; the driver was probably lost. Elliot waited impatiently for Holly to sniff every bush, mark every tree and solicit affection every five feet before she was ready to go back inside. "You're so demanding," he informed her as he hoisted her into his arms and returned through the kitchen. "Honestly, I don't know why I put up with you." She licked his nose, and he smiled, then set her down and walked over to the stairs, butterflies unsettling his stomach.

It wasn't the first time Elliot had had someone to his place for a fuck, but it was the first time he hadn't picked that person up in a bar. He never invited people over that he actually knew. There was living a genuine life and then there was opening yourself up unnecessarily to pain, and Elliot liked avoiding pain. He didn't mix the men he took to bed with the people he knew professionally, but this . . .

They didn't really *know* each other, after all. Lennox had done a job, and Elliot had helped him out of a tight spot. So they'd screw and go their separate ways. It was good. It was all good. Besides, Lennox was in his room right now; too late to be having second thoughts.

Pleased with his mental logic, Elliot went upstairs and into his room. "I hope you didn't get started without . . ." His voice trailed off as he took in the goddamn *display* Lennox was making of the room's picture window. His shirt was off, belt gone, feet bare against the Turkish rug that covered the hardwood floor. The only light in the room was moonlight, and it had turned Lennox's lean, muscular body into a dark silhouette edged with silver. Elliot wanted to trace him with his tongue.

"You don't play fair," he said once he'd picked his jaw up off the floor.

"Who says I'm playing at anything?" Lennox said, fingering the metal zipper of his jeans. "Maybe I always undress this slowly."

I wish. "Keep this up and I'll be blowing you instead."

Lennox's teeth gleamed as he smiled. "As nice as that sounds, I think we'll stick with my plan. Come here."

Elliot went, only pausing long enough to kick his shoes into the corner. They were way too expensive to be treated so casually, but he couldn't bring himself to care about Italian leather right now. As soon as Elliot was within reach, Lennox grabbed his pocket again, only this time he jerked him forward with it, hard enough that Elliot skipped the last foot, collided with Lennox, and rocked him back onto his heels. Elliot's arms wrapped around Lennox's neck as Lennox pressed their hips together, but there was no chance for conversation this time.

Before Elliot could take another breath, his mouth had been claimed in a kiss, hot and slick and coaxing his lips open. This was no perfunctory kiss to warm him up before moving on to something better; this kiss was an event in and of itself, less of a warm-up and more of a bonfire. Stubble rasped against his own still-smooth skin and Elliot groaned at the feel of it.

He tried to hold on to a bit of his reserve, tried to hold a little of himself back so he could figure out his next move. Elliot prided himself on being a thorough lover, even if he never bothered with repeat visits. He satisfied people and then he satisfied himself, not the other way around. Lennox wouldn't let him pull back, though, and didn't seem interested in speeding up or moving on.

This was how he wanted it, then. That was an easy thing to indulge, and took some of the pressure off Elliot. He broke away just long enough to grin when Lennox's hands shifted from where they'd been cupping his ass to tackle the buttons on his shirt. "Multitasker," he muttered before diving back into the kiss.

"Nice to be appreciated," Lennox said. He moved his mouth to Elliot's neck while he tugged his unbuttoned shirt out of his pants.

"Mm, no marks, I have a lot of meetings I have to be pretty for." It was impressive that he was still able to speak coherently while he was losing his clothes and getting what was the start of a fabulous hickey in the crook of his neck. He *wanted* that bruise, but he couldn't afford to have it right now.

"I bet Serena could cover it up for you," Lennox suggested with a chuckle, but he left the spot he'd been worrying with his teeth, hot and tender and tingling, alone.

"Yeah, but I'd rather not have to talk to her about why I have a— Oh *fuck*, oh fuck, shit, you—" Because his belt was undone and his pants were unzipped and Lennox's hand, wonderfully warm and rough, had wrapped around Elliot's dick and stroked him from his slick tip all the way down to the base. Elliot was thick, but Lennox had long fingers, blessedly long fingers, *holy shit*. They clamped around him like a vise and kept a slow, steady rhythm as Lennox swallowed Elliot's incoherent cries. The profanity he usually tried to forget rushed to the front of his brain, because it was deliciously fucking *filthy* for another man's hand to feel this good on him.

With a little help from Lennox, Elliot clawed his clothes off, trying not to move more than an inch or two from where he was grinding his dick into Lennox's hand. He went to return the favor, but only got as far as unzipping Lennox's fly before the other man walked him backward until his legs hit the bed. Elliot went down and Lennox let him go, which was disappointing before he crawled back on top of Elliot and dragged him further up the bed, a wicked glint in his eye that gave Elliot actual shivers.

"Perfect," he said before taking Elliot's mouth in another kiss, using his teeth this time, bruising and harsh and absolutely perfect as he pressed their bodies together. He rubbed the pad of his thumb against Elliot's nipple until Elliot honest-to-God *whined*, because this level of mastery over his reactions shouldn't be possible for a man he barely fucking knew.

"How?" Elliot demanded as Lennox released his mouth and started to kiss a path down his chest. He was still rubbing, scraping the sensitive bump with his nail every so often, and Elliot wanted to shy back and to press into it at the same time. He almost reached up to drag the hand away before Lennox abruptly shifted to the other side, making his toes curl. "How'd you know?"

"From the way you rubbed up against me, leading with the things you liked the most." Lennox's voice was smug as he pinched Elliot's nipple until Elliot gasped. "These."

"I like other things," Elliot protested, but it sounded uncertain to his ears. Fuck it, he didn't care; he was allowed to be overwhelmed under the circumstances.

"I hope so, considering what I'm about to do." The hand on his dick backed off, sliding down to tug at his balls. Elliot spread his legs wider and made room for Lennox to crouch between his thighs, then did his best to hold in his moans as Lennox licked the slick head of his cock. Lennox's touch stayed light just long enough for Elliot to catch his breath, and then Lennox went for it, hollowing his cheeks as he sucked straight down in one smooth motion.

"*Aaah*—ah, fuck," Elliot breathed, sliding his hands over Lennox's gorgeous shoulders and neck, finally sliding into the long, thick hair on top of his head. He did his best not to pull, but it was hard given how tight Lennox's lips were around his dick, how amazing his tongue felt as it licked a line up his shaft before curling around the head. Lennox went down again and again, fucking his own mouth with Elliot's dick as he tugged at Elliot's swollen nipple and tightening sac. He found the round divot in Elliot's side, the spot where the second bullet had ripped into him. The skin in the center was permanently numb, but the skin around it was hypersensitive. Lennox touched the scar more gently than he did anything else, almost reverently, and Elliot's entire abdomen clenched in reaction.

It shouldn't have been long enough for Elliot to come, but he was definitely going to come. "No, no." He pulled Lennox back until he released Elliot's flesh with a wet *pop*. "Fuck," he moaned. "You have to stop."

"You haven't screamed yet."

"But I *want* to, I'm *there*, fuck, I'm there." Any more there and he'd actually scream. "Much further and you'll be the one screaming because you'll have to wait for my refractory period to pass before I can fuck you."

Lennox chuckled from where he was crouching low on the bed. He sounded like the goddamn Devil. "Who says I need your dick to fuck me? You could always just use your hands."

"Oh my god, don't be mean, come here." Elliot drew Lennox up for another kiss, wrapping him up in his long legs and rutting up against his stomach. Elliot wasn't cut like Lennox but he liked to run, and now he was grateful for every mile that had made him stronger, made his grip a little more inexorable. He felt Lennox stop resisting, then sink his weight into the cradle of Elliot's legs, and finally relax.

"You want it," Elliot whispered, and this time it was Lennox who shuddered. Elliot grinned, a glow of satisfaction spreading with the knowledge that he was right, and better yet: he was desired. "You want to sink down on my cock and ride me like a goddamn wave."

"Maybe I'd prefer a bucking bronco," Lennox suggested, but Elliot shook his head. He had Lennox's number now.

"You like to hand it out rough but you're going to take me nice and slow, gonna let me fill you up and stretch you out until you have to remind your lungs to keep breathing," he said darkly, and holy shit, what had gotten into him? He usually wasn't much for dirty talk, but apparently tonight was breaking a lot of his normal sex conventions.

"Lots of talk, not so much doing," Lennox said, but his voice was ragged and his cock was so hard against Elliot's stomach it wouldn't be surprising if it left a bruise.

"I'll back it up." Elliot opened his legs and pushed Lennox away just enough to twist toward his bedside table and awkwardly get to the drawer. He found what he was reaching for after a moment and held them up. "Lube, condoms. Let's *do* this thing."

"You sound like a frat boy," Lennox said, but he was already kicking his jeans off of his feet.

"Fucked many frat boys, have you?"

"Only one, but he was enough for me to know the type."

The mysterious Oliver, most likely. Elliot pushed the thought away. Lennox might be a one-night stand, but by God, he was *Elliot's* to have right now and no one else's. "Come up here." He pulled until Lennox was straddling his chest, looking down at Elliot like he was something novel that he couldn't quite understand. *Good.* Elliot opened the bottle of lube and got his fingers wet. "I'm going to touch you now," he said calmly, "and you're going to fuck my mouth. Try not to come too soon."

"Are you always a cocky little—" Lennox stuttered and went silent as Elliot's finger circled his hole, stroking the tight muscle. Elliot didn't know how long it had been since Lennox had been fucked, but a gentle press of his finger got him easily inside.

"Have you had someone else in here lately?" Elliot asked, his voice husky as he thought about some anonymous dick plunging in and out of Lennox. Elliot wasn't usually possessive, especially not of one-night stands, but something about Lennox made him want to push. "Or have you been riding your own fingers? Maybe a toy or two, a dildo that scratches the itch when you've got to have that feeling of being stuffed? Or maybe you slick up a plug, stretch your pretty hole around it, and walk around your apartment that way, to ride the sensation longer."

Lennox moaned, and Elliot grinned triumphantly. "If you didn't before," he said, hovering his lips over Lennox's dripping cock, "you will now."

Then Elliot closed his lips over the head and went down on Lennox, taking him into his mouth at the same time he slid his finger as deep as it could go into Lennox's ass. He avoided his prostate, pumping his index finger slowly while he bobbed up and down on Lennox's cock. Despite his jokes, he didn't want Lennox to come too soon. His whole body ached with the thought of sinking his dick inside the man.

He got to two fingers comfortably and was about to add a third when Lennox pushed him away. "I'm good, I don't need more."

Elliot licked his lips. "Um." How did he say this with any hint of modesty? He didn't. "Look, you've sucked my dick already tonight. You know how wide I am. You're not stretched enough."

Lennox shrugged. "I like really feeling it go in."

Pain kink. Well, Elliot could work with that. "As long as we're not doing damage."

Lennox slid down Elliot's body until he could roll a condom onto Elliot's cock. "You're big," he said, "but you're not going to do any damage. Trust me."

"I do." It wasn't just a bedroom phrase; Elliot felt reassured by Lennox's calm statement, like he had from the moment Lennox had stepped inside his house earlier to set up the alarm system. It was a bizarre feeling to have for a stranger, this sense of trust, but he wasn't going to fight it. One night. It was only for a night.

Lennox stroked a lube-slick hand over the condom, then shuffled his knees forward a few inches and held Elliot's cock still as he began to lower his body onto it. His dark eyes squeezed shut and Elliot watched, utterly captivated, as Lennox slowly worked Elliot into him, bit by bit, tension reluctantly retreating as Lennox persisted until, finally, his ass was flush to Elliot's thighs.

"Fuck," Elliot said breathlessly. "You're something else."

"Motivated," Lennox said, his voice a little tense but utterly satisfied at the same time. "I'm motivated." He leaned forward, and Elliot couldn't stop himself from touching Lennox's abdomen. He reveled in the bunch and stretch of the muscles even as he let his hands drift closer to Lennox's cock.

Lennox shuddered and began to move, lifting up slightly before he sank back down. He was still tight, tight enough that the movement had to sting, but if he didn't mind, then Elliot wasn't going to bring it up. He had plenty of other things to talk about anyway.

"Do you want my hand?" he asked, scratching his fingertips through the wiry hair at the top of Lennox's groin. "You want me to jerk you off while you bounce on my cock?"

Lennox groaned, and a bead of pre-come appeared at the tip of his dick, sliding slowly down the crown. "Or do you even need that?" Elliot fought to keep his voice level as he thrust up, meeting Lennox's downward stroke in a rhythm that shouldn't have been so easy to find, hard and deep. "You could probably get off like this, couldn't you?"

"Prob'ly," Lennox admitted. Most of his tension was gone, replaced by amusement and hot, pleased desire. "But only because it's been a while."

Elliot chuckled, then groaned as Lennox suddenly clenched down on him, almost too tight for Elliot to thrust, before he relaxed. "I don't believe you," he gasped, determined to get the last word. "I think you've got a slutty streak a mile wide and you love this so much it wouldn't matter if you last got fucked a year or an hour ago, because you like working for it." Lennox started to go faster, and Elliot put his hands on the man's hips, holding him just hard enough to keep him from slipping off in his haste.

"You like having it dragged out of you kicking and screaming," Elliot said, more sure than ever as he rubbed his thumbs into the pockets of Lennox's hips, cut muscle and smooth skin slipping beneath his hands. "You like the fight, don't you?" He leaned up, biting his own lip to keep from coming because fuck, it was almost impossible to feel Lennox like this, to *look* at him, and not come. "You like the fight, but tonight I'm gonna be the winner." He moved one hand to Lennox's dick and stroked him quickly, his grip so tight it had to hurt.

Lennox's breath stuttered to a halt in his chest. His back arched and his head fell back, every muscle in his body clenching as he came, spilling across Elliot's hand and abs. It was more than Elliot could resist. His toes curled so hard they pulled the sheets free as he followed, filling the condom and crying out with bone-melting satisfaction.

Fuck, he thought as he tried to catch his breath, *you would think it had been months for me and not him*. He was shattered, gloriously twitchy, overstimulated, and utterly useless.

Warm hands and a warmer cloth on his stomach perked him up, and Elliot's eyes shot open. "What—"

"You seemed like you were enjoying the afterglow. I didn't want to interrupt," Lennox said with a smile that was only a little smug. He'd already disposed of the condom and cleaned himself up—Jesus, when had all that happened?

"Fuck." Elliot swiped a hand over his face. "I'm sorry, I'm usually way better than this when it comes to sex."

"If that's true, then you're courting an aneurysm every time you get off."

Elliot resisted the urge to smack Lennox's thigh. "Shut up, jerk."

Lennox laughed, and Elliot chuckled with him, slowly sitting and resting with his head on one bent knee for a moment. He couldn't remember the last time he'd laughed during sex. Usually it was a more focused affair, him working to get himself and his partner off before a night of uneasy sleep and a rapid morning-after that ended with no numbers exchanged and no promises to meet again.

"I still maintain that I won this round," Elliot tried. Lennox politely didn't scoff. He did argue, though.

"Seeing as how I was able to get up and move around while you were still practically unconscious, I'm thinking we should call this one a draw."

"You might have a point." Elliot reluctantly got to his feet. "Let me get you a toothbrush."

"Don't worry about it. I saw the spares on the bottom shelf." Lennox's smirk was back. "It looks like you buy them in bulk."

Elliot shrugged. "'Be prepared,' that's my motto." He headed into the bathroom and brushed his teeth, leaving Lennox to make himself comfortable under the covers. By the time Elliot returned, all that was visible of Lennox was the curve of one honey-colored shoulder and the back of his head against a pillow.

"Are you tired?" Elliot asked quietly as he settled onto his own side of the bed.

"After that? Definitely." There was something about the line of his mouth in the moonlight, though, something faintly deprecating that Elliot didn't understand. "Listen, you should know . . . I get nightmares. Bad ones, sometimes. I won't hurt you"—and shit, Elliot hadn't known that was a possibility—"but I might wake you up in the night. So I apologize in advance." He smiled, but it seemed a little grim. "You can always kick me to the couch if you need to. It wouldn't be the first time."

"If I need to I will." *But I hope I don't.* Elliot wanted Lennox to leave on a good note tomorrow, not contemplating an evening marred by things he couldn't help. His assurance seemed to satisfy Lennox, though, who nodded and closed his eyes. He fell asleep while Elliot watched, clearly more exhausted than even their vigorous sex could account for. *Maybe he had a long day.*

Or maybe his nightmares are more of a problem than he's letting on. It didn't matter. Either way, Elliot would give him a morning to remember once he woke up. It was the least he could do for such an unexpectedly entertaining evening.

CHAPTER SIX

Partial transcription of most recent appointment with West, Lennox, Staff Sergeant US Army Rangers (R), January 28, 3:12 p.m.:

LW: What do you expect me to say about my nightmares?

JS: I don't have any particular expectations, Lennox. You can tell me whatever you feel comfortable with. Keep in mind, though, that you can only get as much out of your therapy as you're willing to put in. Making progress in anything is hard work.

LW: I'm no stranger to hard work. That doesn't necessarily mean I want to let you analyze every thought or feeling that flies through my head though.

JS: And that's fine. But for a lot of people with PTSD, talk therapy is one avenue they use to discover coping methods for the challenges in their daily lives. Some of those challenges are severe, others are relatively minor. I'd like to help, whatever it is you're dealing with, and the only issue I know for certain about is your problem sleeping, so it seems like the logical place to start.

LW: Logical. Yeah. (Long pause.) Have you ever been in a position of authority over another person?

JS: I've been a supervisor for several graduate—

LW: No, I'm talking about holding a position of absolute authority. I'm talking about being the literal hand of God here, Doc, making life or death decisions.

JS: I can't say that I have.

LW: Well, I have. I made a bad decision, and now I make it over and over again every night.

ennox woke up from a dreamless sleep to something barking. It took a minute for him to get his bearings: he was in a bed that was twice as soft as his, in a room three times bigger than his own, and he was stark naked under the blankets. That was right; he'd hung around for a rather enthusiastic night at Elliot's, and judging from how relaxed he was, he'd slept soundly. He was alone now, though.

The front door opened and then slammed shut. "Fuck, fuck, *fuck*!" he heard Elliot chant loudly. The barking continued for another moment, then turned to distressed whimpers as the swearing tapered off. Lennox rolled out of bed and grabbed his jeans, not bothering with anything else as he pulled them on and hurried down the stairs.

Seated at the base of the front door, his knees drawn up and back pressed to the wood, was Elliot. He was whiter than the wall right beside him, and wasn't even looking at Holly, who had her front paws on his hip, her muzzle prodding anxiously at his side.

"Elliot?" Lennox took his hand off the pocket where he kept his pistol and knelt on the floor beside Elliot, lightly touching his shoulder. He was relieved when Elliot's gaze tracked over to Lennox's face. "Hey, you okay?"

Elliot's eyes were too wide, his expression too blank, but after a moment he managed a tiny smile. "I . . . Yes. I'm fine. I'm sorry, what a terrible way to wake up."

"I've had worse," Lennox said. "What's going on?"

"There's a . . ." Elliot swallowed hard. "There's a snake on my porch."

That didn't seem like too big a deal. Did Elliot have a phobia? Lennox opened his mouth, but Elliot cut him off. "Wait, I'm explaining this badly. Let me be more specific: there's *half* a snake on my porch."

Before Lennox could ask for clarification, because really, *What the hell?*, Elliot kept going. "It's stuffed inside a plastic bag. You know the ones that come with newspapers to keep the snow off of them? I don't get a paper delivered but some of my neighbors do. I thought it was a mistake, so I bent over to pick it up and Holly was barking and I didn't realize something was wrong until I tried to lift it and it was heavy. I looked inside and . . . there it was. Is. It's still there.

So I dropped it, grabbed Holly, and slammed the door shut." He pressed the heels of his hands into his eyes. "Fuck, I hate things like that. Dead things. Dead animals."

"Ah, wait, hang on." Lennox pulled Elliot's arms away from his face. "We need to clean these before you go touching yourself."

"Why?"

Lennox sighed. "Because there's blood on them."

Elliot stared down at his hands like he'd never seen them before, turning them this way and that and wincing when he saw the dark streaks around his fingertips. "It's cold," he murmured. "The blood. The snake was stiff, close to frozen. Shit, there's *blood* on my *fingers*."

Lennox might be no good at comforting, but he could recognize a panic attack in the making. "Come on, let's go to the kitchen. You could use a hot drink, and we can get you cleaned up."

"I'm fine," Elliot protested, shaking his head. "I don't think I can quite stand yet, but I'm fine. I need a minute or two here, though."

"You've had a minute or two already," Lennox said gently. "Are you sure you want to stay on the floor?"

"Yes. Just for a bit."

"Okay. I'll be right back." Lennox checked that Holly wasn't going to be able to reach Elliot's fingertips, then got up and headed for the kitchen. He added water to the Keurig, popped a pod in, and then let the coffee brew while he hunted down the sugar. It was how Elliot had taken his coffee last night after dinner: black and sweet, whereas Lennox doctored his own with as much cream as he could pour into it, the remnant of dealing with too many years of shitty canteen coffee.

He let the drink cool for a moment as he wet a dish towel near to scalding, then poured some soap onto one corner of it. His mouth twisted a little. Yesterday he'd done this to clean Elliot up after some of the best sex Lennox could remember; this morning he was doing it to clean blood off his lover's hands.

At least it isn't his blood. It wasn't a comforting thought, but Lennox would take what he could get.

He returned to Elliot with the coffee and the cloth. Elliot looked a little better: his legs had relaxed enough to stretch out to the end of the staircase, and his nose was wrinkled with disgust as he stared at his hands. "This is gross," he muttered. "So gross. I haven't touched a dead animal that wasn't food since the class guinea pig died at my house over Christmas break back in the fifth grade."

"Let me have them." Lennox took Elliot's hands and began rubbing them clean with brisk motions. Elliot let him, his demeanor surprisingly docile though his mouth didn't stop moving.

"It's strange. I can handle seeing my own blood, I wasn't alarmed by that even when I got *shot*, but if it comes from an animal?" He shuddered. "I loathe it, I really do."

"I can see that." Lennox wiped over Elliot's skin with the soap-free part of the dish towel, checking for any more dark streaks. There was nothing, not even under his fingernails. "I think I've got it all."

"Thank you." He went to reach for the coffee on the floor, but Lennox kept his hold on Elliot's hands for a moment.

"Wait, hang on." Lennox moved Holly off Elliot's lap, then extended the coffee. "We'll trade. Both at once might be a lot to deal with right now."

Elliot frowned as he watched his hands shake. He gripped the mug with both hands so it stabilized enough that he could take a sip, then hummed appreciatively. "This is just how I like it."

"I know." Lennox waited for Elliot to take a few more sips before he started to ask the questions burning in his mind. "So, do you have any idea who'd leave half a snake on your doorstep in the middle of the night?"

Lennox expected him to say, *I don't have a clue*, or maybe, *Neighborhood kids*, anything except the truth he seemed to keep so close, but Elliot snorted. "I know exactly who did it. Fucking *asshole*."

What, really? "You already know?"

"There's only one person it can be."

"Then we need to report this to the police."

Elliot shook his head. "No, that's not happening."

I knew it was too good to be true. "And why not?"

"Oh, there are so many reasons."

Lennox's jaw tightened. "I'd like to hear a few of them."

At first he thought Elliot was going to refuse. His face was guarded. After a moment, though, he nodded. "We can talk in the living room."

"Once I get a little more dressed." Lennox was willing to give him some extra time now that Elliot had agreed.

"But covering all that up is such a shame," Elliot simpered, the remnants of his vulnerability buried beneath layers of persona. He put one hand down on the floor and levered himself to his feet. "I'll make *you* the coffee this time." He walked off, completely ignoring the dirty dishtowel he left behind. Lennox sighed, grabbed it, and went back upstairs. He'd throw it in the hamper while he was up there.

He reassembled his outfit, glancing longingly at the enormous, rumpled bed as he did. The room still smelled like sex—amazing, bone-shattering sex. Lennox's ass was nicely sore, not painful; he could have gone again this morning. He *wanted* to go again, but it didn't look like that was going to happen now.

When he got back downstairs, it was almost like Elliot's moment of shock had never happened. There was creamy coffee waiting on the living room's low oak table, along with a granola bar and a bright-red apple. Elliot was sitting on the couch sipping from his own cup, Holly lounging by his side. He'd recovered his aplomb so well, anyone else would probably have believed he was fine. As Lennox's last commander had been fond of saying, though, you couldn't bullshit a bullshitter. He could see the slight tremble that made its way down Elliot's arms every few seconds, and how the fingers of his free hand kept rubbing against his jeans, like he was still wiping something off.

Judging from Elliot's smile, though, none of that was fair game to mention now. "Sorry about the lack of food," he said. "I've been so busy this past week I forgot to go shopping."

"It's better than I eat most days." Lennox downed half the coffee in one go, desperate for caffeine at this point, then set the mug down. "Thanks. Now, how about you tell me what kind of person would leave a dead animal on your porch in the middle of the night?"

Elliot sighed, so faintly Lennox almost didn't hear it. "My former boss."

"The CEO guy?" Since when did high-rolling CEOs go leaving dead animals on people's doorsteps? And wait— "Isn't he in jail? Didn't you get immunity for ratting him out?"

"You make it sound *so* admirable," Elliot muttered. "Yes, I did get immunity for testifying against Sheridan Pullman. And yes, he went to jail, but he was recently released. It's amazing how little time you can end up serving when you've got enough resources."

It still didn't make sense to Lennox. "Why would a man with all that power resort to a stunt like the snake?"

"Because he's trying to rattle me," Elliot said instantly. "He's showing me that he can get close to me anytime, anywhere. It's not the first thing I've received from him, though it's definitely the creepiest."

Lennox had the feeling he knew, but had to ask. "What was the first thing?"

Elliot shrugged. "The pictures I mentioned before. A few other items that let me know he was having me watched. I threw them out."

He sounded so glib Lennox wanted to smack something. Not Elliot, but a wall, a couch, *something.* "You threw out your evidence."

"It doesn't matter," Elliot said with exaggerated patience. "Because I'm not going to go to the police."

"You've got good reason to go to the police—you're being *stalked.*"

"But not seriously."

Lennox's jaw fell open. It took him a second to recover enough to speak. "How is your situation not serious?"

"Because I know Pullman, and I know how he works. He's a patient man. He's trying to upset me; he's trying to disrupt my everyday life. He *wants* me to go to the police, and I'm not going to give in to that pressure. Not yet, at least. Not until the special election for district attorney is over."

Of all the fucking non sequiturs. "What the hell does that have to do with anything?"

Elliot's eyes narrowed. He looked like he was an inch away from yelling, but he took a deep breath. "My sister, Vanessa, is one of the candidates for the position. This is the second campaign she's run for DA. The *first* time around, I was shot, indicted, and put on trial right before the election. I got a lot of justifiably bad press, and that bad press sloughed off onto Vanessa. I ruined her campaign and did serious damage to her public image." Elliot set down his coffee and ran both hands through his hair, making it curl a little over his ears. It would have been cute if he weren't so distressed.

"She did a lot for me when I was younger. Our parents . . . they weren't around for most of my childhood, and my older brother left the house as soon as he could. It was just me and her most of the time, and once I hit my teens she had to work hard to keep me in line." He grimaced. "I tried, but I wasn't always the easiest kid to handle."

No kid is, Lennox wanted to say, but he held his tongue. After a second, Elliot continued. "After I was shot, I was in the hospital for longer than I should have been, due to issues with me overmedicating. The last thing Vanessa did for me was sign me up for the Bright Future rehab program in Los Angeles. It's one of the best in the country.

"She let me know before I left that she was done sticking her neck out for me, though. I haven't seen her or her family since. She has two kids; they're great. I'm allowed to send them letters and presents for birthdays and holidays. No emails, no Facebook, but . . ." He shrugged. "It's better than nothing.

"Vanessa put me on a good path, and she did her best to keep me there. It's not her fault I fucked everything up, and I'm not going to ruin her life with my personal issues. If I report what's going on to the police, news will spread up the chain. It always does. Word will eventually get to her, and to her opponents. I won't do that to her, not again."

Lennox couldn't speak for a moment. There was so much to unpack in that explanation he didn't know where to begin, but the thing standing out the clearest was Elliot's absolute determination *not* to call the cops. Lennox considered doing it himself, but he didn't have any evidence apart from half a snake in a bag. Nobody would take him seriously, not without Elliot's corroboration. There had to be something he could do, though.

"Have you tried talking to Pullman directly?"

Elliot shook his head. "There's nothing to say. He's trying to disrupt my life, and I'm not going to let him. Pullman can't do too much—the man's still on probation. This is him being an asshole to me because I'm about to host my Executive Meetup, and he'd love to ruin my business like I ruined his." Elliot picked up his coffee again. "As soon as the Meetup is over, things will go back to normal." He took a sip, then made a face. "Ugh, cold."

Lennox wasn't going to let it end there. "You don't know everything will go back to normal. You don't know he won't keep escalating."

Elliot smiled brightly. It was so obviously fake that Lennox almost hated to look at him. "Well, now that I've got this handy-dandy home security system, I'm feeling a lot more secure."

"A system like this isn't enough to protect you from someone who's intent on doing you harm! A burglar, yeah, it's gonna put them off, but someone like this guy? From the way you describe him, he's not going to care about alarms."

"Pullman won't be attacking me in person. He never does his own dirty work."

It was like being dropped into an alternate reality, where the less seriously something was said, the less seriously it was expected to be taken. "Who's doing his dirty work, then?"

"His favorite fixer, I assume. Jonathan Lehrer."

Lennox wiped a hand over his face and let it briefly rest against his mouth. "The one who forced the wife's car off the road and got her killed?" he asked at last. "He wasn't arrested too?"

"He made bail and fled the country. He's the only person I can think of that Pullman would trust to screw with me. They know too much to betray each other, and Pullman's still very rich. He can afford to protect him."

"This is fucked up." Lennox had had enough of pretending to be calm. "You get that, right? It's seriously fucked up that you're being harassed by a man you put in jail and his—his fucking *henchman*, and you're not even willing to do anything about it."

"I'm not going to let him have the satisfaction of knowing he's getting to me, and I didn't invite you to stay last night so that you could judge my life decisions," Elliot snapped back. "I just have to make it through the Meetup and I'll be fine. It'll all blow over. I can handle it." He wouldn't raise his eyes quite enough to look at Lennox, though.

"What if he takes it further?" Lennox demanded. "What if he decides to say 'Fuck it,' and tries to kill you?"

"He wants to ruin me, not kill me," Elliot scoffed. He almost sounded convinced too, but there was a hint of uncertainty in his expression, the arch of his brows pulling together. "He wants to see me suffer. I can't do that adequately if I'm dead."

"How do you *know* that?" Lennox shook his head as Elliot began to reply. "Don't tell me you're sure. Tell me you're *positive*, because this is your life on the line. You have to do better than sure, and I don't know that you can." Elliot's blithe façade crumpled a little before Lennox's eyes, and he took a deep breath, as though he were about to say something.

Then the doorbell rang and the moment broke. "It must be your tow," Elliot said quietly, standing up and brushing his hands down his shirt to straighten it.

Lennox was lost again. "When did you call me a tow?"

"While you were upstairs dressing. I figured you wouldn't want to stay any longer than you had to, given the events of the morning." He shrugged. "I certainly can't blame you." He walked past Lennox's chair and headed for the door. After a second of stunned silence, Lennox followed him.

"At least check who it is before you open it," he murmured when he caught up with Elliot in the hall.

"I'm not an idiot," Elliot retorted. Lennox bit back his reply while Elliot looked through the door's peephole. "Unless Jonathan Lehrer has lost forty pounds, six inches, and had plastic surgery to make himself appear Latino, we're safe." Elliot opened the door. "Hello."

"Hey." The man at the door wore dark jeans, winter boots, and a heavy red jacket with the words *Mountain View Towing—Juan* embroidered across the chest. "Did you know you got a snake in a bag out here?" He held up the plastic sack and shook it a little.

Elliot went pale. "Yes, right. It's . . . That should go in the garbage, hang on." He stepped away and returned with an empty trash bag a moment later. "Here." Juan set the carcass inside and Elliot tied the bag off with about five knots before he seemed satisfied. "Okay, that's better." He gingerly set it down inside the foyer. "Hi."

"Uh, hi. Did you call for a tow?"

"Yes." Elliot clapped a friendly hand on Lennox's shoulder and pushed him forward a bit. "This gentleman needs help getting his truck back into town."

"Sure, sure." Juan looked at Lennox. "You got a shop picked out to take it to?"

How had his morning spiraled out of control so quickly? "No, not yet."

"What's wrong with it?"

"Fuel pump, I think." He could almost feel Elliot's smirk, but didn't acknowledge it. The time for playful jokes had passed.

"It's an old Nissan, yeah? There's a good place downtown that specializes in them, I bet they could get you in today."

"That's fine." It would do until he could get an estimate, at least.

"Okay." Juan held out his hand. "If you'll give me your keys, I'll get her ready to load."

"Thanks." Lennox handed them over, and Juan jogged down the stairs and over to his tow truck.

"Efficient," Elliot murmured, and Lennox snorted as he faced him.

"Just like you. I woke up half an hour ago and already you're kicking me out."

Elliot wouldn't meet his eyes again. "It's better this way. I've got a lot going on in my life right now, obviously, and none of it should be causing you concern. You set me up with an excellent alarm system, let me enjoy your company for an evening, and I'm grateful. But I think this is the best place to end things, don't you?"

It didn't sit well with Lennox. Avoiding his problems, physical, mental, or otherwise, had never worked out for him. He couldn't imagine it was going to work out very well for Elliot either. "I'm not going to stop worrying about you just because you tell me not to."

"You will," Elliot assured him. "As soon as you get a little distance. Don't let one fabulous night in bed blind you to the fact that we barely know each other." His tone was teasing but his eyes were tired. "Ah, hang on a sec." He came back a moment later with the apple and granola bar. "Don't forget these. You need to eat."

Lennox tugged his coat on and stuffed the food into one of the pockets. "Don't forget to take care of that," he said, waving to the garbage bag. "You wouldn't want Holly to get into it."

Elliot wrinkled his nose. "I don't think I could forget it if I tried. I'll run it out to the garbage in a second."

They stared at each other in silence for a second before Lennox gave in to his impulse. He caught Elliot by the hand, pulled him in close, and kissed him on the mouth. It was a gentle kiss, not passionate, but Elliot's lips went from terse to soft in an instant, and he tilted his head in an effort to deepen the kiss.

Lennox pulled away before he could. "Take care of yourself," he whispered. The next words hovered on the tip of his tongue, and in the end he couldn't resist saying it. "Call me if you need help."

He had to leave before Elliot could cut his offer down. So he opened the door and stepped into the cold morning air. He could feel Elliot's eyes on him as he walked away, but he didn't look back.

After a moment, the door shut.

CHAPTER SEVEN

Excerpt from *Shockwave*'s article:

Of course, for every protestation of Charmed Life's policy of owning your mistakes and opening yourself to second chances, there's no denying it's the things that aren't being said about McKenzie's company that are creating all his buzz. His upcoming Executive Meetup has been widely publicized and should be well attended by his proponents, even though it does take place on the day Denver hosts the Super Bowl. But the crème de la crème of Charmed Life's clientele?

They won't be going to the Meetup, but to the private and completely anonymous Black Box meeting the same night. These are the people who don't openly endorse Charmed Life, people who are too famous to risk their public images by admitting they need help getting over their sordid pasts. It's the information-sharing session that anyone would love to be a fly on the wall for. What does this upper echelon talk about? How do they connect? Just who are they?

McKenzie isn't telling.

One night shouldn't have ruined Elliot's weekend, but by Sunday afternoon, barely twenty-four hours after Lennox had left, he still felt uncomfortably close to pining for his company.

It wasn't because the man was nice. Elliot had had nice lovers before. It didn't matter that he was attractive: Elliot invariably found his bedmates attractive, whether they were long and thin or short and stout.

It wasn't just the sex either, as fantastic as it had been, that was making Lennox linger in Elliot's mind. Fantastic sex was a given when Elliot made the effort, which he always did. So what if Lennox had been the toppiest person who had ever let Elliot fuck him? So what if he'd brought out a talkative side of Elliot that, more often than not, he stifled during sex? So what if he'd been ridden hard and put away wet and satisfied?

It was how Elliot had felt when he was around Lennox that was hard to get over. It wasn't often he didn't have to put on a show; he tried not to with the people he really liked, or with his clientele. Authenticity was part of his brand, after all. But there were only so many smiles you could muster in a single day before they began to feel tired, only so many positive messages you could relay before you stopped considering them and just started saying them.

For now though, he needed to be focused on other things: on his videos, on coordinating the Meetup, on covering up the dead snake in his trash with so much junk he could almost forget it was there. He needed to forget Lennox West, but he couldn't.

With Lennox, his playful overtures had been met, his flirtation had been matched, but Lennox hadn't been calculating. It was clear from how Lennox had been around his daughter: earnest, funny, still trying to understand her when there was no way he could relate to the trials of a thirteen-year-old girl. He'd treated Elliot like that, and it had felt . . . good. Natural, easy. Even their argument hadn't been much of an argument.

Elliot had been prepared to make it easy for Lennox to leave—it was why he'd called the tow early. He'd assumed Lennox would want to get out of there as fast as possible, that he'd be uncomfortable with him, have given him up for a lost cause. Elliot hadn't expected compassion, and he certainly hadn't expected the offer of help at the very end. Elliot could handle a showdown, but what did you do when the person you were ready to brawl with forfeited the fight?

You watched them walk away, apparently.

It had been the right move at the time; Elliot was sure of it. He didn't need to involve anyone else in his situation. Things would either get better, or . . . well. They'd get ugly, but he could and would take care of himself. The fact that he wanted to call Lennox now, not because he needed his help, but just to talk to him?

That was problematic.

Even running hadn't distracted him. Elliot wasn't one of those people who could run and zone out, hit his groove and follow it down a road for miles and miles. In all honesty, he loathed running so much that he had to focus on other things while he did it, so running was also when he got some of his best ideas for his podcasts. Running was supposed to be awful but *productive*, damn it, not awful and made worse by pining like an idiot.

If he'd been a decent cook, Elliot would have thrown himself into a complicated recipe. Stuart called cooking the coq au vin of distractions, but everything Elliot could whip up was far from gourmet. He'd tried to work, but work failed to keep his mind off how much nicer it would be if the only other living thing in his house wasn't a tiny dog who, while great for cuddling, wasn't an ideal conversationalist.

Elliot remembered a conversation he'd had with Willie about why she'd gone through five husbands. "I couldn't stand any of them for long," she'd said, blowing a thin stream of smoke into the warm California air. "But I could stand being alone even less." Elliot didn't think he was quite that bad. He'd lasted with Mischa for almost three years, after all. He wasn't a misanthropist, but he also hadn't had someone he could be himself with since Willie's death. And before that, with his family . . . Elliot shook his head and checked his to-do list. There had to be *something* he could occupy himself with. Or someone.

What the hell. He'd been meaning to call Stuart and check in on the menu anyway.

The man picked up on the first ring. "Elliot! Hi! It's so good to hear from you! I called you a few days ago but I guess you were busy."

Elliot smiled a little. Stuart reminded him of a puppy: tripping over his own ears as he tumbled from subject to subject but always coming back for a scratch under the chin. Elliot didn't often need the adulation Stuart offered, but it was gratifying every now and then. "Things are very intense with the business right now. Speaking of that, did Serena get you the final numbers for the guests at the Meetup?"

"Yeah, she did. Don't worry, I've got the most amazing Super Bowl food that these people have ever tasted coming their way."

"Perfect." It wasn't as haute cuisine as Elliot had originally planned, but Stuart had talked him around to the idea. The Executive Meetup would be half conference, half Super Bowl party, with the game projected on one entire wall of the theater he was renting. It was the perfect thing for his local clients, and would give him the flexibility to leave when he needed to switch venues with few people taking note, as long as the game was good. "How about for the Black Box?"

"Elegant but understated. I feel like we could have gone bigger with that one, though. I mean, you could do a five-course plated meal with the kind of money that—"

"It has to be something I can handle by myself, remember," Elliot said. "That means the food has to stand on its own merits, not rely on presentation to have an impact."

"I could help you serve it. I swear I wouldn't say anything to anyone about who was there."

Coming from Stuart, Elliot actually believed it. But it wasn't a risk he was willing to take. "You'll be there to help me set up and take down, and that's favor enough. I'll make sure they know who the caterer is. Who knows? You might get some business from a few big names."

"Would you like to come over to my house for a tasting?" Stuart's voice went bright and eager. "I could whip up a few of the dishes you approved for each event and you could see what you think about wine pairings!"

And here was where things began to go sour. Stuart was Elliot's most loyal client, and had been one of the first to sign on to the Charmed Life program, paying for all the bells and whistles. He'd come a long way from his early failed businesses, and the allegations of fraud that had gone along with it, into the upscale food empire he was building today. But he didn't understand the line that existed between personal and business relationships, and it was a line Elliot wasn't going to cross. He couldn't afford to, with the extra attention—and scrutiny—Charmed Life was getting these days. "Thanks, Stuart, but I think we'll save the tasting for the office. I need to get Serena to approve everything anyway. I'll talk to you again later this week. Don't forget to hit up the message boards, okay?"

Stuart sighed heavily. "Okay."

"Bye, buddy." Elliot ended the call, then set his phone aside. He was tired, slightly horny, and edgy as hell. Running had failed him, but he still hadn't changed his sheets, so a nap wasn't an option until he felt less lazy, and jerking off would only be frustrating. What could he do that would require all of his attention?

The answer was obvious once he thought about it. Reinvigorated, Elliot let Holly out back for a minute while he shrugged his Burberry wool coat over his sweater. Elliot was a lot of things, but tolerant of the cold wasn't one of them. He grabbed his leather gloves, let Holly inside, and armed the alarm, then headed for his Porsche.

Elliot fired the car up and drove north on his small, two-lane road at double the speed limit. The sky was beginning to drop a few snowflakes here and there, and the ground was clear of packed snow. On a gray Sunday when the Broncos were playing, he wasn't going to run into anyone on this route, and Lookout Mountain Road would connect with the interstate eventually, which he could take home. Elliot opened up the throttle and let his car go. He had fifteen miles of sparse residences, sharp turns, and the occasional deer to play around with. It was enough, finally, to get his mind off of Lennox.

After a few minutes, his phone rang. Elliot checked where it was plugged in—unknown number. Brilliant: a telemarketer. He ended the call and kept going.

The phone rang again. And again. Elliot accepted the call on the fourth attempt, because someone so persistent obviously needed to be told no in person. "Whatever you're selling, I'm not interested."

"But I'm interested in what *you're* selling, Mr. McKenzie."

Elliot started in his seat. The caller's voice was unnaturally deep; it was impossible to tell if it was a man or woman. "Who is this?"

"That's not important. What's important is that you pay very close attention to what I have to say, because if I have to prove to you that I'm serious, you're not going to like it."

"That's an imprecise threat. I don't have time for this." He reached to end the call, but the voice broke in.

"It looks like you do need proof, then. Go ahead, Mr. McKenzie. Try out your brakes."

It only took one tap for the numbing, icy terror to settle over his limbs and in the depths of his stomach. The brakes had stopped working. Or maybe they were working, just . . . not for him. He didn't bother to test the accelerator; he was already heading downhill, speeding up would just make things worse. Elliot took a deep breath. "This is an interesting cry for attention. What do I have to do to get control of my car back?"

"No threats in return? No begging me to restore your brakes to you? I'm impressed by your sangfroid. To the point, then. I want all copies of the Singularity patent information that you stole from Redback Industries."

"I didn't steal any patent information," Elliot said immediately. "Whoever told you that is lying."

"My own eyes can't lie to me, Mr. McKenzie. Careful on that turn up ahead."

Elliot gritted his teeth as the Porsche roared into a sharp turn between two rock faces. The suggested speed was twenty-five; he was going almost sixty. The car hugged the road well enough, but it was starting to get slick out. Pushing in the clutch, he forced the car to downshift. The engine whined angrily at him.

An old VW bus honked loudly as he darted around it, then leveled the car's path out on the next section of road. He snapped, "I'm telling you, I don't have any patent information. Is this Lehrer?"

"You thought no one would notice, in the aftermath of everything that happened at Redback, the chaos of the trial? You thought you could steal the blueprints for the world's most precise viral delivery system and nobody would be the wiser?" It shouldn't have been possible for so much malice to come through a voice disguiser, but this person was communicating it loud and clear.

"Well, I am, Mr. McKenzie. I know you've got them, and I know what your Black Box meeting is really selling. So don't feed me a line about living a genuine life, because I am genuinely telling you right now: if you don't return that information to Pullman, along with a very sincere apology, you might not live to regret it."

"What, the snake wasn't enough of a warning, now you've got to threaten to kill me too?" Elliot demanded. He pushed hard against the shifter, trying to get down to second. Smoke from his grinding gears was stinking up the car. "Come on, *c'mon* . . ." He passed a cherry-red Corvette, narrowly missing its front wheels as he jerked his car back over into the lane to avoid the gravel truck heading up the canyon. And it wasn't the only one. What was a road crew doing working on a Sunday?

His speedometer read forty-five. Better, but not good enough. Still, if he killed the engine, gravity would slow him down pretty fast. He went for it, and waited breathlessly to see if it took. The engine turned off—perfect. He still couldn't use his brakes, though, and if he stayed in his lane he would rear-end a ubiquitous Subaru filled with gawkers who weren't even doing thirty-five. They had a *BABY ON BOARD* sticker on the back window of the car. But now he wasn't going fast enough to pass the semi that was coming up the other side of the canyon. Elliot's throat clenched.

"No more games, Mr. McKenzie. I suggest you hand over everything you've got to Mr. Pullman before your Black Box meeting. If you survive this little outing, of course." The call ended, and Elliot had only seconds left before he either hit the car ahead of him or pulled out in front of a semitruck.

He went with the third option, and jerked his car over to smash its side into the rocky face of the granite hill that framed the road. The impact was like belly flopping into a pool from the high dive; he couldn't move, couldn't even breathe. The scream his car made as it scraped the bare rock stabbed into his skull like an ice pick through the eye. He was almost grateful when the car began to spin, then roll, and the noise finally stopped.

Then his head hit the ceiling, and everything went black.

Was this the third or fourth person to shine a fucking light in his eyes? Elliot wasn't sure, but he was damn tired of it. It had been bad enough getting it from the paramedics who'd picked him up, and who had patently refused to listen when he said he was fine, no really, he'd walked out of the wreckage of his car with hardly a scratch on him! As if looking at the carcass of his Porsche hadn't made him want to cry, he had to be subjected to the medical equivalent of musical chairs now?

"You're a very lucky man, Mr. McKenzie," Dr.—his name tag was a little blurry, Elliot had to tilt his head to make it out—Chen said as he pulled back and finally, blessedly, turned the fucking light off. "Apart from the cut on your scalp, what seems to be a mild concussion, and a few deep contusions, I can't find anything wrong with you. You're going to be incredibly sore for the next week or so though, as your chest heals." Right, where he'd slammed against the seat belt. "But overall your car did an excellent job of protecting you."

"So it did," Elliot said mournfully. The cut on his head had bled badly, but was small enough that it had been sealed with glue, not stitches. Thank God for that; the last thing he needed to deal with was a wound that everyone could stare at to go with the gaping hole in his self-confidence.

"The police have already been here to take your statement?"

"Yes." And to administer a breathalyzer—the second one, actually, on top of the one he'd had done in the ambulance. No, he'd said, he wasn't drunk. Yes, he'd lost control of the vehicle. No, he didn't know where he wanted the wreckage towed yet.

Elliot needed to know what had gone wrong in his car. It had been hacked, obviously; he needed to know *how*, but he didn't want the cops involved any more than they already were. Word would go up the chain, he knew it; his sister would hear about his accident before the day was out. He let himself muse for a second on whether or not Vanessa would break her silence to check and see if he was all right. He could text her, and maybe she'd finally answer. He could *call* her, and maybe this time she'd pick up.

But Elliot wanted to reach out too much for it to possibly be a good idea. He was so close to exonerating himself, to making up for ruining everything for her five years ago. He couldn't falter now. He couldn't bring her into this, couldn't risk entangling her. Not until she won the election. He sighed.

"Tired?" Dr. Chen asked sympathetically.

"Very." He tried to muster a smile, but it probably wasn't half as charming as it should be. "I'd really like to go home." Call a cab, get back to Holly—she had to be losing it now—and fall into bed with some over-the-counter painkillers. A night to remember.

"I'd like to do a CT scan first, just to make sure there's no brain damage. After that, though, you're welcome to go home, as long as you have someone there to supervise you for twenty-four hours."

That didn't sound good. "Supervise?"

"You've been in a very serious accident, Mr. McKenzie. It's only reasonable that you have a family member or friend stay with you to ensure you don't suffer any complications. I'm prepared to make it a condition of your release," he added when Elliot indignantly opened his mouth. "You can think about it while you're in the CT."

Dr. Chen had vastly overrated the comforts of a damn CT machine if he thought Elliot was going to be doing any quality consideration inside of one, but it wasn't hard to narrow down his options. The only person off the top of his head that he could think to call was Serena, but that would mean he'd have to explain to her what had happened tonight.

Any other person, any other night, and Elliot would be able to bullshit his way through the facts until they believed it really was an accident. But Serena knew him, the *real* him, or as close as he ever got. She'd never buy that he'd been joyriding up Lookout Mountain and lost control of his car. And even if she did buy it, and agreed to stay with him for a while, what if something else happened at the house? What if Lehrer left the other half of the snake hanging out of his mailbox? What if things escalated further?

Not to mention, he needed someone to look at his car and figure out what the hell had gone wrong. Hacking a car: that was the sort of thing that happened in spy movies, not in real life. Elliot almost wanted to check for tiny cameras. That had to be the concussion talking. But who could he go to that he could trust to keep quiet about it?

"Call me if you need help."

Elliot groaned. A voice came in over the speaker: "Mr. McKenzie, you need to be quiet and hold still while the CT scan is going."

Elliot cut off his simultaneous urges to apologize and say, "Fuck you." Oh god, he was going to be that guy, wasn't he? The one who showed somebody the door and came sniffing back the very next day, looking for a favor from Lennox and his MIT friend. This favor might entail saving his life, but he felt like an idiot just considering it. *You'll feel like more of an idiot if you die out of stubbornness.*

Eventually he was let out of the machine and returned to the examination room. Dr. Chen joined him a few minutes later, and cheerfully pronounced him brain-bleed-free. "Only a little swelling, like we thought," he said. "Hold still for a moment, please." He injected him with a syringe so smoothly Elliot barely noticed it.

"What was that?"

"Just a little morphine. It should keep the pain down for now, but I'll write you a prescription for some Percocet to help manage your pain over the next few days."

Morphine. Of course they'd give him morphine. Elliot had abused morphine to the point where it had reduced effectiveness these days, but he'd still get some side effects: a touch of dry mouth and upset stomach as well as the beautiful dreaminess that had always helped him to forget his fuckups. That made it even harder to stay clean of it.

And Percocet on top of that? "I'd rather stick with aspirin."

"Tylenol might be better. I'd rather you didn't take anything that thins your blood, just in case. You'll start coming down from this shot before too long, and I think you'll want something stronger than over-the-counter drugs anyway." He wrote the prescription and held it out toward Elliot, who couldn't quite make himself take it as he absorbed this unwelcome information.

After a moment the doctor simply tucked the prescription into Elliot's coat pocket, probably chalking up his sudden slowness to the concussion. "Have you thought of someone who can keep an eye on you for a few days?"

Elliot made himself nod. "I guess I have." He retrieved his phone and wiggled it. "Can I call from this room?"

"It shouldn't be a problem. I'll let you go as soon as they get here, then."

"Great." Elliot waited for the doctor to leave, then reached into his pocket, pulled out the prescription, and dropped it into the trash can before gingerly lying down on the hard exam bed. Being on his back felt better than trying to stay upright, given the way his head still ached despite the drugs.

Elliot forced his eyes open, turned on his phone, and stared at his contacts list. Fuck. He was going to do it, he had to. He couldn't do this alone, not if he was going to get through the next few days without falling back on old, bad habits. Not for the first time, he wished he'd followed his program's advice and hooked up with a mentor to help him handle the rough patches that came with dealing with his addiction. Elliot hadn't trusted anyone enough to rely on them back then, though.

You don't have to share all the details, he reminded himself. The nature of the threat, the gravity of theft he'd been accused of—that could stay private. He hit Send and hoped that Lennox wouldn't refuse his call.

CHAPTER EIGHT

Partial transcription of most recent appointment with West, Lennox, Staff Sergeant US Army Rangers (R), January 28, 3:15 p.m.:

JS: What decision did you make?

LW: The decision to fire.

(Long pause.)

JS: Why did you have to make this decision?

LW: Because I was in charge.

JS: I meant to say, what were the circumstances that led you to have to make a decision to fire?

LW: Ah. My squad, we were running a patrol near Ripley. We were spread across four vehicles. It should have been routine, but we ended up taking heavy fire from enemy units and got separated. The tracker that let us see who was where had been damaged. It was dark out, it was snowing . . . we couldn't get visual confirmation of who was shooting at us. My gunner detected movement and asked if he should fire. We were still taking shots, so . . . I said yes. Turned out it was a friendly unit. We wounded two of our fellow soldiers. They later died.

JS: I see.

LW: No, you don't.

"You look like hell."

Lennox winced almost as soon as the words slipped from his mouth. As greetings went, he could have done a lot better. Especially since the last time he'd seen Elliot, he'd figured it really would be, well, the *last* time. He certainly hadn't expected to get a call as he was leaving the boxing gym, less than an hour ago. When he'd seen whose name popped up, he'd actually done a double take.

The conversation had been brief, mostly because Lennox had cut things short as soon as he'd heard that Elliot was in the hospital. He'd agreed to come and pick him up, take him home, and hear him out. He was still in his sweats from the gym when he got to the hospital, but he felt positively fastidious next to Elliot, who had on a thin cotton hospital gown; the see-through plastic bag next to him had his ruined clothes in it. Now Lennox understood why Elliot had asked him to bring any spare clothes he had on hand.

"I promise you, I feel just as good as I look," Elliot replied with a thin smile. Thin with pain, Lennox saw, not with anger. He held himself gingerly on the end of the table, one hand pressed lightly to his chest. His hair was a mess of dried blood, and midway up one of his shins he had a nasty purple bruise almost the size of a dollar bill.

Lennox dropped his gym bag and came over to the bed. He carefully framed Elliot's face with his hands. "What's the damage?"

"Mild concussion. Mild," Elliot repeated with a little snort. "Like the other concussion flavors are medium and extra spicy. I've also got some bumps and bruises, my chest hurts where my seat belt caught me, and I cut my head. So no showers for a few days. Which is bad," he added, "since I've got to be on camera for work."

"Work might have to wait," Lennox said. He didn't realize he was still holding Elliot's face until the man leaned into his palm with a heavy sigh.

"Thanks for coming," he murmured. Lennox's heart twisted.

"I told you I would if you needed me."

Elliot shrugged. "Yeah, but I bet you didn't think I'd take you up on it so fast, did you?"

"No," Lennox admitted.

"It's because you already know," Elliot said drowsily. "You know, and you're better at this stuff than I am. It won't surprise you."

"What won't surprise me?"

"That someone tried to kill me." Lennox barely had time to register his stomach dropping before Elliot went on, his words tripping over themselves in his haste to get them out. "Or scare me, I guess. They *said* they weren't trying to kill me, but I think it was just luck. I couldn't make my brakes work. I had to drive my car into the mountain." Actual tears welled up in Elliot's eyes. "I *broke* her. She was new and beautiful and perfect, and I broke her so I wouldn't hit the car in front of me."

"Oookay," Lennox said, forcing himself to stay calm. Freaking out right now wouldn't help anyone. "They've got you on some good meds, huh?" Elliot probably had no idea what he was saying.

"Just a little morphine. Which is bad," he added. "Because I shouldn't have it. I used to want it all the time and then I finally forgot how it felt to want it like that, and it felt so good to forget. But now I remember and I *hate* that I do. It makes me want to do stupid things. I think it's making me a little loopy too," he confessed.

Addict. Rehab. Shit. "I bet it is," Lennox said gently.

"The tow company wants to know where to haul my car, but I can't let them get rid of it because I have to know how it was hacked. The voice on the phone took my brakes away." Elliot glared at Lennox indignantly. "Do you know how important those are?"

"Pretty important." Lennox glanced around for Elliot's shoes. Lennox hadn't brought another pair, they were screwed if— Ah. Different bag.

"Really fucking important," Elliot agreed. "Can we take my car to your place? Your work? So someone can figure out how it was hacked?" He covered one of Lennox's hands with his own, holding on too tight to be comfortable for either of them. "I know I sound like I don't make any sense but it's true, I swear. I got a call and I couldn't tell who it was, and they threatened me and took my brakes and I had to crash my car to stop it in time. I have to know how they did it! It's driving me crazy, Lennox, please."

Lennox wished he wasn't inclined to take Elliot so seriously, but . . . the snake. He hadn't imagined that, or the fallout from it. "I'll tell them to drop the car at Castillion's lot," Lennox promised. And boy, would he have groveling to do tomorrow when Rodney found out.

On the other hand, Kevin would literally kill for the chance to root around in a Porsche, even a destroyed one. He was their auto-security-systems expert; Castillion didn't sell car alarms, but some people liked their cars to be linked to their home systems on Castillion's app. Kevin would figure it out. If it turned out to be nothing, great. If it didn't . . .

"Thank you," Elliot said sincerely. "You're far too nice for me."

"I'd say you're far too pretty for me, but right now I'd be lying."

"*Ooh*, mean."

"I know I am; I hear it all the time from Lee. Come on, let's get you into actual clothes." Which, in this case, were the ones Lennox had worn to the gym. They fit Elliot pretty well, although the way the denim stretched across Elliot's ass was almost impossible to look away from.

Elliot carefully tilted his head and sniffed at his shoulder. "These smell like you."

Nothing Lennox could do about that now. "Yeah, sorry."

"I like it."

"Well, you're kind of a strange guy," Lennox drawled, earning a glare from Elliot. "Good thing I like strange," he added. "Let me get your socks and shoes on and we can go."

"I can do it."

"Not without bending over," Lennox pointed out. "And then your head will hurt even more."

"You and your stupid . . . logic. Fine." Elliot sat back and waved a hand at his bare feet. "Be my ballet."

Lennox pursed his lips as he knelt, fighting to keep the smile in. "I think you're thinking of a different word."

"Probably." Elliot didn't seem overly concerned.

Lennox got the socks onto him, lingering a little over his toes before he covered them up. They were surprisingly cute. "Do you get pedicures?"

"I love pedicures," Elliot confided. "They make my feet feel amazing. The hypermasculine posing that says that pedicures can't be for guys? It's bullshit."

"You can spit out 'hypermasculine' on a whim but you can't remember the word 'valet.'" Lennox put Elliot's shoes on him and straightened up. Elliot grinned broadly at him.

"That's the word! Ha, I didn't need to remember it, because you remembered it for me."

"I guess I did." Lennox helped ease Elliot off the table and into his coat, then grabbed his sealed bag of clothes. "Come on, let's go spring you."

Elliot stayed close to Lennox all through his discharge, actually touching him for most of it, leaning into his side whenever they stopped walking. Lennox worried he was getting dizzy, but he seemed to be moving fine, he just . . . wanted to be close, for some reason.

By the time they got out to the truck it was dark, and the slush on the pavement had refrozen into solid ice. Lennox helped Elliot into the truck, then got into the driver's seat. The vehicle started with a purr.

"Fuel pump," Elliot said sleepily. "I knew it."

"You were right."

"The way I sent you away yesterday was wrong. I didn't handle the snake thing well, but I didn't want you to know how freaked out I was. I should be able to deal with my own messes."

Lennox sighed as he pulled out into the street. "It's not the worst morning-after I've ever had."

"How many others have included dead wildlife?"

"None," Lennox admitted, "but one involved a very sharp knife, so at least nobody tried to stab me this time around."

Elliot chuckled. "Was that Gaby?"

"No, thank god. We wouldn't have lasted as long as we did if she was that kind of crazy. Are we going to your place?" He'd actually prefer to, but— "My apartment's not as far."

"*Hmm* . . . no, I have to get back and take care of Holly," Elliot said. "She's probably made a mess, and she'll be hungry, and worried."

"That's fine. Your place is fine." Lennox kept his speed low; his tires weren't the best, and the last thing Elliot needed was to get into another accident. The other man was fading fast. Lennox would be lucky to get him into bed before he fell asleep.

Lennox left his headlights on when they got back to illuminate the stairs to the porch, then slid an arm around Elliot's waist and helped him climb them. Fortunately his wallet, phone, and keys had been put in his coat pockets; it was easy to fish out his key ring and open the door. Holly danced around their feet as they entered, barking madly for a few seconds before she darted into the night.

"She can't go alone," Elliot mumbled. "Something might eat her."

"I'll get her in a second," Lennox promised as he typed in the security system's code. The blinking red light turned solid green. "Do you think you can get to your bedroom on your own?"

Elliot blinked at him owlishly, then straightened up with a grimace. "Sure. Just let me pick a bannister."

"There's only the one."

"It looks like there's two." Elliot successfully grabbed it, though, and started to make his way up the wooden stairs. Lennox watched long enough to be sure he wasn't going to fall over, then grabbed his flashlight and headed outside again. He killed his car's headlights, slammed the car door shut, and almost tripped over Holly, who had apparently finished her bathroom break and had decided to roll around until she was whiter than a snowball.

"You're ridiculous," Lennox said to her, shivering a little as a gust of wind blew ice crystals down the neck of his jacket. "You ready to go inside, then?" *Are you expecting her to answer?* he thought to himself as he headed for the porch. Holly followed.

A few minutes with a kitchen towel cleaned the worst of the snow off. Lennox topped off her food bowl and toed off his own shoes by the door before going to make sure Elliot was okay.

To Lennox's surprise, Elliot wasn't only still awake, he was standing in the bathroom, half-naked and inspecting the massive bruise on his chest left by the seat belt. "It seems like something in there should be broken," he mused as Lennox joined him, Holly at his heels. "Nothing is, though. It doesn't even feel that bad, but it's definitely not pretty, is it?"

"Good thing nobody's going to be able to see it," Lennox said.

"Except for me. And you."

Lennox shrugged. "I don't care. I've seen worse."

Elliot turned his reflection's tired gaze to Lennox's face. "I care, though."

Lennox couldn't help himself. He set a gentle hand on the back of Elliot's neck and kissed the point of his shoulder. "Care tomorrow. You should be sleeping now."

"You believe me, don't you?" Elliot covered his hand and didn't look away. "You believe that someone sabotaged my car?"

"Kevin will tell us what's going on," Lennox promised.

"But you believe me."

He didn't even have to think about it. "Yeah, I do."

"Thank you. For that, and for coming and getting me, and for . . . helping." Elliot smiled crookedly. "Like you said you would."

"You're welcome."

Adrenaline, even when it stemmed from someone else's trauma and not his own, was more than enough to fuel Lennox through getting Elliot home and dealing with the cleanup that came next. He'd talked with the tow company and Elliot's insurance, texted Serena to not expect Elliot the next morning, then he called his own workplace and talked to Kevin.

Kevin Cooper was, in some ways, Castillion's best employee. He was an MIT graduate, a brilliant programmer, and could do any aspect of the job almost perfectly, whether it was dealing with customers or installing software updates. He lived on site—he was Rodney's nephew and he liked the rent there, which was dirt cheap—and covered the phones when no one else was around. He was eager to help, naturally friendly, and everyone liked him. Even Lennox, when he could get the kid to shut up. Kevin was almost impossible to shut up when he got going, and he had certainly been *going* about the Porsche.

"A Panamera, that's awesome! Do you know what those retail for in Germany? Your friend must be sick loaded, man. Is he there? Can I ask him about the—"

"He's asleep," Lenox broke in. "You can ask him questions tomorrow once he's awake, and only if they pertain to the car."

"Sure, but this is the guy who knows the mayor, right? He's friends with the mayor, isn't he? I thought I read that on his website. Can he get me an introduction? I want to talk to him about—"

"Kevin. Tomorrow."

"Yeah, sure. Tomorrow. I'll check it out first thing."

"Thanks, I appreciate it."

"No, dude, *I* appreciate it," Kevin exclaimed. "Do you know how boring it's been here lately? I haven't had to connect anyone to the cops all week, there haven't been any emergencies, and there aren't any trade shows to get ready for. It's *so dull*."

Lennox pressed his thumb to the spot between his eyes that always seemed to ache when he talked to Kevin. "That's how it's supposed to be."

"God, you sound like Uncle Rodney," Kevin moaned. "Oh hey, there's the truck—I've got to go direct them to the pad out back, I'll talk to you in the morning, okay?"

"Thanks, Kevin."

That phone call went brilliantly compared with how the next one would probably go. Tonight had been Sunday dinner at Gaby's house and Lennox should have been there for it. Gaby had left two messages on his phone while he was taking care of Elliot, and by the time he called back he could have set fires off the sparks that suffused her voice.

"What the *hell*, Lennox?" she demanded. "Where have you been? Your *daughter* was expecting you to be at dinner tonight."

"Gaby—"

"You can't do this, Lennox, you can't refuse to even *try* to be a part of her life! Eventually it's going to get to the point where we don't want to bother accommodating your issues anymore. Do you understand me?"

"I've got a good reason, Gaby," he insisted.

"Oh yeah?" She couldn't have crammed another ounce of disbelief into those words. "Does this reason have anything to do with the fancy black car you showed up in the other night? Or more specifically, it's owner?" *Is she psychic?* "Because if you skipped out on dinner to get some tail, so help me *God*—"

"It's nothing like that," Lennox interrupted. "Can you give me the benefit of the doubt for two damn seconds before you go thinking the worst? A friend got into a car accident. He didn't have anyone else to contact, so I picked him up from the hospital and took him home. I'm sorry I didn't call, but I lost track of time. Can you put Lee on now?"

There was a long pause. "That's it?"

"Yes."

"Since when have you had a friend?"

"Gaby..."

"Fine, fine." She called for Lee. A moment later his daughter was on the phone.

"Dad?"

"Hey, sweetheart," he said, the tension in his neck easing at her friendly tone. "Sorry I missed dinner."

"What happened?"

Possibly against his better judgment, Lennox decided to tell her the truth. Some of it, at least. "Elliot got into a car accident. He's okay, but I had to get him from the hospital. Do *not* let your aunt know," he added sternly. "He's not fit for visitors yet, and she'd want to take over everything. Nobody else knows the details, Lee."

"Really? Just us?" Lee sounded hushed but pleased.

"Just us," Lennox said. "I'll make it up to you this week, okay sweetheart?"

"Okay, Dad. And you could invite Elliot again too, if you want."

Did Lee have a little crush? "Yeah?"

"Yeah. He was fun the other night, and you seem to like him."

If only she knew. "You're right, I do like him. I'll pass the invite along. I love you, Lee."

"Love you too, Dad." She hung up before Gaby could get back on, which was a relief.

It wasn't that late, but Lennox decided to try sleeping anyway. Not in Elliot's bed this time; he hadn't been invited. He grabbed another spare toothbrush, then made his way to the second bedroom, which Elliot clearly hadn't extended his personality into. The room was wallpapered in rows of pale-pink roses, the bedspread was edged with white lace, and the air smelled like desiccated lavender, too old to do much more than vaguely scent the drapes.

The bed was small, the room cold. Lennox left the light on and the door open in case Elliot called out, then tried to get some sleep. He got that far, but it didn't last long.

Dark, cold . . . the reverberating crack of bullets penetrating metal at high speed, Davis taking a shot to the thigh, and Lennox's hands are finally warm but it's Davis's blood on them, not his own heat, and he's trying to stop the flow but feels like he's stealing all Davis's warmth instead, and Martinez is calling out to him, asking whether he should shoot, should he shoot, Sarge! *And Lennox says—*

He woke up with the comforter thrown to the foot of the bed, his torso half fallen off the mattress like he'd been trying to lean on something that wasn't there. Lennox groped for his phone and checked the time. Two sixteen. He'd slept for almost four hours.

Not bad, especially not in a strange room. Lennox lay back on the mattress and stared up at the ceiling for a moment before he decided that he really wasn't going to get to sleep again. His hands still tingled from applying pressure to Davis's leg—lord knew what he'd actually been doing to them to make them feel that way. His shirt was damp with sweat, and his mouth was dry.

Yeah, that was it for tonight. Lennox rolled off the bed and halfheartedly drew the comforter back up; he'd have to change the sheets in the morning anyway. He washed his face in the bathroom, washed his hands until they were bright pink from the heat of the water, then crept down the hall into Elliot's room to get a change of shirts. He didn't mean to get distracted by the quiet scene on the bed, but . . . well. He wasn't made of fucking stone.

Elliot was lying on his side facing the empty half of the bed. He'd pulled the spare pillow into his arms at some point, and drawn his legs up until he was lying in almost a fetal position. Holly had tucked herself in the pocket of his knees, and she looked up but didn't bark at Lennox. Elliot appeared surprisingly peaceful, given what he'd gone through today. Or maybe not everyone was as prone to reliving every trauma in their life as Lennox was.

Lennox had no real reason to stay there after he'd changed into one of Elliot's shirts, a V-neck with long sleeves that felt almost shockingly soft. He stayed anyway, though, slipping into the chair on the far side of the room and leaning back and just breathing. Holly held his gaze for a while, her tiny eyes shining green in the dark, before she finally turned around and resettled in her nest. Elliot stirred but didn't wake up, and Lennox let himself slump down a little.

Just a few minutes. He'd stay a few minutes, then head downstairs and start composing his apology to Rodney for filling part of his lot with a busted-up Porsche.

CHAPTER NINE

Excerpt from *Shockwave*'s article:

Given how little we actually know about Charmed Life's inner workings, from its inception to how it grabs and holds the high-rolling elite, it's astonishing it's been the runaway hit that it has.

McKenzie disagrees with me, naturally. "No one is perfect, and therefore no one is immune to the need to recover from their mistakes," he says, sipping from a bottle of Evian. "The urge to confess and be absolved is written into humanity's most venerable institutions. Unless you're a psychopath, you're going to want to share your errors and earn forgiveness at some point. Holding your wrongs inside of yourself is toxic, and it will poison everything you do. Everyone needs release. Charmed Life is one avenue for it."

I concede that's possible, but have to ask: "How many of your subscribers do you think get accounts with Charmed Life just so they can watch videos of you?" Because it seems clear to me that the biggest asset this company has is its CEO, and not because he's a canny businessman. He knows how to lead people in the direction he wants them to go, how to give them just enough to make them hope for more.

McKenzie smiles, shrugs, and changes the subject.

Elliot's breath hitched with pain the moment he woke up. His hands, which he'd started to extend above his head for the sort of full-body, back-cracking extension he always craved, curled instantly back down to his chest. Every breath ached, and his shoulders and neck felt like they'd been strung through with piano wire that had been tied into a bow right between his shoulder blades.

His skin was raw and tender underneath the Army Rangers T-shirt he wore, which— Ahh, *right.*

If it was possible to drown in a flood of memories, Elliot might not have minded at that moment. A phantom voice had stolen his brakes, he'd crashed his car, gotten concussed, and called *Lennox* to come and get him out of the hospital. He'd stolen the man's clothes. He'd been loopy from the morphine, which, as nice as the reduced pain had been, wasn't really something he wanted to think about now. And, to top it all off, it was Monday morning, which meant he needed to get to work. Wonderful.

Elliot gritted his teeth and grunted as he rolled over and up onto his hands, then blinked his eyes clear of sleep to see Lennox slumped down in the cushy wingback chair Elliot usually hung dirty shirts on. He blinked again, to make sure he wasn't imagining things.

Nope: there was Lennox, hands folded, legs going on forever out in front of him as he snored gently, his head on his chest. Holly had abandoned her usual spot with Elliot in favor of Lennox's lap. He couldn't blame her. Elliot reached for his phone, which had been silenced and set on the nightstand, and held it up to take a picture. He had to preserve the surprising level of cuteness that this man was showing.

The faint *click* of the camera was enough to wake Lennox up. "Elliot?" He started to straighten, then paused to set Holly on the ground before he pushed his way out of the chair. He stretched the way Elliot had wanted to, complete with a quiet symphony of cracks from his spinal column, then ran a hand through his messy, gorgeous hair as he asked, "How do you feel?"

"Like I got run over by a mountain," Elliot said honestly. "But I'll survive. Why were you sleeping in the chair?"

Lennox frowned, but it seemed to be directed at himself instead of Elliot. "I didn't mean to fall asleep there."

"Was the bed in the guest room not comfortable? Or is it that you missed me?" Elliot tried on a smile. It felt far more natural this morning than it had in the hospital yesterday. "You could have hopped in the bed. I wouldn't have minded."

"Trust me, you'd have minded," Lennox said. Elliot was prepared to argue the point, but his voice dried up when Lennox came over and sat down next to him on the bed. "How's your head feel?"

Elliot cleared his throat. "Fine." *Like a herd of elephants is tangoing around inside my skull.* "I mean, it could be worse."

"I'll grab you a pain pill." He got up, but Elliot grabbed his hand before he could go far.

"What kind of pain pill?" Had they filled the prescription last night after all? It was a little fuzzy. "Because I can't have Percocet. Addict here, remember?"

Lennox nodded calmly. "I know. It's just some Tylenol that I keep in my gym bag. Extra strength."

Tylenol. That would probably be fine. "Sounds good." He sighed and ran one hand carefully over his head. His hair was crispy in places. *Gross.* "And then I need to shower. I've got things to do today and I can't afford to be out of it."

Now Lennox's frown was *definitely* directed at Elliot. "Your things can wait."

"I've got to get to work—"

"You've got to take it easy," Lennox said gently. "Serena already knows you're not coming in."

"You talked to her?" Elliot asked, horrified.

"Not directly. I left her a text. I didn't get too specific, but she knows enough that she won't expect you to show up."

"*You* left her a text about *me* not coming in to work? That's like waving a red flag in front of a bull. She's going to think I'm taking the day off to get over a weekend of crazy, amazing fucking when really I only got a single night of that before everything went to hell." Elliot sighed. "This was the worst weekend, seriously. You're the only good thing that happened to me."

"Well, I'm glad I qualify. And if you're that worried . . ." Lennox nudged the phone. "Call her and see what she has to say. If it's anything other than 'Don't come into the office,' I'll be stunned. I'll leave the pills in the bathroom for you, make some coffee and call my work, then we can talk about the rest of the day."

"Okay." Elliot watched him leave, then bit the bullet and checked his messages. There was only one from Serena. *Call me when you get this.* Oh no, that wasn't ominous at all. He called her up before he could convince himself to fall asleep again.

"Elliot! Tell me you're at home and you haven't been whisked back to the hospital for a life-saving emergency surgery!"

"I'm at home," he parroted obediently. "No surgery of any kind required, I promise. What on earth did Lennox say to you?"

Serena grunted like she'd just tried to shoulder the world for Atlas. "Oh, that man! He said, and let me quote this text to you because it's absolutely ridiculous—it's so like him; he used to drive Gaby crazy with this stuff: 'Elliot in accident. Doing fine. I'm looking after him. Don't call tonight—his head hurts. No working tomorrow, doctor's orders.' Which tells me everything and nothing, and then he wouldn't answer my texts!"

"I like his commitment in the face of extreme pressure," Elliot joked. "We should hire him to do all the social media posts; people would go crazy speculating."

"Elliot." It was the voice she used on telemarketers who wouldn't quit. "This isn't funny. Tell me what's going on."

Part of him wanted to spill the whole story, to unburden himself to the person who knew him best these days. The other parts, though? Those parts of him knew it was a bad idea. Serena would react like any sane person would react, just like Lennox had: she would ask him to tell the police and then, when he didn't, do it for him. Serena had little in the way of understanding and compassion for Elliot's sister, and wouldn't give a shit about ruining Vanessa's chances to become Denver's DA. She would put Elliot first, and he couldn't have that. Not right now.

"I crashed my car on Lookout Mountain Road," he told her. "I wasn't drunk and no one else was involved—I just lost control. I was taken to the hospital and Lennox came to get me because," and here was a lie he hadn't discussed with the man, but it was only to save Serena's feelings, "he was staying over at my house anyway."

There was a moment of silence, and then— "Oh my God, I knew it! The two of you got along like a house on fire! Are you the reason he missed the family dinner yesterday?"

"I was treated for a concussion, and he wanted to stick around and make sure I was okay."

"Oh, Gaby was so mad at first! But Lee, she was fine—because she knew, didn't she! She had to know. Otherwise she'd be furious too. How did all this happen?"

This seemed like a good place to stop things cold. "*Aaany*way, can you tell Ted we need to postpone the shoot to later in the week, when I can wash my hair again?" Elliot said loudly. "And reschedule my meetings? I can handle any paperwork you send along from home—"

"What, no! No, you do nothing, you need to rest and recover! I'll take care of everything, don't worry about work, it's just a tasting and a few final contracts to review. And Elliot," Serena's tone changed. "I'm so sorry about your car. Do you think you can get it fixed?"

He had no idea. He couldn't even remember what it looked like, post-crash. "I hope so. Thanks, Serena."

"Thank me by being good for Lennox."

"I'll do my best." He ended the call and set the phone down, then carefully got out of bed and headed into the bathroom. The Tylenol were on the sink, two innocuous little white pills. They'd barely be enough to take the edge off, but he didn't have any other choice. Except for the morphine he'd been unable to avoid last night, he hadn't touched anything stronger than aspirin since getting out of rehab.

Elliot stared at himself in the mirror. He could vaguely remember doing this last night, and the purple expanse on his chest was even more livid in the cool lights of his vanity today, especially where his seat belt had cut into his skin. His eyes were bloodshot and baggy with exhaustion, and his hair was *literally* a bloody mess. The urge to pop a few pills, crawl back under his covers, and sleep the rest of the day away was so strong it almost made him nostalgic for the brief period when he'd done that every morning.

Those days were gone, though. Elliot swallowed the Tylenol and rinsed them down with a palmful of water, peeled off Lennox's clothes, turned the shower to as hot as he could stand it, and got under the spray. He was desperate to dunk his head, but resisted for the sake of the super glue that was holding his scalp together. The worst of it would come out with his comb.

Thirty minutes later he was clean, dressed in one of his suits, and had straightened his hair out to the point where he wasn't ashamed to meet his own eyes any longer. He wasn't bleeding again, at least, so that was a good sign. He folded up Lennox's clothes, took one last surreptitious sniff of them, then carefully made his way down to the kitchen.

Lennox was standing with his back braced against the counter, one hand holding a cup of coffee while the other was occupied with his phone. It took a moment for Elliot to realize what was different about him—Lennox was wearing one of Elliot's favorite shirts, a maroon Henley that complimented his bronze skin. Seeing it cling to his biceps was a lovely distraction, almost enough to make Elliot forget that his lungs felt like going on revolt and refusing to keep up this breathing bullshit.

The only problem with the pretty picture was how Lennox was glowering at his phone. "Is something wrong?" Elliot asked as he sat on one of the barstools.

"My boss isn't too happy with me."

That didn't sound good. "Is he unhappy as in, 'I'm going to make you work nights and weekends for a month to make up for this,' or unhappy as in, 'Pink is the new black and you'd better keep an eye on your inbox.'"

"The first. Pretty sure, anyway," Lennox said. He didn't sound sure, though. Elliot had to beat back the hot niggle of guilt that was trying to worm its way into his gut. "I'm basically being ordered to show up and explain why I'm not there this morning, but a beat-up Porsche is."

Oh, perfect. "I'll go with you."

"You could stay here and rest," Lennox said. "Your doctor said that's what you need most of all."

Elliot did his best to exude health and well-being through his smile. "I also seem to recall something about needing to be looked after while I'm recovering, so we'd actually be following his instructions. Besides, I want to talk to your coworker about the car and see if he's found anything amiss."

Lennox's lips quirked in a little smile. "'Amiss.' What are you, a detective novel?"

"It could be worse, I could have said 'nefarious,'" Elliot pointed out, delighted to get a positive reaction out of the man. "Or dastardly! 'Dastardly' is a good word—it sounds exactly like what it means. Everyone should strive to use 'dastardly' as often as possible."

"That's ridiculous."

"*You're* ridiculous. Let me come to work with you since I can't go to my own." He tried to bat his eyelashes but failed, since any rapid movement of his face provoked a wince. "I really do need to talk to . . . Kevin, was it? So I can find out if anyone has done something dastardly and nefarious to my car." The grin ached a bit, but he couldn't hold it back. "Do you see what I did there?"

"I can't believe people pay to listen to you," Lennox said, but his tone was one of capitulation. "Fine. But I'm making breakfast first."

"I didn't know you could cook."

Lennox shrugged before opening the fridge and rooting around inside. "I'm not fantastic, but I have a kid to feed and I have to provide something marginally healthy for her when she's over at my place." He paused for a moment, like he was going to say something else, then sighed and pulled out the butter, eggs, and some shredded cheese that Elliot had intended to turn into quesadillas and then forgotten about. "Pan?"

"To the right of the oven." Having seen Lennox's hesitation, Elliot felt the urge to press. "How often is Lee over at your house?"

"Not too often."

Nightmares. Elliot remembered Lennox mentioning them before they fell asleep together. Nothing had happened that night, or last night as far as Elliot knew, but maybe when they manifested it was a lot worse than normal nightmares. Not the sort of thing a kid could sleep through, perhaps. He watched in silence as Lennox broke the eggs into the pan, scrambled them up, and threw cheese in. It was quick, simple food, the kind that Mischa used to make for them on the weekends when they'd been too tired to go out. He'd dressed it up with chives and Himalayan rock salt, but in the end it had just been eggs, greasy and delicious.

Lennox sat down on the other stool as he set a plate in front of Elliot, jolting him from his reverie. "Bon appétit."

"*Merci.*" He took a careful bite, and then, when his stomach didn't kick up a fuss, another. "It's good. Thank you."

"It was easy to make."

"That's not what I'm . . ." Elliot shook his head. "Thank you for being here. I know I said it before, but I mean it. I don't want you to risk your job over taking care of me, especially when you have no good reason to, but I'm really glad you're here."

Lennox put his fork down. "I don't think the fallout's gonna be that bad, but even if it is, I'd rather be here and know you're okay than hear about it secondhand from Serena when you're not and wonder why you didn't call me. I need—" It was his turn to seem frustrated. "I've got a need to verify, these days. Check and double-check. If I wasn't here, I'd just be thinking about you anyway, so. Thanks for letting me stay." He picked up his fork and ate determinedly, as if his discomfort could be buried beneath activity. Elliot let him have his distance, and treasured the blossoming warmth in his chest that had nothing to do with his bruises.

Lennox took Holly out before they left, which was nice because it gave Elliot a chance to moan and groan without an audience as he got into his shoes and jacket. He moved like an old man, evaluating every body part before he shifted it, but his head was clear and he was ready for some answers. Or barring answers, at least a chance to evaluate whether his car could be saved. He carefully didn't allow his mind to ramble down the path of *who, why, what if?* Instead he waited for Lennox to bring Holly in from the cold, then gratefully took the man's hand for support as they went out the front door.

In true Colorado fashion, it had snowed half a foot overnight. Equally true to Colorado, the sun was now out and it had to be close to forty degrees, because the snow was already starting to melt. "I love it here," Elliot sighed, looking out over the plains as Lennox began to drive back into Golden. "Nowhere else has ever really felt like home."

"It has its charms," Lennox allowed. "I'm not sure I'm sold on the whole 'ice and snow and mountains' thing, though."

"This is the South in you rising up in rebellion, isn't it?" Elliot demanded. "You've got to fight the good fight here, Lennox. Don't let the memory of warm winters blind you to all the other shit that you get down there: humidity, bugs, incoming tropical diseases, and pure chaos whenever the gods *do* bless the place with snow."

Lennox took a left at the light, heading away from downtown and toward the warehouse district. "You make a strong case, advocate."

"I do indeed. If I wasn't a businessman, I'd be a lawyer—oh wait, I was."

"And how did that turn out for you?"

Coming from any other person, that question would have been loaded with sarcasm and Elliot would have responded in kind. But Lennox just sounded slightly amused, which was a state of being Elliot could get behind. And the question deserved his honesty. "It wasn't the best, I'm not going to lie. But I enjoyed it for quite a while, and knowing how to present my point of view persuasively has certainly helped me get to where I am today." He shrugged a little. "Despite the fact that I clearly haven't won *everyone* over, I don't regret my life."

"Just some of your decisions," Lennox said softly. He seemed a thousand miles away.

"A few," Elliot agreed. They had been big decisions, with correspondingly big regrets, but he couldn't dwell on them without drowning in them. Better to push them aside and press on.

They sat in silence for a few minutes before Lennox turned onto Castillion Place. "You know you've arrived once they're naming streets after you," Elliot murmured, coaxing another smile out of Lennox.

"It's because of the factory. This was an undeveloped part of town before Rodney bought part of it and started making knives here. He's brought a lot of attention and revenue to Golden, so they gave him props. It's not that impressive though," he added as they pulled to a stop in front of a single-story brick building with *CASTILLION* written in wide white letters over the front door. The *T* in the word was shaped like a dagger. Lovely. "The city council almost named a street Dunkin around the same time." He stopped the truck. "You need help getting out?"

There was no judgment there, but there was also likely no fooling the man. "I can get out," Elliot said. "I'm just not sure how far I can go from there."

"I'll be here if you need me."

I know you will. It was a comforting promise, even if Elliot hated that he might need to rely on it. He managed to get his feet onto the pavement okay, though, and after the first few steps, his soreness eased to the point where he barely limped.

Inside, the store was surprisingly large, with rows of glass display cases filled with knives, handguns, and all sorts of weaponly ephemera that Elliot couldn't identify. A man who looked like a skinnier version of Santa Claus was ringing up a customer at the front desk, but as soon as he saw Lennox his cheery demeanor fell into something grave, disappointed even. This was the boss, then. The customer left, bag in hand, and the white-haired man waited expectantly.

Lennox took a deep breath. "Let me talk to Rodney and go get Kevin. I'll be right back."

"Take your time." Elliot turned to the nearest display case and surveyed the contents. Nothing in there was explosive or edged; good, these were more his speed. *ASP: Airweight Expandable Baton*, the card beside one of the things read. Apparently they came in black, silver, or camouflage. A color for every occasion, whether it was beating people at a black-tie event or clubbing bunny rabbits as they ran through the woods.

"Are you interested in a baton?" a salesperson asked, coming up on Elliot from behind. Elliot almost startled, but his body wasn't in the mood to comply, thank god. The man was youngish, had thick, dark glasses framing a round face and a beard you could have lost small animals in. Elliot glanced at his name tag. Ah, this was the infamous Kevin. He seemed like Lennox's polar opposite.

"I don't think I've got the appropriate skill set to use one well," Elliot demurred. "I was never much of a baseball player."

"Oh, dude, no, you totally don't have to be any kind of athlete to use one of these! I mean, I carry a baton myself and look at me." Kevin patted his slightly rounded stomach. "Of course, for me it's just a backup weapon, but I still really like having it on hand. It's comforting, you know? Like having a tactical flashlight, but without the flash."

"I have no idea what a tactical flashlight is," Elliot said.

Kevin's face brightened further, and he led Elliot to another case. "Oh, they're great! They're super bright—it's all about lumens, mostly, but they also make a great fist pack to support your hand when you're throwing punches, and there are crenellations on the end so that if you impact *that* way, you do extra damage. See?" He opened up the case and pulled out a four-inch flashlight. It did, indeed, have teeth carved out of the end. Elliot shuddered.

"This one has a strobe function too, and the back glows red in case you want to leave it out as an emergency beacon, and if you pull it apart like this—" he demonstrated "—it's like a lantern! It's so useful. I've had one of these going since four o'clock this morning."

"Why so early?"

"I've been checking out some wreckage, trying to determine whether or not there was any foul play."

"Foul play." Good phrase, I should have remembered that one. "And was there anything foul at work in my car?" Elliot asked.

Kevin's reaction was gratifyingly enthusiastic. He could give Holly a run for her money. "Holy shit, you're the dude! Oh wow, you— It's your car? Dude! How did you walk away from that? The damage is fucking sick!"

"Kevin." Santa Claus—or Rodney, Elliot presumed—was walking their way, looking embarrassed. Lennox came with him, avoiding eye contact even though Elliot tried. "Please don't use that kind of language with a customer."

"Yeah, but Rodney, it's his car! This is the guy with the car!" He turned back to Elliot and stuck out a hand. "It's so nice to meet you, dude!"

"Likewise." Elliot shook, then rerouted Kevin's wandering attention. "And what did you find out about the car?"

"Oh, yeah. It was totally hacked."

It shouldn't have been such a huge relief to Elliot; he'd *known* that his car had been hacked—it was the reason for the crash. Still, hearing someone else verify it so readily lifted off one particular weight, while another surged in with a vengeance. Elliot wasn't crazy and he had hard evidence to prove it: excellent. Someone wanted to screw with him badly enough to actually hack his car: frightening. "Would you mind showing me how?"

"Showing all of us," Lennox interjected.

"Dudes." Kevin grinned like it was Christmas morning. "I'd love to."

CHAPTER TEN

Partial transcription of most recent appointment with West, Lennox, Staff Sergeant US Army Rangers (R), January 28, 3:19 p.m.:

JS: You're right, I don't understand how you feel. But I can see that this decision weighs heavily on you, and I want to try and help you come to terms with what happened, so you can move forward.

LW: There are some things you don't move forward from. You don't deserve to. The men who died, they were under my command. They'll never move on. The guy who did the shooting did so on my orders, and it's fucked him up for life. Yeah, we were acquitted of any wrongdoing, but that doesn't matter.

JS: It does matter, Lennox. You made the best decision you could at the time.

LW: It was still wrong. Friendly fire . . . isn't that the worst name you've ever heard of for killing a teammate?

The first thing Lennox thought when he saw the car was, *Thank fuck Elliot survived.* His second thought was, *Thank fuck there were no passengers in there.* The driver's side was banged up from rolling, but seemed largely intact. The passenger's side had been scraped along the canyon wall, and it was . . . well, it mostly wasn't there anymore. The door was missing, part of the roof was gone, and the tires had practically evaporated. It was the worst damage he'd seen on a vehicle up close since an IED exploded under a convoy two tours ago. He shivered.

Kevin never had time for anyone's discomfort, and was rambling on without a care in the world. "I was worried at first that I wouldn't be able to find anything because there's so much damage to this side, but when I found the dongle I knew I was going to get lucky." He pointed at the tiny black device inserted into the car's USB port, almost out of sight on the passenger side.

Elliot frowned. "That's from my insurance company."

"Yeah, that's what it *looks* like," Kevin crowed. "But it's a *fake* dongle! It's got some amazing software on it that tapped right into your car's computer and handed over essential functionality to whoever was controlling it."

"So someone had to break into my car to put it there."

Kevin waved a hand. "Yeah, but that was probably the easy part. It's not hard to break into a Porsche, I've—" he glanced back toward Rodney, who was standing in the doorway, and cleared his throat "—never done it before *myself*, obviously, or like, not for years, y'know? Definitely not. But it takes about ten seconds."

"Interesting," Elliot murmured before turning back to Kevin and putting on a pleasant face. "Is there any way to trace the signal to whoever was controlling my car? Or track the software?"

Kevin shook his head. "The signal leads to a dead end, probably a burner phone. And the software . . . man, it's good but it's not *signed* or anything. You'd have to know a lot more about hacking than me to get a clue about who might have made it just from the code."

"Kevin?" Rodney called out. "If you're done here, someone really ought to be minding the store."

"Right." Kevin nodded, one hand still caressing the dented side of the Porsche.

"I mean *you*, Kevin."

"Oh. *Oh*, sorry. Sorry! I just . . ." He turned a beaming smile at Elliot. "It's so interesting. I never could have imagined yesterday that I'd get to root around in a car like this! With permission and everything!"

"*Kevin.*"

"Right, sorry, sorry." Kevin scooted, and Lennox got ready for round two with Rodney. He hadn't been fired—not quite—but the man didn't approve of his business being dragged into what looked like an enormous mess, and he appreciated Lennox aiding and abetting that mess even less.

"I thought you finally had your head on straight," he'd said fifteen minutes ago, disappointment suffusing his voice. "What are you getting out of this? Some sort of penance? You have nothing left to pay for."

"I know that," Lennox had replied, as convincingly as he could. "This has nothing to do with me. This is about helping someone in need."

Rodney had arched an eyebrow. "Our assistance doesn't extend as far as allowing customers to stow their compromised cars on company property. It doesn't extend as far as getting my employees wrapped up in their troubles, either. What's really going on here, Lennox? What have you gotten yourself into?"

Lennox had sighed. "Sir, with respect . . . that's not something I can talk about right now."

It had been nicer than saying *none of your business*, but Lennox hated the thought of disappointing the man who'd taken a chance on him, especially since he wasn't going to back down. He had no intention of leaving Elliot alone until things got resolved. That meant taking unpaid time off from work, which Gaby would surely find out about, not to mention making rent tight next month. That was the silver lining to Lee not spending nights at his place: if he had to cancel his internet and television for a month, and maybe cut the heat off as well, at least she wouldn't know about it.

He started to turn to Rodney, but Elliot caught his arm. "Actually, can you give me a few minutes with him?" he asked. "I'll catch up with you inside as soon as we're done."

"What do you plan to talk about?" Lennox asked warily.

"It's nothing, it won't take long. Go on, I'll be right there. Mr. Castillion!" Elliot walked to the back door before Lennox could stop him, better now than he had when they first arrived, almost normally. "May I have a moment of your time?"

Rodney raised an eyebrow in Lennox's direction but responded politely enough, and Lennox took that as permission to postpone their confrontation. He dodged around them and went back into the building, stopping in the break room to wave through the office window at Rebecca, who was monitoring the system. She had Rodney's round face and comfortable build, and if Lennox hadn't seen her fieldstrip her Glock 19 in under twenty seconds, he wouldn't have suspected she even knew what one was.

It was a shame she was on a call; he could have used their conversation as an excuse not to go into the store and deal with Kevin's exuberance head-on. Fortunately, his own phone provided one by ringing a moment later. He glanced at the caller and answered before the second ring. "Oliver?"

"Who else would be calling you from this number?" his best friend asked.

"A Nigerian oil smuggler holding you for ransom."

"Once. That happened *once*—will you never let me live it down?"

"Probably not." Oliver was one of the few people he could tease with impunity, he wasn't about to relinquish that pleasure. "What's up?"

"The price of ammunition in the Sinai Peninsula, but you don't care about that."

"Not at all."

"I tried," Oliver said with a dramatic sigh. "Lord knows I tried to make a businessman out of you. You're just resistant to anything remotely interesting."

It said something about the strength of their relationship that they could joke about this now. For years Lennox had been carefully ignorant of Oliver's business, and then, very briefly, he'd jumped into it feetfirst in an effort to forget his mistakes. But it wasn't just deciding to battle his latent suicidal tendencies that had made Lennox decide to get out. There was illegal and then there was immoral, and Lennox wasn't entirely sure where he categorized Oliver's work. He'd only known he couldn't keep doing it.

That didn't mean he couldn't give Oliver shit about it, though. "Really? Interesting? Three gun battles in six months, that's interesting to you?"

"It keeps the blood pumping, doesn't it?"

Lennox rolled his eyes. "Unless your blood is pumping *out*, you'd better have a reason for calling when you know I'm working."

"Are you rolling your eyes at me? That's what you usually do when you're delivering ultimatums."

"*Oliver*. Kind of busy here, so get to the point."

"Right. I have a layover in Denver two days from now at three in the afternoon. Would you like to meet me at DIA, get a beer?"

Christ, would he ever. As annoying as Oliver was sometimes, being with him relaxed Lennox in a way almost nothing else did. It reminded him of being around Elliot, actually. In which case, Lennox had to seriously question his taste in men, because well-dressed, incredibly frustrating jackasses were a recipe for trouble. Still . . . it would be nice to see Oliver again. He didn't know where things would stand with Elliot by then, though.

"Does silence mean no?"

Lennox blinked, then shook himself. "Sorry, I was just thinking . . . do you mind if I bring someone along?"

"Who, Lia? Wouldn't she be in school?"

"Yes, she would, and no, not Lia. It's Lee now, by the way."

"*Lee.* Lord. It'll be metal bands and eyeliner twenty-four seven before you know it."

"Don't mistake her teenage years for yours," Lennox chided him, but he had to smile. He remembered Oliver in eyeliner. It had been startlingly sexy.

"Fine, K-pop and Nicki Minaj, then—I don't know. And if it isn't her, who do you have in mind?"

How did Lennox explain Elliot? "I'm sort of . . . looking after someone at the moment. He's in a difficult situation, and I want to make sure he gets through it okay."

"Oh, *he* is, is he?" Oliver sounded way too interested.

"It's not like that," Lennox protested, even though it sort of was. "I'll try to be there, all right? Text me when you land."

"I will. Lennox—remember to take care of yourself too, all right?"

It was only the genuine edge of worry in Oliver's voice that prevented Lennox from ending the call instantly. They had agreed *not* to talk about Lennox's personal issues, had practically signed a contract in blood after the clusterfuck of their last month together. Oliver had been as enthusiastic about him getting a shrink as Gaby by then, the traitor. "I'm fine."

"I don't doubt you think that." And then, before Lennox could go after him, "Hopefully I'll see you in a few days. Don't freeze to death in the meantime!"

Lennox snorted. "Who's the Canadian here?"

"I'm a Canadian who hates snow, why do you think I spend so much time in the Middle East? *Au revoir.*" Oliver was gone before Lennox could tell him exactly why he spent so much time in war zones. He tentatively put the appointment into his calendar, then went back into the shop.

Elliot was already inside, and was buying something from Kevin while he chatted with Rodney. They all appeared totally at ease, and Rodney actually smiled at Lennox when he saw him. Lennox approached warily.

"Lennox!" Rodney clapped him on the shoulder. "Why didn't you *tell* me about the sponsorship deal you were negotiating?"

"I'm sure it's just because he didn't want to mention it before the paperwork was on the way," Elliot interjected with a smile, covering nicely for Lennox's utter confusion. "Which I'll have my secretary complete and send to you before the end of the day. In the meantime, I can't thank you enough for letting me steal away your best employee for the rest of the week. Once the Meetup is over, I'll be sure to return him in perfect condition."

Rodney chuckled, his amusement clearly tempered by relief. "It seems the business we're going to get from this will more than make up for his *temporary* loss."

"I can virtually guarantee it," Elliot said, taking a black bag with the Castillion logo on it. "Kevin, thank you so much for your help. It was invaluable. My insurance company will send a tow truck later today for the car."

"Dude, you're totally welcome! Like I said, I never get to play around in quality vehicles like that, so I was all about it."

Somehow Elliot was able to get them out of there in a flurry of well-being and delight instead of the recriminations that Lennox had been preparing for since last night. And it wasn't even lunchtime yet.

"What did you say to Rodney?" he asked as he opened up the truck. Elliot managed to get in by himself with only a little grunt of effort.

"I said that you were hard at work negotiating a Castillion sponsorship of my Executive Meetup for free, in exchange for your assistance in prepping for the event and looking into installing systems in my business for the rest of the week," he said flippantly. "It has a ten-thousand-dollar value: you're welcome. Are they really called *dongles*?"

"Elliot . . ."

"Because that doesn't sound like a real word to me. Was Kevin screwing with us?"

"No, *dongle* is the word. Elliot, I didn't *do* any of that."

Elliot stared at Lennox like he was being deliberately slow. "I know. But it was the easiest way to get him off your back and keep you with me at the same time. I figured you'd choose to stay whether Rodney wants you to or not. I just had to give him a reason to be happy about it."

Lennox shook his head. "You didn't need to do that."

"It's my business, my call. If I want to hand Castillion a sponsorship that everyone else has paid out the nose for, I'll do it. Now, seriously though. *Dongles*? Because that has to be a joke."

"Not really, you're just concussed."

"I'm not *that* concussed," Elliot argued, but he shut his eyes a moment later. "I am tired, though."

"Yeah, that would be the concussion," Lennox said gently. "Sit back and get some sleep; we'll be back at your place soon."

"I have to call Serena and tell her to send a contract to Rodney and change the adverts first." That didn't take long, and by the time they'd pulled back in to Elliot's house, he was drowsing against the headrest, his grip on his phone loose enough that it threatened to release entirely.

The affection that surged through Lennox as he looked at Elliot made goose bumps rise up on his arms. He couldn't possibly feel so strongly about this guy so soon. They barely knew each other, and though Lennox had come out on top, he didn't like lying to his boss to get himself out of trouble. Elliot was an unknown quantity, not someone he'd grown up with like Oliver or trained with like Gaby. He was a rock making ripples in Lennox's already-turbulent life, and Lennox didn't need further ripples to deal with.

It didn't matter. Good idea or not, Lennox was committed now, at least to helping Elliot get rid of his stalker. Which was definitely a situation he needed more information on.

He helped Elliot inside, put him to bed—with only Holly for company, despite Elliot trying to pull him down beneath the covers—and started searching for information on Sheridan Pullman. There was plenty to read up on. He'd gone to MIT, worked for a few other big companies to get experience, before starting up Redback Industries on his own. He was a good scientist but a better businessman, who had kept his ear to the ground in search of new technologies to patent in the name of Redback in addition to all the in-house research the firm did.

The articles Lennox read were split when it came to Pullman's personality. The company had been nothing but profitable until its untimely demise, but Pullman himself, well . . . writers couldn't agree on whether he was Satan in a suit, or just a lesser Machiavelli. It was a biography that spoke of ruthlessness either way, and Lennox could definitely see him doing unscrupulous things in the name of business. But . . .

The snake didn't fit. It didn't seem *elegant* enough for a guy like that. Sheridan Pullman might be an ex-con now, but he was still a millionaire, still a genius. He could still afford to hire the best, and probably wouldn't resort to Godfather-like tactics to instill fear. The snake had been gross, but it was crass, the angry act of a person sending a simple, gory message. Remotely hijacking the car, on the other hand? Smart. Very smart, and something that required skill to pull off. An action like that instilled reasonable paranoia in the victim.

Then again, maybe Lennox just wasn't scared enough of snakes. Elliot had certainly responded badly to it.

Lennox's phone rang. He checked the caller and answered. "Hey, sweetheart."

"Hi, Dad."

"What's happening?"

"Not much."

Oh boy. Now they were going to play the *let me pry this information out of you* game. Lennox checked the time: already after three. How had it gotten so late? "How was school?" he asked as he got up to stretch his stiff muscles.

"Fine. Boring. I don't have homework, if that's what you're getting at," Lee added.

"Okay, good."

"Yeah." *Oh, this is going fantastically.* Fortunately, Lee got tired of stalling. "So, remember when you said you'd make up for missing dinner to me this week?"

"I do remember, seeing as I told you that yesterday," Lennox replied. "You calling your chip in already?" It wasn't the best night for it, but then, things would probably only get more frantic as it got closer to the weekend and the Executive Meetup. Lennox didn't want to stand up Lee again.

"I'm *bored*," Lee complained. "Mom is going to be out late at a business dinner, the twins are at their mom's and Marcus is traveling this week. Mom left me some food, but it's gross."

"Too healthy for you?"

"Too many beans." Lennox could picture the disgust on her face. "Why does she have to put so many beans in the chili? Why can't she just use more meat?"

Personally Lennox agreed, but he wasn't about to say so. "You could make it yourself next time if you don't like it."

"Stop it, Dad, now you sound like her. Can't we do something tonight? Maybe go to a movie?"

"Not on a school night," Lennox said automatically, but his free hand was already flexing as he thought about what he'd really like to be doing—burning off some energy in the ring. He could bring Elliot, even. That way he could get a workout in with Lee and keep Elliot in his sights all at once. "How about we go to the boxing gym? We can see how much you remember from last time."

There was a long moment of silence, but it didn't seem like a bad one. "It's been a while," Lee said at last. "What if I suck at it?"

"You won't suck at it."

"People might make fun of me."

"Nobody will make fun of you at my gym." *Or I'll make them regret it.*

"Is Elliot coming?"

Lennox had thought that might come up. "I'll bring him along, but he's in no shape to box right now."

"No, I get it," Lee said quickly. "That's cool. Sure. Let's do it."

"Let me check with your mom first."

"She won't care," Lee said. "She'll be happy you're not neglecting me."

That sounded awful. "Is that how you feel?" Lennox asked.

"Not exactly," Lee said, but her voice was a lot smaller. "It's just . . . Why won't you let me come back to your apartment?"

Lennox squeezed his eyes shut. "Lee . . ."

"It's not like you hurt me! Mom said I shouldn't have tried to wake you up like that anyway, so it was *my* fault—"

"No, it wasn't your fault at all," Lennox insisted. "It wasn't mine either; I was asleep—" his therapist had been useful for pounding *that* into his head, at least "—but it still wasn't safe for you. I don't want to take any chances until I've got things under a little better control, okay? It's not you, sweetheart. I swear it's not you."

Lee took a deep, hitching breath, then sighed loudly. "Dad?"

"Yeah?" he said tentatively.

"I really want to punch something now."

Lennox smiled despite himself. "That's my girl. I'll be there soon."

"Don't forget to bring Elliot!"

"As long as he feels up to it." He ended the call and turned toward the stairs only to see that he'd been beaten to the punch: Elliot was standing on the lowest stair, seeming way more alert than he had that morning.

"So, we're getting together with your daughter?" he asked with a smile.

"If you don't mind, yeah."

"Not at all. She's incredibly easy to get along with—it's hard to believe you're related."

"Someone woke up with a smart mouth," Lennox said, going over to the stairway. He leaned against the bannister and looked up at Elliot, who stared back like he knew everything Lennox was thinking.

"My mouth isn't the only clever part of my anatomy," he said. "I've got lots of clever parts."

"That doesn't make any sense."

"It will once you see what I can do with my hands."

"Ah." Lennox glanced down at the front of Elliot's slacks, then back up. He slowly slid his arms around the other man's waist, pulling him a little closer. "I see. You didn't wake up smart, you woke up horny."

Elliot shrugged. "Guilty as charged. Chalk it up to my astonishing powers of recuperation."

"Well, I'd love to help you with that," Lennox said earnestly, leaning in until Elliot's erection was pressed to his stomach. He felt it harden further, and smiled. "But . . ." He placed a kiss on Elliot's collarbone as he rubbed against his groin.

"But?" Elliot asked breathlessly.

"But now we've got to go." Lennox smacked Elliot on the ass and then pulled away entirely. "I'll get your jacket." He left Elliot gaping as he headed for the coatrack.

"Wha— No, hold on," Elliot protested. "That— You—"

"We have places to be. If you're good, though, and if you feel up to it later tonight, we can revisit the issue." He brought Elliot's coat over and held it open for him. Elliot reluctantly turned and let Lennox pull it over his arms and shoulders. "But for now, we're in a hurry."

"You are an unexpected tease," Elliot said as he turned back, full of aplomb again.

"Gotta keep you on your toes." Lennox pulled on his own coat and zipped it closed. It looked cold out there.

"We'll see if you can, later." Elliot smiled like sin as he slipped his shoes on. "Let me take Holly out and we can go."

"Hey." Lennox caught his sleeve. "Thanks." *Thanks for understanding that I have a kid, thanks for humoring her, humoring both of us, and coming along.*

"It's my pleasure," Elliot replied. "I like kids." His smile crumpled a bit as he turned away, but Lennox didn't push it. It wasn't the time for that. He got his phone out and called Gaby instead.

An hour later they were at the gym, Elliot seated on the bleachers and watching with every indication of interest as Lennox put Lee through her paces. They'd started slow, reviewing the basic punches and making sure she wasn't going to hurt herself when she made contact. She was a fast learner though, and while it had been years since they'd boxed together, back before his last tour they'd done it every weekend.

Lennox held the punching pads and called out combinations, and Lee, with a fierce focus that reminded him of her mother, hit every one of them. He threw in slips and she moved like water, sliding under the pads and then coming back around for a perfect hook or uppercut. Lennox had expected her to call it after half an hour but she held out for nearly forty-five minutes before she finally dropped her hands and didn't pick them up again.

"I need . . . a break . . . Daddy . . ."

"You need a freaking medal, is what you need," Lennox said with a grin, but he put the pads down and walked her over to the bleachers, where she collapsed next to Elliot without taking off her gloves.

"Water . . ."

"Here." Elliot handed over her bottle, which she somehow managed to hold long enough to down half of. "You were fantastic," he told her, then looked at Lennox. "If this is the kind of self-defense you teach, I don't think I'd survive it."

"This isn't self-defense," Lennox said automatically. "It's boxing. Different skills."

"Self-defense has groin strikes," Lee added. She seemed tired but bright, happy. It wasn't an expression Lennox had seen on her a lot lately. "It's way easier to learn."

"The basics are, at least," Lennox agreed. Carl waved at him from the rear of the gym, and Lennox raised a shoulder in question. Carl just raised an eyebrow and disappeared into his office. *Subtle.* "I'll be back in a second, okay?" Lennox tapped one of Lee's gloves. "Get these off before they start to smell."

"*You* smell," she replied, but she put the water bottle down. Elliot began to help her with the gloves, and Lennox went to meet with his cryptic coach.

Carl's office carried the same scents of sweat and leather as the rest of the gym, but underneath them was a hint of stale tobacco, leftover from before Carl's brush with lung cancer. He didn't waste any time. "Your kid needs to be on our team."

Of all the things Lennox hadn't expected to hear today. "You want to train her to be an actual boxer?"

"She's got a good grounding in it, and she looked hungry out there. She'd eat the other kids her age for breakfast."

Lennox shook his head. "She doesn't have time for boxing, she's got school, and ballet, and . . ." *And she hates ballet. And it would give you something to do together.*

"Ballet helps teach good footwork," Carl said nonchalantly. "If I could get more of my guys into ballet, there'd be more Golden Gloves champions in this place. Hell, I dated a ballerina in the seventies. She was, shit, Ukrainian, I think?" His eyes went a little hazy. "She could kick like a mule in pointy-toed slippers. Put me flat on my back for a week once."

Lennox held up a hand. "TMI."

"I'm just sayin', maybe talk to her about it. I've got two other teenage girls training here, both a bit older, but they'd be good sparring partners. Boys too, and I don't put up with macho bullshit when it comes to my team."

"I'm sure you don't." He couldn't deny that the idea had a certain appeal. But the last thing he wanted was for Lee to do it just because she wanted to please him. "I'll talk to her about it. Promise."

"Good."

Lennox headed back out to the gym, and wasn't as surprised as he should have been when he saw Lee giggling over something on Elliot's phone. "What's so funny?" he asked as he rejoined them.

"Dad, how did you fall asleep like that?" Lee marveled. "And the dog is so cute, oh my God! I want one."

"Talk to your mother," Lennox said automatically before his body caught up with his brain and he snatched the phone out of Elliot's hands. "What— I didn't even know you took this."

"I didn't want to tell you, for fear you'd delete it before I got a chance to show it off," Elliot said blithely. "I was waiting for the most appreciative audience."

"It's so cute," Lee advised him. "I asked Elliot to send it to me; I'm going to use it for your contact picture."

"You're a strange, strange girl," Lennox told her. "You feeling better now that you're all punched out? Not too tired, not too sore?"

"I'm fine." Lee tilted her head in assessment. "Although I'd really love pizza for dinner."

"Your mom left you chili."

"And the beans are *gross*, Dad, how many times do I have to tell you?"

"I could really go for pizza tonight," Elliot agreed. "And I've been unwell, so you should humor me."

Lennox stared back and forth between them for a moment, then sighed loudly to cover up the sudden surge of warmth in his chest. "You two are menaces when you get the same idea."

"Ooh, counselor, I object to your hideous slander," Elliot teased. "The only possible reparation that can be accepted at this point is pizza."

Lee nodded regally. "I concur."

"Well, then." One night of avoiding her mom's chili wouldn't hurt her. "Pizza it is."

Naturally, Elliot knew of an Italian restaurant that did a thinner, more authentic pizza instead of the deep dish, oil-drenched fare that Lennox was used to. It was still good, and Lee agreed to think about joining the boxing team as long as Lennox talked to Gaby about getting her out of ballet either way. Most of the conversation was between her and Elliot: Serena, movies, what kind of superpower they'd pick if they could have one.

"Telekinesis," Lee said at once. "So I could do all my chores with my mind, and when someone bothered me at school I could shove them and they wouldn't know it was me."

That was the first Lennox had heard of an issue at school. "Who's been bothering you?"

"Just a stupid idiot who thought it would be funny to snap my bra strap in gym class," Lee replied. "I told the teacher," she added in an attempt to mollify him. "And he got in trouble, which is good because if he hadn't I was going to—"

"Ah-ah, never confess to hypotheticals," Elliot interjected. "It gives people the wrong idea about you for no reason. Since you didn't do it, it doesn't matter."

"I'd rather know if my daughter is thinking about punching some jackass in her gym class," Lennox said, but Lee was nodding along with Elliot.

"It was fine. The teacher took care of it," she said firmly. "What would your power be, Elliot?"

"Telepathy, no question. Reading minds would have made my first job so much easier."

The mere thought of somebody else being able to look into his mind gave Lennox chills. "Good thing telepathy doesn't exist, then," he muttered.

"I'm pretty good at telling when people are lying, even without a superpower," Elliot said lightly. "And don't think you're getting out of playing. What would your power be?"

"Time travel." He said it without thinking, but the idea of being able to go back in time and unfuck everything he'd done wrong . . . he'd dwelled on that thought way more than was probably healthy in the past. His hand tightened around his glass of water, and he had to force himself to let go.

"Like in *Doctor Who*!" Lee exclaimed, for once perfectly oblivious. "Wibbly-wobbly timey-wimey!" Lennox breathed a silent sigh of relief as the topic turned to television shows he hadn't seen.

Gaby still wasn't home by the time they dropped Lee off, which spared Lennox a conversation he didn't particularly want to have about the other person in his truck. Elliot was uncharacteristically quiet on the ride back, probably due to fatigue. They got all the way inside the house and took a moment to deal with a frantically happy Holly, who was equally frantic to go outside and pee, before Elliot turned to Lennox with clear intent in his eyes.

He wrapped his arms around Lennox's neck and pulled him in close. "You are stupidly sexy even in the rattiest outfits," he murmured as he trailed his lips over Lennox's neck, tongue flicking out to taste. "Your gym clothes could belong to a hobo; they should *not* be sexy. Holes aren't hot."

Lennox huffed out a laugh. "Some holes are hot."

"No, don't attempt innuendo, you're terrible at it." Elliot kissed the point of Lennox's jaw. "Fortunately you have other sterling qualities."

"I thought you might be too tired for those other qualities."

Elliot laughed and straddled Lennox's thigh, grinding his erection against the muscle. "I'm bruised, not *dead*." There was a note of genuine desperation in his voice that Lennox hadn't counted on. "You have no idea how you look. None at all. I bet there are always people watching you when you're working out in there, aren't they? They can't take their eyes off you either."

Well, sure, but that was because people liked to watch the sparring. It didn't matter who was in the ring. "You're biased," Lennox told him, but his blood heated as his body responded to Elliot.

"Biased in favor of your mouth on my dick, definitely," Elliot said. "We should do that. On the stairs, because you were cruel earlier and I haven't been able to get them out of my mind since."

"We'd be more comfortable in a bed," Lennox argued.

"Whatever." Elliot kissed him, hard and needy. "I'm not going anywhere until I come, unless you carry me."

That sounded like a challenge. Lennox hadn't worked out nearly as much as he usually did tonight, so it was easy to slide his hands down beneath Elliot's butt and lift his feet off the floor. "Wrap your legs around my waist," he said, and Elliot obeyed, wide-eyed.

"Nobody has picked me up since high school," he remarked as Lennox walked them over to the stairs. Elliot wasn't a small man by any means, but Lennox barely felt his weight as he climbed, absorbed by the heat Elliot gave off, and how good it felt to hold him like this. "Not since I tried out for wrestling. I was awful at it, but it was worth the pain to be pinned by Ricky Otero."

Lennox reached Elliot's unmade bed and gently tipped him onto it, careful to remember his bruises as he followed Elliot down. He bracketed Elliot's torso with his arms, leaned in, and murmured, "And how does it feel to be pinned by me?"

"So much better." Elliot tried to press up against him but winced. "Except for that, *fuck*."

Lennox sat back and placed a hand on Elliot's shoulder. "Okay. I'm going to blow you, and you're going to lie there and take it like I want you to. Sound like a good plan?"

Elliot's eyes were dark. "It sounds even better than being pinned."

"Oh, that's not going to stop just because I'm not covering all of you." Lennox let the edge of the pure, smoldering *want* that was coursing through him come out in his smile and long, slow look. "Because the way I want you to take it? Is without moving a muscle."

"Except to touch you."

Lennox shook his head as he stripped his T-shirt off and threw it over the side of the bed. "Nope. No touching anything, not even yourself, until I'm done with you. I want to be the only thing you think about." *Not your pain, not your car, nothing but me.* It was nice to see Elliot being friendly toward Lennox's coworkers and daughter, but there was something thrilling about being the recipient of all of his attention. Lennox wanted to pass that feeling along.

Elliot gestured at himself. "I'm still dressed."

"I'll take care of that. Although next time?" Lennox leaned down until his chest barely brushed Elliot's, tilted his head, and whispered, "You should wear clothes you don't mind having ripped off."

"Holy shiii . . ." Elliot's voice trailed off as Lennox got started on his belt after checking his shoes were gone. Few things killed the mood like getting tangled in clothes. It wasn't easy, but he stuck to his guns about not letting Elliot help with anything, pulling back the moment Elliot's hands moved. Being bitched out had never been so satisfying before.

Lennox took his time and told Elliot everything he wanted to do to him, now and later, as he went. It was torturous for both of them, but Lennox liked it. "I can't play with these tonight." He brushed Elliot's nipples with the backs of his fingers after he'd finally bared his chest. "It's too bad, because I'd love to bruise them up, pinch them until you're begging me to either let go or do more."

"How is it possible," Elliot demanded, "that I'm the one who reads people for a living, and yet you're able to play me like a fucking flute in just two dates?"

"Two dates with my kid around, no less," Lennox agreed. He stroked his hand down Elliot's stomach, curling his fingertips under the edge of the soft cotton briefs. "You forget I was a sergeant for a long time. It's an interesting job." He slid his fingers inside the front of the briefs. "You've got to be able to interpret orders in the field, work with young lieutenants, keep your enlisted men from fucking up. You think I didn't read people for a living?" Lennox drew Elliot's silky cock through the gap and bent over it, rubbing his stubbly face along the shaft. Elliot shivered, but Lennox gave him a pass for involuntary movements.

"I can read you, Elliot, because I want to. You have all . . . my . . . attention." Elliot's cock was leaking now, a slow, pearling bead sliding down the side. Lennox lapped it up, and Elliot groaned. "Keep your hands down," Lennox reminded him.

"Such a control freak," Elliot grunted, but lowered his arms back onto the bed.

"You say that like it's not a turn-on, baby." Lennox gave in and closed his lips around the head, sucking slowly. It wasn't the easiest thing to do hands-free, but he needed them to hold himself up—as much as he wanted to grind down on top of Elliot, it wasn't going to happen right now. He remembered how it had felt, being on top, fucking his mouth while Elliot fingered him open.

That wouldn't be tonight, but maybe he could spare a hand after all. Lennox shifted his weight, then slid his fingers over the cotton covering Elliot's hole. Elliot bucked up like he'd been tased. "Oh, fuck, touch me like that—do it again."

"If you keep bouncing around, I will tie my hand behind my own back before I use it on you," Lennox warned him.

"Interesting kink." Elliot gave a wide, exhilarated grin. "Fine, fine, no moving, just . . . I like it. I like that."

"Good." It was good to know it; it was better to *use* it, rubbing his thumb across the tight fabric until Elliot's muscles quivered like they wanted to reach out and grope him. Lennox kept sucking, kept fondling him, didn't stop until Elliot, with a drawn-out groan, came in his mouth.

It seemed like forever since Lennox had gone so far with a guy that he could actually taste him. He wanted to wring Elliot dry, wanted to suck him until he had every last drop, but Elliot was already a quivering mess and Lennox needed to get himself out and relieve his own pressure. He needed a touch, just a tiny touch . . .

He jerked his jeans down, pulled his underwear off, and cupped his aching balls with a sigh of relief. Just a little further—

"Fuck, get *up* here." Elliot made grabby hands at him and Lennox went with it, crawling on hands and knees until he was bracketing Elliot's torso. He couldn't touch himself now, but he didn't need to: Elliot did it for him, stroking his cock with both hands. Lennox fucked Elliot's grip, less than an inch above his mottled skin, breathing in every one of Elliot's exhalations as he strove to come, a bit more and he would come, he could—

Elliot leaned up and kissed him like he wanted to devour him, hungry and sharp. Lennox shouted into the kiss as he came, *finally*—it felt like he'd been waiting forever—and now he was painting Elliot in his mess, covering his hot hands with slick release and it was perfect. He let himself go, only enough to brush their bodies together, and Elliot smiled against his slack mouth. The urge to settle in and hold on was almost too strong to resist.

He hummed happily, then nipped Elliot's lower lip before pulling back. "You're fucking fantastic, you know that?"

"I'm also a fantastic fuck."

"I can't argue with that." Lennox kissed him again. "Now, bathroom."

Elliot shook his head. "I think I'll stay here and enjoy this thing some of us like to call the afterglow. You can go be responsible."

"You're probably going to pass out in five minutes," Lennox said. He knew he was right; Elliot could barely keep his eyes open. "You should stand while you still can, brush your teeth, clean up."

Elliot lifted a haughty eyebrow. "You realize that you aren't *my* father, yes? You're *a* father, but if being called 'Daddy' is another one of your kinks, I'm afraid I'm going to have to pass."

Lennox made a disgusted face and got off the bed. "No, Jesus. I just don't want to wake up to morning breath that's any more hideous than it has to be."

"Oh yeah?" Elliot sounded pleased. "I take it you're planning on sleeping in here tonight, then."

Lennox nodded. "If that's okay with you."

"Of course it is. I was going to offer anyway, but handsome men who suck me off definitely get to stay in the bed."

"Good." They shared a little smile. "So, brushing your teeth . . ."

"Yeah, fine."

It wasn't until they were under the covers, close but not quite touching, that Elliot pulled the trigger on something Lennox had hoped he hadn't heard. "So, the nightmares you warned me about last time . . . that's why you won't let Lee spend the night at your place?"

Fuck. Lennox didn't want to talk about this, but Elliot would probably keep asking if he tried to shut him down. In his defense, it was a pertinent situation, since they were in bed together. "Yeah. I, ah . . . I woke her up the last time she stayed over. She came in to check on me and when she shook my shoulder, I woke up—abruptly. I didn't hurt her," Lennox insisted, because damn it, he hadn't lost that much of his mind. "I shoved her back, and I was loud, but I didn't hurt her. But the rest of the night was . . ."

Awful. God, it had been so rough, trying to comfort a daughter who'd only wanted to help him before he'd literally pushed her away. Lee had cried for over an hour and it had taken Gaby coming to pick her up to really calm her down. She'd been horribly embarrassed afterward, but by then Lennox had already decided it wasn't worth disturbing her like that again just for her to spend every other weekend with him. He simply had to make an effort to see her more often, that was all. She'd understand, and maybe one day the nightmares would stop and she could come back.

"It sounds rough. But at least you're talking about it, and trying to do something about it." Elliot's tone was somewhere between intimate and expository, like he was used to saying these things in front of a camera. "The effort is important, trust me."

"Are you using your psychobabble wiles on me?"

"Oh, you haven't seen wiles until you let me do some neuro-linguistic programming," Elliot said, but Lennox heard the smile in his voice.

"Remind me not to make bets with you, then." He could have let things go there, but as long as they were delving into uncomfortable territory . . . "Do you like hanging out with Lee because she reminds you of your sister's kids?"

"Not only because of that," Elliot said after a moment's pause. "She's interesting all on her own, not to mention that being in your company is obviously going to involve her. But I'd be lying if I said that certain similarities never crossed my mind."

"Have you ever thought about flat-out asking to see them?"

"No. I respect Vanessa's decision." Though he clearly didn't like it. "Someday, after I've treaded carefully enough, she'll relax the rules.

I just have to be patient." Elliot rolled over to face the wall. "Sleep well, Lennox."

It was as good as a gag on further conversation. *Probably for the best.* "You too."

CHAPTER ELEVEN

Excerpt from *Shockwave*'s article:

Thirty minutes into my interview, I found out two things: one, I'm not going to get any clientele names out of McKenzie, which stands to reason since confidentiality is a promise of his. Two, and more surprisingly: he's comfortable contracting out his network security. This is unusual because most startups like to keep their proprietary information as close to themselves as possible. Elliot's explanation?

"I'm not a computer whiz," he says with no hint of self-deprecation, just a man stating a fact. "But I know people who are. One of them offered to help me when I was getting started, and they've done an excellent job in providing a safe, secure forum for members to talk in."

"Aren't you afraid that, as your company grows, they'll be under pressure to sell you out?" I ask. Corporate sabotage is a growing industry, especially in the digital age.

He smiles confidently at me. "Everyone who has anything to do with the running of my company is also a member. They have a personal stake in maintaining our security."

In other words, keep your friends close, keep your business partners closer.

Going back to work the next morning was a relief. While being alone with Lennox felt oddly comfortable, it felt perhaps almost too comfortable for his own good. It wasn't that Elliot didn't feel safer with him around—there was no doubt of that. He knew his own strengths, and defending himself wasn't anywhere near the top of that list. Not to mention, he'd already requested Lennox's presence during preparations for the Meetup. But the two of them alone together?

It felt too close to something Elliot hadn't had for years, something he had long since convinced himself that he didn't *want* now. Mischa had been an eye-opener for him, and even if he had fewer regrets about his former lover, he didn't want to repeat the experience. It made him nervous that Lennox fit so well into the empty places he tried hard not to dwell on these days. He didn't want to make himself more vulnerable—he was vulnerable enough to his sister, who wasn't around. He didn't need to worry about any relationship riskier than that right now.

So, coming back to work with a full day ahead of him was a relief. The second, bigger relief, was his meeting with Serena.

She met them at the door to Charmed Life's part of the building, just an inch shorter than him in her ridiculously high heels. Her dress was fire-engine red, and her demeanor was the kind of brisk Elliot needed.

She thrust a set of keys at him. "For your rental car, which is parked out front. You have to send the paperwork to the company in the next half hour."

Elliot perked up as he took them. "The Camaro?"

"The Camaro," she agreed. "You have it through next Monday, at which point you can extend or we can go car shopping. And yes, I've seen the photos the insurance company sent of your Porsche, and I agree that it's unsalvageable." She handed over a plain manila folder. "Car paperwork is on top, schedule of meetings for today is underneath. Ted is available first thing tomorrow morning for a video shoot, and if all goes well, you can put it up by Friday. There's also a list of vendors we've confirmed for the events, the finalized list of attendees for the Meetup, and new graphics for your approval that include Castillion."

"You're the light of my life," Elliot told her seriously.

"And you're the bane of my existence," Serena replied, but then her impersonal demeanor melted away, and she almost crushed him in a hug. "You *idiot*, oh my God, I'm so glad you're all right!"

Elliot actually couldn't draw a breath, his chest had contracted so painfully, but Lennox was there to gently pull Serena back.

"He's tender," he said. "I recommend holding off on the full-body tackles for now."

"Oh shit! I'm sorry." Serena looked Elliot over anxiously. "I didn't even think about that. Of course you're sore, good lord. You were in a car crash."

"The hug was worth it," Elliot assured her. "It's good to be back."

"It's good to have you back. Plenty of people have been anxious to talk to you." She rolled her eyes. "Stuart practically camped out here yesterday."

Elliot winced. "Is he one of my meetings?"

"No, he's got a big corporate event today, but I promised he could come tomorrow for a tasting. He'll bring everything here, so we can call it a lunch meeting."

"Sounds good." Elliot opened the folder and glanced inside, flipping past the first few pages to the schedule. "You booked Quantum Imaging at nine thirty? That hardly leaves me any time to prepare!"

"Then I suppose you better get started," Serena said, one long-nailed finger tapping her hip. "Chop-chop. I'll handle things out here, including—" She turned a bright smile on her ex-brother-in-law. "Lennox! Can I get you some coffee, or something to eat?"

Lennox returned Serena's smile with an easy, gentle one that Elliot got a little too much pleasure out of seeing. "I made sure we ate before we came in, but coffee would be good."

"Excellent! Sit and stay for a while, you can tell me all about why my sister called me at ten last night bitching about Lee joining a boxing club."

Lennox winced, and Elliot left him to Serena's inquisition as he headed into his office. He kept the door open a crack, so that Lennox would know he was welcome to come in if he wanted to, but honestly Elliot hoped Serena would keep him busy. He needed a little distance for the moment.

It's only for this week, he told himself. *Pullman will get bored after the Meetup, and we can go back to our old lives.* Even if the former CEO proved persistent, the special election for DA was happening this weekend as well. Once his sister had won, he could take things to the police.

Everything would be fine.

He spent the morning and most of the afternoon reviewing the last fine details with his vendors, and meeting with clients who were coming to the Meetup. After going through numerous layers of firewalls and verification, he sent out a message to the Black Box subscribers, telling them he'd be releasing the location of their event twenty-four hours before the event itself, and to be careful who they gave that information out to.

It was all so clandestine Elliot almost wanted to roll his eyes, but this was the sort of secrecy his clients demanded. These were people in power, people in the public eye, entertainers and politicians and CEOs; if they wanted to play spy games, then Elliot would take them seriously. It wasn't as though *he* wanted what they were doing exposed to more scrutiny either.

It took until almost seven, but Elliot managed to catch up despite his forced day off. By the time he finally emerged from his office he was dragging though, and Lennox took one look at him and put the kibosh on what sounded like Serena's nascent dinner plans. "You need dinner, a bath, and sleep, in that order," Lennox told him.

"I'm fine!" Elliot protested, but Lennox and Serena exchanged doubtful glances. "I'm also an adult, fully capable of judging my personal state of health and well-being."

"Which is why I'm letting you drive yourself home instead of insisting we carpool," Lennox said mildly.

Elliot grinned and spun the Camaro's keyring around his index finger. "When it's a choice between this beautiful machine and yours, there's truly only one option."

"My truck's not so bad."

"The most expensive part of your truck is its new fuel pump," Elliot said. "Which makes it quite serviceable, but not nearly as much fun as my new ride. I'll see you at home, then."

His plan to drive off like he owned the thing was delayed by Lennox pulling out his flashlight and doing a thorough check of the Camaro's underside before he'd let Elliot inside. "You can't seriously think I've got to worry about a car bomb or something," Elliot said. Pullman wasn't that stupid.

"I think anything is possible," Lennox said, standing up and brushing slush off his knees. "But it looks clear." He stepped in close to Elliot and patted him on the hip. "Be sure to check for dongles, though."

Lennox's hand might as well have been made of molten iron, given the way his touch seemed to sear right through Elliot's slacks to the skin beneath them. Elliot swallowed and forced his voice to be nonchalant. "I still say that's not a word."

"Just because it's funny doesn't mean it isn't real. I'll follow you home."

Home. His home, and Lennox's temporary one. Only temporary, which was right, no matter how it felt. Elliot nodded and got into the car.

He wished he could have enjoyed the ride a little more, but he really was tired. Sunday had been a roller coaster of first the crash, then the hospital. Monday had been the exhausting trip to Castillion while his body and brain had still been freshly pummeled. Today would have been normal any other week, maybe, but after his unexpectedly busy weekend, Elliot wanted nothing but to shut down for a while.

It was almost eerie how Lennox seemed to read his mind. Not five minutes after they arrived at the house, Elliot was seated in front of the television with *Breakfast at Tiffany's* playing, Holly firmly settled in his lap and a mug of tea on the table in front of him. By the time Lennox came with dinner (soup and grilled cheese sandwiches, which Elliot hadn't eaten since he was a teenager and enjoyed far more now because of that) he was ready to be gracious.

"This is my favorite movie," he said as Lennox handed over the plate before joining him on the couch. Holly moved to snuggle between the two of them. "Willie was considered for the role, but it went to Audrey Hepburn. Willie didn't mind," he added as he watched Holly Golightly meet her neighbor Paul for the first time. "She was a big fan of Audrey's."

Lennox glanced at the black-and-white picture of Audrey Hepburn arm in arm with Wilhelmina VanAllen beside the door. "Looks like they knew each other."

"Willie knew everybody in the business."

"Everybody who was anybody," as she used to say.

Lennox nodded but didn't try to continue the conversation, which was perfect. Elliot relaxed and zoned out, eating and watching and gradually sinking further and further into the couch. Once Lennox shook him awake again, Paul had just flung the ring into Holly's lap before leaving her to search for the cat.

"I can see why this is your favorite movie," Lennox said as he prodded Elliot up the stairs, Holly the dog following close at their heels. "She reminds me of you."

"You might think you're being insulting, but I take any comparisons to Audrey Hepburn as compliments," Elliot said around a yawn. "God, I'm so tired."

"You have good reason to be." They got ready for bed, and as Elliot slipped under the covers he contemplated, for a brief moment, asking Lennox to sleep in the guest room tonight. After all, they weren't going to be having sex and it might be better to put up some boundaries now, while they could still be enforced.

But he remembered how Lennox had ended up sleeping in the chair last time, and how much better he'd seemed when sleeping alongside another person. No nightmares yet, as far as Elliot knew, and that was good.

It couldn't hurt. It was a friendly gesture. It was … Elliot resolutely shut his eyes. It was something he could deal with later.

Being around Stuart Reynolds was like standing in a sunbeam, Elliot thought. The overall sensation was warm and pervasive but if you weren't careful, you'd get burned. Stuart was a brilliant chef with a big personality: outgoing, social, and friendly to a fault, which got him a lot of business. He also clung like a burr, and after a few initial missteps in dealing with him, Elliot had carefully framed their relationship as primarily a business one, and stuck to that ever since.

That didn't mean he didn't ever enjoy Stuart's company though, especially when Stuart brought enough food to feed the entire building with him.

"Seven-layer nachos, all organic ingredients, in tasty, red hot and 'oh dear God, get a fire extinguisher!'" he said, pointing out the dishes on the table he'd set up in the front office. "Mini quiches in regular, gluten-free, vegetarian, and gluten-free vegetarian, for our selective eaters. Baked brie with a cranberry compote and my special seed-bread to serve it with, various dips and crudités—try the spinach artichoke, Elliot, you'll *love* it—and Swedish meatballs for the meat lovers. You look like a meat lover," Stuart added saucily to Lennox, whom he'd absorbed into the tasting without a fuss. "Try the meatballs, they'll hit the spot."

He turned to Serena. "And for you, there's an array of flavored macarons, miniature cheesecakes, and custom sugar cookies frosted in orange and blue, because we have to support the home team even though we're not in the Super Bowl this year, right? Oh, and," he reached into the pastry box and withdrew a red and white cupcake with a flourish, "*this*. Red velvet with cream cheese frosting, on the house."

"You're a god among pastry chefs," Serena declared, snatching the cupcake out of his hands. Stuart preened a bit under the attention, but his eyes kept darting back to Elliot. It was his itchy look, and it heralded a barrage of questions that would inevitably be asked, one way or the other. Elliot vastly preferred that they be asked in private, so he spent a while longer tasting the food, gave everything the okay, and then asked Stuart to join him in his office.

Everything okay? Lennox mouthed from the other side of the table.

Fine, Elliot replied, waving his concerns off. He shut the door and barely took a breath before Stuart was speaking at a thousand miles a minute.

"I heard about the car accident," Stuart said, wringing his hands a little. His face was flushed almost as pink as his shirt. "And I know, I know, personal boundaries and all that, but I just have to ask if you're okay."

Classic Stuart. He worried more about Elliot than Elliot's own mother ever had. "I'm fine," Elliot said. "Who did you hear about the accident from?"

"Serena. Oh no, was she not supposed to say anything? Forget I mentioned it, I don't want to get her in trouble!"

"No, it's fine." He hadn't told her to keep it quiet, after all. She must have given it as a reason for rescheduling their Monday meeting. "I don't mind you knowing. I got a bit banged up, but I'm on my way to a full recovery."

"Thank *God*." Stuart cast his eyes heavenward as he heaved a sigh. "I'm so glad to hear it. And who's taking care of you during all this?"

"Stuart—"

"Because I would happily come over and help you out. You know I would. That's what friends do, isn't it?"

"Stuart, listen—"

"And I know you were serious about taking a step back, but you're letting me help with your *Black Box meeting*." Stuart whispered the words with quiet emphasis. "So I know you trust me."

"That's true," Elliot agreed, because, well, it was. "But I don't need any more help at home. I've already got one person doing everything for me except tying my shoelaces." And actually, Lennox had helped with that this morning because Elliot had been so stiff, but it had been a one-time deal.

"Hmm." Stuart pursed his lips doubtfully. "He seems like a bodyguard instead of a nurse."

Elliot forced a laugh. "Lucky for me, I don't need a bodyguard."

"But you do need a nurse?"

"I don't need either," Elliot said. "Now, I've got to leave the office early today, but I can't pass up the opportunity to sample a little more of your amazing food before I go."

"Oh." Stuart shook his head, then smiled. "Oh! Well, of course you can't. Come on, come on, I held back a few things for you in the chafing dish."

"I appreciate it." And Elliot did: he appreciated having a good working relationship with one of the best caterers in Denver, and a small, darker part of him appreciated having the man's undivided admiration too. Mostly though, he appreciated from a distance, and that was the way it had to be with people like Stuart.

Serena had apparently split her cupcake with Lennox, a shocking concession on her part, and when she saw Elliot again, her face lit up. "Listen! What do you think of Lee coming to the Executive Meetup with me?" She winked slyly. "She can be my date."

"She?" Stuart looked confused as he bustled around the table, filling a plate. "I didn't think you dated women."

"She's my niece," Serena explained, then poked Lennox's shoulder. "And this one's daughter, and I gave her a dress for Christmas that she's been dying for an excuse to wear."

"That was you?" Lennox frowned. "It's tiny. She's thirteen. It'll be cold. That dress barely covers her butt."

"It's fashionable, she'll be inside, I'll be with her, and as long as she's standing, the length won't be a problem," Serena retorted.

"It's fine with me if she comes," Elliot interrupted as he took the salmon croquettes and crab salad that Stuart handed him. "But do you really think she'd enjoy it?"

"A big, fancy party with some of the city's biggest movers and shakers? What's not to enjoy?"

"We can ask her, as long as we clear it with Gaby first," Lennox said. "No promises, though. And she wears a different dress."

Serena rolled her eyes but dropped it, discreetly tapping her watch in Elliot's direction as she walked back to her desk. Yeah, timing—they had to leave soon if they were going to get to the airport to meet the intriguing Uncle Oliver. Lennox had asked if Elliot minded tagging along, and Elliot couldn't think of anyone he'd rather meet. He was interested in sizing up the only man he knew of that Lennox had been with apart from him.

After sending Stuart on his way, Elliot drove them to DIA. Lennox had already arranged a meeting point in one of the airport bars, and five minutes after they arrived and were seated at Red Rocks Bar and BBQ, Lennox got up again to greet a shorter, dark-haired man with a briefcase who was heading straight for them. Elliot stayed seated, both to give them a moment and to give himself time to appraise the situation.

Oliver Morin looked like he'd just come from the beach. His suit was made of light linen, a sandy color that complimented his sun-kissed complexion. He wore a narrow goatee and had expensive aviators slung over the third button down on his cream-colored shirt. His face was friendly—not exactly handsome, but there was an unrestrained energy in how he moved that was captivating. Elliot could see why Lennox liked him.

It didn't follow that Elliot had to like those things too, of course.

Their hug was long, but when they separated Lennox immediately led his friend back to their table. "Oliver Morin, this is Elliot McKenzie. Don't be a dick to him."

Oliver extended a hand, which Elliot shook politely. When he took it back he turned to Lennox and said, "Oh, it's 'not like that,' is it?" And *fascinatingly*, Lennox blushed.

"Don't be a dick to me either," he warned as he sat down—next to Elliot, gratifyingly, leaving the other side of the table for the newcomer.

"Nonsense, I've got permanent leave for that." Oliver's accent was hard to place, almost unnoticeable except for the tenor of his speech. "Good friends get to act however they want to each other as long as no one loses a limb and we all walk away happy in the end."

"Is that the criteria for friendship with Lennox?" Elliot asked, deciding to test the waters. "Because that's a pretty low bar."

There was complete silence for a moment, and then Oliver started to laugh. "It is, isn't it? I've told him he's got to be more selective about his company but no, he'll take any old thing that acts pathetic and bleeds all over him. Aren't we lucky?" He signaled the waitress before Elliot could reply. "We'll have a pitcher of something crafty, because this is Colorado, isn't it, and you can't tell me a bar in the middle of the airport doesn't have a craft brew. My treat, boys. So!" He clasped his hands in front of him on the table and looked Elliot straight in the eyes. "What did you do to attract this one's notice, hmm?"

Elliot smiled as charmingly as he could. "I hired him to secure my house, took him on a dinner date with his daughter, seduced him into staying the night, kicked him out in the most awkward morning-after imaginable, and then, to make a long story short, basically bled all over him. He decided to keep me after that."

To his credit, Oliver dropped the veneer of sociable asshole by the end of the explanation, his shoulders relaxing as he looked between the two of them. He nodded at Elliot like he'd just slotted a piece into a particularly frustrating puzzle. "Tried-and-true method, my friend, tried-and-true. Len, you can't resist a good rescue."

"I don't remember you ever complaining." Lennox's blush had faded, but he seemed half a second away from rolling his eyes.

"Or didn't you want me to carry you out of the last mess you got yourself into?"

"Far from my last," Oliver scoffed. "Just my last with you. I had to hire four people as your replacements, do you realize that? Four people! You've completely screwed with my bottom line."

"You should hire more competent people, then."

"No, no." Oliver sat back as the waitress arrived with the beer. "It's personal investment that's the problem. None of my hirelings are as invested in keeping my hide whole as you were. It's not as though there's a Yelp site for black-market bodyguards, you know?"

"That sounds like a problem waiting for a solution," Elliot remarked before he could help himself. "Surely there'd be an interest in that, wouldn't there? If it could be managed in a way that kept authorities from gleaning too much information."

Oliver smiled slowly. "Spoken like a true visionary. And it would be rather helpful, I admit, but the darker side of the internet is constantly being trawled by the fishing boats of freedom, justice, and the desire to interfere with very necessary international commerce. It would be challenging to make such a rating system stick."

Elliot leaned forward. "Challenging, but not impossible. I've got some friends in Silicon Valley who—"

"Oh, hell no," Lennox broke in. "You," he pointed at Oliver, "no discussing the details of your job in a public place where anyone might hear you, and *you*." Now he pointed at Elliot, who held up his hands innocently. "Don't encourage him. Holy shit, what was I thinking, bringing the two of you together?"

"And plying us with alcohol, nonetheless." Oliver took a long drink from his glass. "Mmm, that's good. Why don't I live here? I love the beer."

Lennox snorted. "You hate the cold."

Oliver snapped his fingers. "Ah, that's right, got it in one. If you won't let me discuss personal security in the internet age with your new friend here, maybe I should start telling him embarrassing stories about you?"

Lennox crossed his arms. "Go ahead. I wasn't the one who got into trouble with the goat."

"You always bring that up," Oliver muttered before drinking again. At this rate he'd down most of the pitcher himself.

Oliver was, Elliot had to admit over the next hour, pretty personable once they'd established that there was no reason for either of them to be territorial. Oliver and Lennox were very friendly with each other, but whatever passion there had been between them had long since cooled. And Lennox, for all that his work kept him firmly on the right side of the law, didn't get worked up, while no one else was sitting too close, talking about Oliver's less-than-legal occupation, which seemed to involve weapons dealing. He hadn't expected that, and his surprise must have been evident, because Oliver chuckled and leaned in.

"Who'd ever suspect a Canadian, eh?" he asked. "Never mind that our country exports more ammunition than anywhere else in the Western Hemisphere."

"Isn't the US a bigger manufacturer when it comes to—"

"Guns? Absolutely, you're number one there," Oliver said. "But guns are only as good as their ammo, and we deal in the best, for the best. We being *me*, for the most part."

Elliot nodded. "I appreciate your lack of false modesty."

"I dislike being false in anything, but especially when it concerns my own excellence." They toasted each other and drank.

"You're both seriously delusional," Lennox said, but he looked like he was trying to hide a smile. "Since you do get around though, have you ever heard of a guy called Jonathan Lehrer?"

Oliver frowned. "The name isn't familiar. Who is he?"

"He's a former corporate fixer who used to work for Redback Industries," Lennox explained. "In the employ of Sheridan Pullman. He was arrested for vehicular homicide five years ago but he made bail and vanished."

"Huh." Oliver traced the top of his glass with his index finger. "And your interest in this man is . . . what, personal? Because if you need a fixer, Lennox, then we should be having another conversation altogether."

"He's after me," Elliot supplied. "Still working for Pullman. Or at least I assume so."

"And is he any good, or are you just very lucky?"

Elliot shrugged. "We're not out of the terrorizing phase yet, I don't think."

"Aren't you blasé?" Oliver stared at him for a long moment, then shrugged his shoulders. "I don't know of the man, but I'll see what I can find out. You're sure it's him?"

"No," Lennox said firmly. "We're not. It would be good to have confirmation one way or the other."

"I understand."

Lennox got up a few minutes later to go to the restroom. As soon as he was gone, Oliver leaned forward and put his elbows on the table. "Actually, I'd heard of *you* before today." He didn't sound pleased.

Elliot's hackles rose, but he forced himself to stay relaxed. "Really? From whom?"

"From someone who's trying to make a deal with Mischa Kovalin." Elliot's expression froze—he couldn't help it.

"You and Mischa were together, weren't you?" Oliver went on. "His firm worked with Redback Industries, correct?"

"Yes," Elliot managed. "We were together. We haven't spoken in years, though."

"Hmm. I hope for your sake things stay that way. Mr. Kovalin is developing a rather *intractable* reputation in some dangerous circles, and you don't want any part of that."

"No." Elliot lifted his own glass and drained it in one go. Whatever Mischa was up to, it was none of his business now. Mischa had made that very clear, and Elliot had more than enough of his own affairs to handle. "I certainly don't."

"One other thing," Oliver continued. "Lennox is doing a lot better since being here. If whatever you're drawing him into fucks him up again, you and I will have a problem."

Elliot was too intrigued to be offended by the threat. "Better than what?"

Oliver shrugged. "It's not my place to say. He's just better. Let's keep it that way, all right?"

"That sounds fair."

By the time Lennox came back, the tension between them had dissipated. Oliver didn't mention what they'd discussed, and Elliot certainly wasn't going to if he didn't have to.

The meeting ended on a friendly note, with a fleeting promise from Oliver to find out what he could as he ran off to make his next flight. Lennox had skipped the beers, so he drove them back. If he was a little heavier on the pedal than usual, hey, it was a brand-new Camaro. Elliot understood.

Holly was her typical enthusiastic self when they returned to Elliot's house, and he still felt energetic enough to take her for a walk himself. "A walk" basically meant following her out to the yard, but he handled the back stairs pretty well and strolled around a few feet behind her as she made her usual circuit from tree to tree, sniffing and digging through the snow and fallen pine needles to uncover canine treasures.

Elliot's thoughts kept returning to Mischa, even though he was the last person Elliot wanted to be stuck on right now. Oliver's warning had been pretty pointed, and part of Elliot wanted to call up his ex and tell him to lay off whatever he was up to. That had been Elliot's role for years: trying to rein Mischa in until the only option Elliot had had left was either to take part in what his lover was doing or leave him.

Elliot wasn't good at leaving people, and he'd been far *too* good at lying to himself. Becoming a criminal had been easier than it should have, and Mischa, in the end, had only opened the door. Elliot had been the one to run through it.

Mischa had been so much more *careful* than Elliot back then, though. It was surprising to hear he was making waves now; that wasn't the sort of thing Mischa did. He was as soft and silent as a snake, and just as dangerous as one.

It was only when Elliot actually bumped into Holly that he noticed she'd stopped moving. In fact, she seemed to be eating something.

"What have you found, silly thing?" he asked, kneeling down next to her. Hopefully it wasn't part of a snake; she'd been way too interested in the last corpse to grace their grounds.

The light was poor, but as he leaned in, Elliot could still make out the shape of— "What the hell? Holly, no." He pushed her away from the cube of beef she'd been attacking. "*No.*" What on earth was fresh-cut meat doing out here? Elliot picked up the meat—it felt oddly gritty. He held it a bit closer to his face and sniffed. It smelled like garlic.

"Oh shit." He had Holly in his arms in a second, running back to the house at full speed. "Lennox!"

The door banged open. "Elliot! Jesus, what's going on?" Lennox helped him inside, and Elliot dropped the piece of meat onto the counter before sitting down and starting to examine Holly closely. "What happened?"

"There was . . . that, the meat, it was outside and she ate some of it and it smells like fucking *rat poison*, and I don't know how much she ate." Holly didn't appear sick, but he had no idea how long it took for rat poison to take effect.

Lennox went over and examined the piece of meat, then grimaced. "I can see the powder on it. We've got to get her to the vet."

"She seems okay . . ." Holly began hacking, bits of partially chewed meat winding up on Elliot's lap. *Spoke too soon.* "Fuck, yes, we have to go." Good thing Lennox hadn't bothered to take off his coat. Elliot slung his own on and led the way to the Camaro, but let Lennox drive so he could keep holding Holly. Lennox started it up and peeled out of the driveway, heading back into town at a screaming speed.

"Where's your vet's office?" Elliot barely heard him; Holly was lying down now, making a whimpering noise that hit him straight in the heart. He stroked her head and held her close, helpless to do anything else. "Elliot, your *vet*, where is it?"

"Ah . . ." He reengaged his brain with difficulty. "Fifth and Main. Friendly Paws Animal Hospital. God, who would *do* this to a dog? Holly's the sweetest thing in the world! She's never hurt anybody!"

"I know." It wasn't an answer, but the sound of Lennox's voice helped calm Elliot down a bit. "I know, and she's going to be fine. We're almost there."

"I don't—I don't even know if they're open." It was after six at night. "What if they're closed?"

"Then we find a vet with emergency hours that's open," Lennox said. "There are bound to be some close by."

"But will we be in time? She ate rat poison, and she's not a lot bigger than a rat. Oh my god." Elliot felt more panicked now than he could remember being when he crashed himself into the side of a mountain. His fingers were numb, and his stomach roiled with nausea. "What if she dies?"

"Elliot." Lennox grabbed his arm, not hard but with a reassuring firmness. "She's not going to die. Look." He nodded toward the side of the road. "Here we are."

Friendly Paws was still open, thankfully, and the staff reacted to the emergency with gratifying speed, Dr. Navarro gently taking Holly out of Elliot's hands and assuring him she'd do everything she could, but they couldn't come back right now. The receptionist handed over a sheaf of paperwork, probably to act as a distraction, but before he could start on it his hands were claimed by Lennox, holding a wet wipe he'd stolen from the counter.

"You always forget the mess," he said, calmly wiping away blood and dog drool.

"You always seem to remember it," Elliot replied weakly. He was shaking, and his own voice sounded like it was coming through a layer of cotton. "I don't— This is—"

"Let's sit down, yeah?" Lennox led him over to the benches along the wall of the waiting room, away from the overly interested receptionist. "Are you okay?"

"I'm fine." And it was awful, but now that Holly had been whisked away, Elliot *did* feel better, physically. Mentally, though, he was nowhere close to fine. "How . . . my *dog*. She's a dog, for fuck's sake, she has nothing to do with anything. Who the fuck would try to hurt my dog?"

"Someone who knows you love her and is interested in hurting you," Lennox said with a grimace. "Someone who's not afraid to trespass on your property, either. *That*, at least, I can do something about."

Elliot shivered. "You can't keep people from approaching the house. We're surrounded by open space in the back, I couldn't put up a fence even if I wanted to, and there isn't time to—"

"Not to stop them," Lennox amended. He was gently rubbing his hands up and down Elliot's arms, and though he couldn't sense their heat, Elliot still felt warmed. "Just to give us a heads-up. I'll relocate some of your motion detectors, set them up to ping a warning. We'll know if anyone else gets within twenty feet of the house."

Elliot snorted. "You'll get a lot of false positives, then. I get whole herds of deer in the backyard."

"And I'll check out every single one of them," Lennox said with a smile. "Even if it's only a bunny rabbit."

"My hero." Elliot would have teased a little more, but Dr. Navarro appeared in the doorway and he shot to his feet instead. "How is she?"

"It's a bit early to say for sure," she began, and Elliot's stomach dropped so suddenly he thought he might be sick, "but I think she'll make a full recovery. You got her here very quickly, and fortunately she was able to purge most of what she consumed before she arrived."

His knees went weak, but he stayed upright. "Can I see her?"

"Sure. Follow me." She led them to the kennel, where a chorus of barks greeted them as they walked in. Holly wasn't one of the barkers; she was on her side in a bed on an exam table, a vet tech gently inserting an IV line into a shaved section on her leg, but she licked comfortingly at Elliot's hand as soon as he was close enough.

Dr. Navarro smiled. "She's a trooper. You're lucky the poison wasn't on something easily consumable, like hamburger. Otherwise she could have eaten a lot more than she did. I assume the poisoning was deliberate, not an accident?"

"No," Elliot murmured, stroking Holly's head. Soft orange fur parted under his fingertips. "It wasn't an accident."

"Are you going to be filing a police report?"

Lennox stepped in. "We'll make sure it gets taken care of."

"How long do you want her to stay?" Elliot asked.

"At least for the night," Dr. Navarro replied.

"Actually, could she stay a bit longer?" Lennox broke in before Elliot could say anything else. "If not for medical reasons, then just . . . boarding?"

Elliot raised his eyebrows. "Why should I—"

"So we can make sure she's well taken care of while we finish up our business," Lennox continued. "We could come get her Monday morning."

After the Meetup is over. It made sense; if this was an example of what Pullman was capable of, Elliot wanted Holly as far out of the line of fire as possible. "Good idea." Elliot nodded at Lennox, then turned back to the vet. "Is that doable?"

"I think we can work something out." Dr. Navarro's mouth tightened in sympathy. "I don't think it'll be necessary for her health, though."

"I appreciate it regardless," Elliot said.

They left half an hour later, Elliot's wallet light but his heart lighter. Holly had been standing again by the end, which the tech had said was a good sign. Elliot slumped into the car seat and didn't speak as Lennox drove them back to the house, his head spinning. It shouldn't have come as such a surprise that Sheridan Pullman and his lackey were willing to kill his dog to fuck with him. They'd almost killed Elliot when they hijacked his car; why would they balk at killing a dog? But it still stunned him, hurt on a deeper level than any violence or animosity directed at himself would have. Holly was the definition of an innocent bystander. She had nothing to do with any of this.

Lennox was right. It was best for her to be out of the way until the Meetup was done, Vanessa's election was over, and Elliot could go to the police without fear of endangering her.

"We have to go to the police now."

Never mind, Lennox was completely wrong. "No."

"Elliot, think about what just happened to Holly!"

How can the man be so obtuse? "What happened to Holly wasn't a random poisoning in a city park," he snapped. "It was a calculated attack by a sadist who's trying to spread his wings now that he's out of prison, but he's not going to kill me, and I'm not going to go after him until everything else is finished."

Lennox's hands were so tight on the steering wheel that Elliot could hear the leather creak. "You're making a hell of a lot of assumptions there."

"You don't know him like I do."

"I'm not even sure *he* is who you think he is."

"I repeat: because you don't know him," Elliot said. "You don't know how he thinks. I worked for this man for over a year. I saw him screw people over again and again, and no, usually it wasn't this extreme, but he kept a fixer on the books for a reason. I can weather him, and I will, and then I'll get his ass arrested once I've got enough evidence to do it. He's sure to try something the night of the Meetup, and that's when I'll take him out."

"Oh, you will?" Lennox turned sharply down the road to Elliot's house, the tires squealing on the road. Elliot would be paying for damages to the car if Lennox kept this treatment up. "How, exactly, are you gonna do that? What's your brilliant plan?"

"Get him before he gets me."

"How, by stalking him with rat poison in your back pocket?"

"No," Elliot said quietly. "He'll wait until the Black Box meeting to make his big move. He wants to ruin me at the apex of my career, just how *he* ended up ruined. I'll find a way to expose him then, once nothing that happens could hurt my sister." Lennox pulled to a stop in front of the house, and Elliot looked at his profile. "You don't have to stay. You helped me out when I needed it, and I'm grateful, but I'm not going to make you a part of anything you don't want to be part of. Although I hope that you still want to help."

Lennox was silent for a long moment before he finally spoke. "So you don't have a plan."

"I don't have a plan *yet*, but I will. Whatever it ends up being, it won't work unless I hold off until the night of the Meetup, though." Elliot knew that; he knew it like he knew his own mind. Pullman was in many ways a more extreme version of himself, and a better showman. He'd wait until the last possible minute. "I honestly don't think it'll get any more dangerous than this."

Lennox shook his head. "Don't say that. That's begging for the universe to give you hell."

"Yeah, probably," Elliot said. "So . . . will you stay?" *Please stay.*

"I'll stay." There was an implicit *for now* in there that Elliot didn't like, but he wasn't going to push his luck. "Come on, let's get in. I need to reset those motion detectors."

"I'll clean up in the kitchen," Elliot said. Mmm, poisoned meat and dog vomit. He'd never be able to scrub the floor, or himself, hard enough. He got out of the car with a sigh. It was going to be a long, uncomfortable evening.

CHAPTER TWELVE

Partial transcription of most recent appointment with West, Lennox, Staff Sergeant US Army Rangers (R), January 28, 3:25 p.m.:

JS: Are you still in contact with any of the people who were in your unit?

LW: I keep in touch with all of them. Facebook, emails, that kind of thing. Just casually.

JS: Do you think it helps them, to know that you care about their well-being now?

LW: I'm not sure. A couple of them never write back. I don't know if I'm shooting my thoughts off into the void when I send them messages, but if they want to block me, that's their call. If they want to read and not respond, that's their call too. Whatever they have to do to take care of themselves.

JS: And how do you feel, about putting your interest out there and having it disregarded by some of your soldiers?

LW: It's my job to take care of them, not the other way around. Even if it gave me a heart attack every time, I'd still do it.

JS: Why?

LW: Because I told them I would.

The motion detector went off at six the next morning. Lennox was out of bed and on his feet before Elliot had opened his eyes, shutting the alarm down with a quick press of the fob on Elliot's keychain.

For the first time since they'd shared a bed, Lennox hadn't been able to sleep. Too many thoughts, too many issues, swirling together like a hurricane inside his skull, until it was all he could do to keep from rolling over and pummeling his pillow. He needed to do something, he needed to *move*. The alarm's siren was like a godsend to his nerves.

"What the hell?" Elliot mumbled. His freshly cleaned hair was a total mess, sticking up on half his head. Lennox had to resist the urge to run his fingers through it.

"I'm going to go check it out," Lennox told him. "It might be nothing, but I'll lock the door behind me."

"Oh . . . kay?"

That semiconscious acknowledgment was all Lennox was waiting for. He jogged downstairs, grabbed his Kahr pocket pistol from the drawer Elliot had reluctantly designated as the "if you've got to have a freaking gun, at least keep it out of my bedroom" drawer, slipped into his shoes, and headed to the back door. He opened it quietly, stepped outside, and stared into the gray predawn light.

Lennox held still as he scanned the area, shielding his steaming breath from his face with a hand while he searched for movement. One sweep . . . another sweep . . . he was about to go for a third when on the left side of the backyard, farther into the woods, something shifted. Something tall—taller than a deer.

Lennox didn't waste time second-guessing before darting off the porch and across the brief stretch of snowy lawn, keeping his gun down but ready at his side. He paused at the edge of the woods, half-crouched, and looked again. It was freezing out, but he felt hot, the surge of adrenaline an old, familiar friend. He'd seen *something* in the depths of the trees. He took one slow step forward, then another.

The figure he almost thought he'd imagined took off like a shot twenty feet ahead of him, apparently heedless of the noise he or she was making. Lennox followed, building to a sprint. Dead branches cracked and broke, pine needles crunched underfoot, and the remnants of most of a winter's snow made sprinting hard, but Lennox was gaining on the intruder. He was gaining *fast*. He could shoot the figure, but bullets meant cops. It didn't matter. He could catch them without a gun.

The figure turned suddenly, left arm rising in a familiar arc, and Lennox swore and ducked behind the nearest tree. *Bang-bang-bang.*

Three shots were fired in rapid succession, only one of them actually hitting anything: a tree about fifteen feet to the right of Lennox's. He heard splinters of bark scatter across the ground, and had to stifle a gleeful laugh. For the first time in a long time, he felt *vital* again, vibrantly alive in a way only nearly dying could make him feel. His heart beat a war song through his chest, and he readied his Glock. After a few more bullet-free seconds, he peered around his tree for any sign of the lurker-turned-shooter.

Nothing. He or she had taken off, probably not even waiting to see if their shots had done any damage. The road was close; once Lennox got there, the intruder would be long gone.

"Shit," he muttered. Was Jonathan Lehrer a left-handed shooter? Because this person certainly had been, and a poor one at that. Or had they been deliberately bad?

Elliot might know, but—the thought crystallized in his mind before Lennox could put words to it—Lennox wasn't going to ask Elliot anything, because Elliot wasn't going to know anything about the shooter. Unless he'd heard something, Lennox wasn't going to enlighten him.

Dead snakes, car crashes, poisoned pets: these could possibly be explained as acts of simple intimidation, but firing a weapon? That brought things to a new and lethal level, and Lennox knew without a doubt that despite that, Elliot still wouldn't involve the police. He might, however, think better of having Lennox stick around if he thought he was putting Lennox in danger, especially after their argument last night. And if someone *was* turning up the intensity, then Lennox was exactly where he needed to be. Not only that, it was where he *wanted* to be.

He turned and started walking back to the house, going slow to give himself time to come up with a believable story. *Flexible morality*, Gaby had scolded him after she'd found out that he'd been briefly arrested in Nigeria, *isn't much better than no morality at all. You have to follow the laws even when you've got something personal at stake, you* idiot.

She'd been talking about him helping Oliver with his ammo-smuggling operation, which . . . yeah, had been very illegal, but the part of Lennox that put ideals ahead of people in his mental hierarchy? That had been broken, irreparably, after Afghanistan. Oliver had offered him a purpose after he got out of the service, something he'd been desperate for. It might not have been a pretty purpose, keeping Oliver alive while he did his illegal deals, but Lennox hadn't cared back then. He'd been desperate for diversion, for anything to distract him from the darkness inside himself. He almost hadn't survived that time, but he didn't regret it.

Elliot might not be doing the right thing either, but to hell with it: right now Lennox's purpose was keeping Elliot alive. If he could do that and get the cops to come into it on their side in the end? Great.

If not? Well . . . he wasn't going to let people start shooting at Elliot without shooting back. *Your hero complex*, he heard Oliver tease. Fuck it. There were worse complexes to have.

Elliot was waiting for him at the back door, his body silhouetted behind the glass. He opened the door for Lennox as his foot hit the first step of the porch. "What was it?" he asked, his eyes full of concern.

Lennox shook his head. "Only a deer. I followed a ways to make sure." He shrugged. "Just me jumping at shadows."

"You're bleeding." A warm thumb brushed across his cheekbone and came back smeared red. "What, did the deer chase you into a thorn bush?" Elliot smiled a little. He had a tiny dimple in his right cheek when he smiled. Lennox suddenly couldn't look away from it.

"I don't have night vision, give me a break," Lennox said, before brushing a kiss over that dimple.

Elliot laughed. "Running through the woods in the dark and the cold makes you horny? Really?"

"I don't have to want to fuck you to want to kiss you." Lennox pressed another kiss onto the side of his neck. "Although I've gotta say, I could use a shower now. You should join me."

Elliot raised one eyebrow. "Oh yeah? How are you going to make it worth my time?"

All Lennox's capacity for being suave was buried under his fight-or-flight reaction. He gripped Elliot's lower back, pulled him close in a way he wouldn't have yesterday, when he had still been so mindful of his bruises. He pulled him in *hard*, slotting his leg between Elliot's thighs and grinding up against his groin. Elliot groaned, but it sounded about as removed from pain as possible.

"Does this feel worth your time?" Lennox asked, voice almost guttural as he slid his hands under the band of Elliot's soft, cotton sleep pants. "Or should I tuck you back into bed and take care of things on my own?"

Elliot's multicolored eyes sparked with heat. "You don't want to go to bed with me?"

"I told you." Lennox bent his head to Elliot's neck and inhaled, slow and deep. He smelled a bit like the fabric softener Elliot used on his clothes, a bit like sweat, but mostly like warm, inviting skin. "I need a shower."

"Then I need to join you." Elliot leaned back and smirked at him. "Since you're making it worth my time."

"So fucking gracious," Lennox snarked, right before he bit down on the smooth curve of Elliot's shoulder. Elliot stiffened in his arms, but didn't jerk away. If anything, he pressed closer, and humped the top of Lennox's leg shamelessly.

Lennox pulled off before he made any lasting marks. "If you weren't already black and blue, I'd pretty you up some," he rumbled.

Elliot actually whined. "Oh god, don't talk like that unless you're planning on bending me over the counter and fucking me right here."

"Maybe in front of the bathroom mirror instead," Lennox offered, then let go of Elliot and prodded him toward the stairs. "March."

"Sir, yes, sir," he said mockingly as he led the way. Lennox swatted him on the ass.

"If you were one of my troops, I'd have you on the ground giving me push-ups until I thought you were sorry enough for sassing me," he said as they got to the bathroom. He reached into the shower—an epic affair, all glass and marble, with a convenient bench on the far side—and turned on the water. He stripped off his clothes, then leaned over the sink and looked at the cut on his cheek in the mirror. It was hardly more than a scratch.

Behind him Elliot's eyes were wide, his reflection completely entranced. "I'd happily get on the ground for you," he said. "Or did you change your mind about who should be fucked in front of the mirror?"

Lennox smiled. "Nope." He straightened up and got into the shower. The warm spray felt amazing; why hadn't they done this in here yet? "But you might want to make sure we've got supplies."

Elliot was gone and back in a heartbeat. He took off his own clothes without ceremony and joined Lennox in the shower. Seeing him naked was a stark reminder that no matter how much Lennox wanted to fuck Elliot until he screamed, he was still covered in purple from the top of his shoulders to his hips. That seat belt hadn't been kind to him.

"No, no, no." Elliot grabbed Lennox's face in both hands and kissed him insistently. "Don't look at me like I'm broken," he murmured when he drew back to take a breath. "I don't want nice. I want you to want me like you did downstairs, like you're so wound up you want to hoist me up against the glass and fuck me until I can't breathe without saying your fucking name."

You asked for it. Lennox kissed him savagely, sinking his teeth into Elliot's lower lip until he cried out, then soothing it while he slid his hand down and curled his fingers around Elliot's balls. Elliot's moan of pleasure turned into a gasp of dismay as Lennox pulled down, hard enough to sting.

"No coming until I'm in you."

"Then fucking *get in me* already!"

Lennox spun him around to face the wall. Elliot pressed his hips back invitingly, and Lennox had to remind himself that jerking off over that luscious ass could wait for another day. He opened the door and grabbed the lube—silicone-based, perfect for the shower—slicked his fingers up, then swept them over Elliot's hole. Elliot shivered as his breath caught, and that was enough for Lennox.

There was no slow, teasing play like the last time. He remembered how much Elliot had liked being touched here, how he'd quivered and moaned when Lennox pressed in on his tender skin. Now there was no cloth to stop him, and he smoothed his slick index finger over the tight muscle, then began to penetrate Elliot.

Elliot bore down, almost sucking Lennox's finger in. Lennox chuckled darkly and placed a hand on Elliot's neck, keeping him bent and exposed. "So ready for this, aren't you?" Elliot took the second finger just as easily, biting off swear words every few seconds. He tried to thrust back, but Lennox held him firmly in place. "My speed."

"I thought you were desperate," Elliot gasped.

"Mmm, I am." Lennox leaned in close and added, "But I like feeling desperate."

He didn't push, curling his fingers until he could tap against Elliot's prostate. Elliot whimpered.

"I like needing something I can't quite have. I like hovering at the edge, ready for whatever's going to happen. I like the thrill of it, the danger. I like the rush."

"Lennox, please . . ."

"Say that again and maybe I'll say yes."

"Lennox, *please.*" Elliot clenched his hole around Lennox's fingers, clearly hungry for more, for anything. Lennox grinned but didn't move, stroking slowly over Elliot's prostate until he was barely intelligible. Elliot smacked his palm against the tile. "Fuck you, oh my god, I'm going to come like this and you'll *miss* it, and then where'll your edge be?"

"I'm sure I can get off fucking you after you've already come," Lennox assured him as he added a third finger. Easy, still, and for a moment he honestly considered finishing Elliot off this way.

"No, god!" Elliot kept his head down, but managed to turn far enough to catch Lennox's eye. "Please, *please*, get your dick in me and let me come on it. Please, I want you to fuck me so hard I can't breathe, I want to think about you every time I sit down, I want— Ahh, please—"

Lennox stroked him once more, then pulled his fingers out. "It'll be rougher in the shower," he warned as he reached for the condom. Silicone lube could only do so much.

"We can save fucking me in front of the mirror for when I'm pretty again."

Lennox covered his cock in lube, hunching to avoid the worst of the spray. He leaned in close and slid inside, slowly but steadily. Elliot hissed but didn't try to move away. He pressed both hands flat to the wall, then brought one foot up on the bench, spreading his cheeks apart and making it easier for Lennox to bottom out.

"Goddamn," Lennox swore. He pulled back, added lube, then pressed forward. It was easier this time, and Elliot relaxed into it. *Good enough.*

It was simplest to stay in close, bodies touching so the water couldn't wash the slick away. Lennox rolled his hips in rough, short bursts, covering Elliot's outstretched hands with his own as he licked drops of water off Elliot's shoulders. He nipped at the base of his neck as he fucked, and Elliot's hands turned into fists.

"Harder," Elliot breathed, and Lennox gave it to him harder. Every thrust went deep, into a more welcoming heat than the hot water provided. Elliot groaned and tried to free his hands, but Lennox held fast.

"You think you're not pretty now?" he breathed into Elliot's ear. "Whiny and eager and spread apart like this? I think you're the one with the slutty streak, you pretty thing. You're so pretty right now I can barely stand it."

"Nnn-not—not to look at," Elliot gasped. "Oh fuck, please touch me, I've got to come, Lennox—"

"Come on my cock or come after I'm done, one or the other," Lennox said. He was too keyed up to make either of them wait much longer, for all that he wanted to. "God, Elliot . . . you feel so fucking good." He drew back and pushed in hard, one last time, and that was it. His hands clenched around Elliot's as he came in a rush.

Elliot laughed shakily. "You bastard."

"I'm only a bastard if I don't follow through," Lennox said breathlessly before letting go with one hand to stroke Elliot's cock from base to tip. His grip was rougher than he knew Elliot liked it, too harsh without fresh lube, but Elliot was so ready that a few strokes was all it took before he cried out and came, spilling over Lennox's hand and onto the bench below.

"Holy shit," Elliot said with a groan, leaning against Lennox as he pushed himself upright. "Ugh, I have to go to work now? Why do I have to go to work now? I want to go back to bed, not to work."

"It's a nice thought, but Serena would kill you if you didn't show up." Lennox kissed the side of Elliot's neck, then slowly pulled out, securing the condom as he went. He threw it away, then reached for the bodywash. "We can make this part quick."

Elliot turned around and wrapped his arms around Lennox's neck. "But not too quick."

"Nah. Not too quick."

By early afternoon Elliot had been swamped with client teleconferences and vendor meetings. Serena was firing on all cylinders, unlikely to go anywhere, and with everyone else there, Lennox finally felt comfortable leaving Elliot, to run an errand of his own. He was able to explain it away as something for work, and went before either of them could question him in detail. In reality, Lennox had decided it was time to learn more about the enemy.

He was going to meet with Sheridan Pullman.

Reading about the man didn't do justice to the situation. Listening to Elliot speak about him was no better than any other witness statement: irreparably biased through the lens of Elliot's perception. If Pullman was a man capable of every nefarious action that Elliot said he'd done, then Lennox introducing himself wouldn't change what the man might do to him. If he was being talked up, well, then Lennox wanted to know that too. Personally, he had his doubts about Pullman. Something just wasn't sitting right, with the mix of extremely high-tech manipulation and very low-tech intimidation tactics. They seemed too disparate to be the work of just one person.

Sheridan Pullman had relocated after his release to a private, closed community in the foothills, complete with video surveillance and a guard at the gate. If Lennox had been a little more like James Bond, as his daughter would have loved, he might have shot out one of the security cameras and scaled the gate in a single jump. If he'd been Elliot, he would have convinced the guard that he was visiting a resident and had forgotten to call ahead, and oh, could he let him in? Lennox was neither a super spy nor intensely charming, but he didn't have to be.

It was amazing what you could get away with if you had a decal.

Lennox stopped on the side of the road half a mile out and took a moment to plaster a few Castillion stickers onto the doors of his truck. As he slapped one on the tailgate, a text came in. He pulled out his phone and checked the sender: *Oliver*. Excellent. Lennox opened it.

Unconfirmed sighting of Jonathan Lehrer in St. Petersburg this morning, but my source is generally reliable. Looks like he's found a position with the Bratva. Not the bad guy you want.

Well, that was helpful, but also a little disappointing. It would have made things simpler if Elliot's suspicions had been correct. *Thanks,* Lennox replied before climbing back into his truck. He put his work hat on and drove up to the community's gate with the slightly weary air of one blue-collar worker to another. "Hey."

"Hey there," the man said. He wore his uniform open at the collar, his tie long since abandoned to the desk he sat behind. *Perfect.* "What can I do for you?"

"I've got a call to inspect a system in here. Some problem with the keypad."

The man peered at his hat. "Castillion, huh? The knife people?"

"We do security systems too," Lennox assured him.

"Why does somebody in here need a private security system?"

Lennox spread his hands. "Hey, man, it's none of my business what some rich guy decides is worth the extra trouble."

"Yeah, I hear you. Who're you seeing?"

"Pullman."

"Huh." The guard checked the screen in front of him. "He didn't call ahead about you."

"He probably forgot. The guy seemed . . ." Lennox tightened his mouth into a grimace. "Well, let's just say he was kind of pissed over the phone."

"Uh-oh. Not a good guy to annoy."

"You're telling me. I'm hoping I can get in, get out as soon as possible." He rambled ahead before the guard could think of another reason to doubt him. "He didn't even bother to give me directions to his place in here, and of course my phone isn't getting any reception." He held up his darkened phone. "Can't check the map."

"Oh, Mr. Pullman lives in the rear loop. Number two fourteen. It's the biggest house on the block, you can't miss it."

Lennox smiled broadly. "Thanks, that's really helpful of you. I'll be out of your hair in half an hour, tops."

The guard smiled back. "Sure, okay." He pushed a button and the gate rolled open.

"Thanks again, man." Lennox waved and drove through, driving around to the rear loop. The community was one of those places that had been intensely manicured, but designed to look as if it hadn't.

Like nature created pine trees in the shape of near-perfect cones, and every bush was a decorative one that featured red or white berries during the winter. As soon as spring came, Lennox was willing to bet that every lawn would magically sprout Kentucky bluegrass too.

The houses were all expansive, but the biggest on the rear loop by far was two fourteen. It had a circular driveway in front of the house, cobbled, not paved, and a portico that cars could park under to the right of the actual garage—a four-car garage, from what Lennox could see. The house itself was made of rough-hewn sandstone and smooth, dark wood, with a glass A-frame in the front. Well. They'd certainly see him coming, but then, Lennox's strategy had never relied on stealth. He got out of his truck, walked up to the front door, and knocked twice.

The man who met him at the door looked almost nothing like the photographs that Lennox had seen. That man had been in his early fifties, with a head of thick, silver-gray hair and an angular, handsome face. He'd been broad-shouldered and tall, and as sleek as a shark. This man?

He walked with a cane, painfully stooped. His head was bald on top now, and the rest of his hair had thinned to the point where his scalp was visible through the wispy white strands. His skin was slack around his neck and wrists, and he wore a housecoat and slippers even though it was the middle of the day. The only things that remained the same were his whiskey-brown eyes, sharp and assessing as they skewered Lennox where he stood.

"Ah," Pullman croaked with evident satisfaction after a moment. "McKenzie's new bodyguard. Here to try your luck?"

"I'm not an assassin," Lennox said, slowly and distinctly in case someone was listening. "My name is Lennox West. I'm a friend of Elliot's. I'm just here to ask you a few questions, that's all."

"A friendly chat, so to speak?"

"I'd certainly like to keep things cordial," Lennox agreed.

Pullman snorted. "You've got a hint of Southern hospitality in you, 'keeping things cordial.'" He turned away and limped back into the house. "But fine, fine. You'll hand your weapons over to Martine before you come any farther, though."

A woman seemed to melt into existence beside the door. She was a hard-faced redhead packing a Walther PPK in her holster. Lennox suppressed a smile. At least *someone* here was getting into the spy persona. He handed over his Kahr PM9 by the barrel, which she took wordlessly before looking him up and down.

"Yeah, okay." He handed over both his Castillion folding knives as well, one from each pocket. She eyed him again. "That's it, I swear. You can pat me down if you need to."

"Not interested." Her voice was husky and heavily sarcastic. "Go on, then. And don't get any ideas."

Lennox nodded and walked after Pullman, who'd turned from his massive foyer into a room on the left. It was like a library, but instead of books it was filled, floor to ceiling, with file folders. Each folder had a number at the top of the spine, but no other visible identification. There was also a desk with a computer, and a massive, highly ergonomic chair behind it. It was all very monochrome and intimidating, except for the *Happy Birthday, Brother* card propped up beside the keyboard. Pullman was lowering himself into the chair as Lennox entered the room. He waved toward the only other seat in the place. "Make yourself comfortable."

"Thanks." Lennox sat down and waited silently while Pullman poured himself a drink. He didn't offer one to Lennox, which was fine as far as he was concerned. They stared at each other for a long moment before Pullman broke the silence.

"So, why did he send you here? To beg on his behalf, or is he finally ready to negotiate?"

"Do I need to beg for something?" Lennox asked.

Pullman shrugged. "I assume he's rattled. Elliot's a smart enough kid, but he's never been very brave."

So it is him. Lennox was relieved. One person behind it all simplified things immensely. "Well, anybody would be rattled after some of the stuff you've done."

Pullman waved a gnarled hand. "Please, it didn't hospitalize him for long. I knew he'd wriggle out of the wreck. Elliot is an expert at setting himself up to survive, which is something you should know about him if you plan on spending much time in his company.

Don't trust that little shit, because he'd as soon stab you in the back in private as kiss your ass in public."

"That's pretty rich, coming from a man who's just admitted that he hijacked Elliot's car."

"I didn't admit anything. Expressing knowledge of a particular event in no way correlates to admitting culpability." Pullman squinted at Lennox. "You haven't spent much time with him yet, have you?" He took another drink. "You'll learn to listen for his doublespeak, same as I did. He was always better at it than Kovalin."

Pullman leaned forward intently. "Which is why I see right through his act. Bettering other people's lives? Ha! Elliot McKenzie has always been and will always be only concerned with himself. Don't be fooled, Mr. West." His tone implied that he didn't really think Lennox was capable of that much insight, but that he had to try to educate him regardless, like a bad dog who needed his nose rubbed in his own mess.

"I'm convinced that Elliot's the one who stole the patent information for my Singularity project. Not only digital copies, but the hard copies as well. He's one of the only people who had the opportunity before the whole company got broken up for scrap." He gestured at the walls of file folders. "Very few people had access to where I kept them at my headquarters, but my lawyers were among them, and Elliot had the sharpest eye. And if he thinks I'm going to let him auction off my golden goose without putting up a fight, he's got another thing coming to him."

This was all news to Lennox. "What's the Singularity project?"

"I'm not surprised he hasn't mentioned it. Why would he tell you the truth? I'd be shocked if he knows the meaning of the word. But that Black Box meeting? It's not clients coming to drink from the wellspring of that lying fuck's wisdom." Pullman snorted derisively. "Not that he couldn't make a living selling sand to Saudis, but what he's selling this time is significantly more valuable, and I want it back. Either he gives it to me, or I ruin everything he's built up over the past five years." He smiled thinly. "His choice."

None of this made sense to Lennox, but he didn't need to let Pullman in on that. The smug expression on Pullman's face intimated that he probably already knew, anyway. Still, Lennox had to ask. "Why not just kill him, if you've got the means?"

"I'm sure I don't know what you're talking about," Pullman drawled, "but if I did, I'd say that the satisfaction of killing someone only lasts for as long as they're dying. But killing their pride, destroying their self-worth? That's satisfying for a lifetime. He'll be the one going to prison next, if he doesn't cough up my patent before his auction." His smile came back. "I doubt he'll do well in there, pretty little thing. He's smart, but he's soft. That's why he hired a goon like you, isn't it? To hide behind?" Pullman's phone beeped, and he glanced at the screen with interest.

"You're not a man without your own soft spots, Mr. West. You're in therapy, it looks like. And you have—one daughter, I see. She lives with her mother?"

Lennox's blood chilled. "You don't need to know anything about them."

"I agree. And if Elliot gives back my research before Sunday evening, I won't. If he doesn't, well." Pullman shrugged. "Collateral damage happens."

"Yes," Lennox agreed flatly. "Yes, it does."

Pullman sighed after a moment and lifted his glass.

"Touché. To be honest, I never liked the idea of threatening a man's family," Pullman went on. "It hits too close to home."

"That didn't stop you from doing it before."

"I've come to see the error of my ways on that front," Pullman said. "Family is precious, and no one should be without. The fact that Elliot McKenzie's won't talk to him anymore, despite his supposed turnaround, speaks volumes about his character, doesn't it? They turned their backs on him. He had to charm a batty old broad he met in *rehab* to fund his resurrection. Does that seem like the action of a good man, someone who's seen the light?"

He looked Lennox straight in the eyes. "Let me be frank, Mr. West. I don't want a fight, and I know beyond a doubt that Elliot doesn't want one either. He's not a fighter, he's a negotiator, and he'll try to talk himself out of any corner you put him in. But he's also a thief, and a liar, and he's about to try to make a lot of money on some very proprietary, very dangerous information. If you're smart, you'll convince him to give it back, and we'll go on our merry ways. I won't even ruin his company."

"Gracious of you."

"Old age is making me mild, what can I say?" He drained the last of his drink. "I appreciate you stopping by. It makes sending a message so much easier."

"I think poisoning his dog did a decent job of that," Lennox said as he got to his feet. He was more than ready to head out and have a heart-to-heart talk with Elliot about everything he'd just learned, but then Pullman . . . *froze* for a moment, his face completely blank and his gaze unfocused before he recovered himself. *Interesting.*

Pullman seemed torn over what to say, finally settling on, "Good-bye, Mr. West."

Lennox left without looking back. The sour-faced redhead gave him his weapons at the door—using her left hand for everything— and didn't hesitate to slam it shut behind him as soon as his feet passed the threshold. Lennox resisted the urge to run to his truck and speed back to Elliot, just kept his pace steady as he thought about what he knew now.

One: Sheridan Pullman was a cold-hearted, vengeful son of a bitch who wasn't afraid to threaten people.

Two: There were potentially a lot more layers to what was going on with Elliot and his upcoming event than he'd let on to Lennox, and that had to change.

And three: Either someone was taking independent action on Pullman's behalf, or there was another hostile in play whom Lennox couldn't place yet. Either way, Lennox was going to have to take steps.

And the first step? Cornering Elliot and getting the truth out of him, no matter how hard he squirmed.

CHAPTER THIRTEEN

Excerpt from *Shockwave's* article:

It's a funny thing, the desire to be part of something bigger than yourself. McKenzie's business plan cultivates an air of elitism, by acknowledging some of the worst mistakes he and his clients have ever made. A lot of his videos are about forgiveness. Not just forgiveness of others, but forgiveness of yourself. They would be disgustingly cloying if it were directed at any other population, but under the circumstances, he sells it. He sells it well.

Charmed Life's CEO borrows from religion, new-age mysticism, and classical philosophy in a lot of his directives. If he elevated his language a little more, if he altered his tone, if he changed his message a bit, you'd think he was running a cult.

Then again, I'm not a member of Charmed Life. Maybe he is running a cult.

"Aaand take two . . . go."

Elliot smiled into the camera, his nerves finally subsiding now that he was going. He'd made close to a hundred of these videos, and he still got anxious just before they rolled. "Hey, guys. It's Elliot at Charmed Life, here with your weekly insight. This is my last chance to talk to you before the Executive Meetup this weekend, so I figured I better make it count. For those of you who are coming to Denver to take part, I'm very thankful, and I can't wait to meet you all. I know that you're going to make connections here that will help transform your life. If you can't make it this year, don't be afraid of being left behind. I'm sure that the most interesting stuff that happens will make it onto the forums, and I'm planning to massively extend both the time and the offerings for next year."

Elliot sighed. "Life doesn't turn out the way we want it to sometimes. Maybe you wanted to come this weekend and you couldn't manage it, or you were planning to and something unexpected came up. Maybe you're hoping your team will win the Super Bowl, in which case, you're fifty percent likely to be disappointed. Maybe things have gotten hard again recently. Maybe you've backslid on some goals, or gone back on some promises.

"I know how you feel. Trust me," he laughed a little, "I try to hide it, but I'm always making mistakes. It happens to the best of us, and I've stopped pretending to be the best at anything. I'm imperfect, and no matter how hard I try, I'm never going to get everything right. That's why it's so important for me, for everyone, to have a team. We need people in our lives who we can count on, people to help pull us through the tough times. It could be friends, or family, or a newcomer that you've got a good feeling about. Your best support might come from a canine companion, for all I know. And that's fine.

"If your team isn't what you need it to be, then I want you to try and do something about that over the next week. Reach out to new people, go to a new place, and try to expand your circle. Or maybe you need to revisit old acquaintances that you might have thought were lost to you. Forgiveness can take time, and we can't force anyone else's heart to work on our schedule.

"So!" Elliot clapped his hands together. "Last week I talked about letting people go, now I'm talking about bringing people back in. Out with the bad, in with the good. If you have a strategy for attracting the right kind of people to your life, share it on the forums, unless it involves drugs, blackmail, or bribery, in which case." Elliot shrugged. "You've got bigger problems to be working on, my friend. Good luck this weekend, and may the best team win."

"Aaand . . . done."

"What do you think?" he asked Ted, who gave his usual one-shouldered shrug.

"Pretty good. We've probably got enough footage to put together something nice. You want it out tomorrow?"

"With the newsletter," Elliot confirmed. "Send it to Samar by this afternoon so he has enough time to do all the formatting."

Ted nodded. "I know the drill."

"I don't mean to sound like I'm doubting you. I just want everything to go smoothly for this weekend."

"What could go wrong?"

Elliot grinned at him. "Let's not tempt fate, shall we? Thanks, Ted." He headed upstairs and toward his office, but Serena intercepted him before he could get through the foyer.

"Lennox is back."

"Good, I wanted to talk to him about his suit situation."

"No," Serena hissed, somehow making it simultaneously stern and surreptitious. "He's here and he is *pissed*. He didn't say anything, but the last time I saw that face on him, Gaby had run his old car into a fire hydrant. He said he needed to talk to you and slammed the door to your office behind him before I could ask why. What's he been doing?"

"Something for work, he said." But that didn't seem to have been the truth. "Well. I guess I'd better see what's up."

"I hear screaming, I'm calling the cops."

"If things get that far, it'll be too late for me," Elliot joked, but he was uncomfortably aware that his joke was probably right on. Disregarding Lennox's gun and the knives, the man likely knew a dozen ways to kill him with his bare hands.

But now he was just being dramatic. Elliot rolled his eyes at himself as he turned to the door of his office. Everything was going to be fine.

He walked in, shut the door behind himself, and stopped dead in the face of a man he'd never seen before. It was *Lennox*, but this was a Lennox that Elliot didn't know. He stood stock-still against the far wall, his expression so hard it could have polished diamonds. There was no feeling in his eyes, no hint of shifting or movement to give away his state of mind. All Elliot could read was a cold, fierce fury, and he swallowed nervously.

"Lennox," Elliot said cautiously. "What's wrong?"

"What's the Singularity project?"

Elliot's mind exploded in a hundred different directions. How had Lennox learned about Singularity? Who had he been talking to? Had he gone to Pullman, had he— Oh, of course.

"You talked to Sheridan."

"Yeah."

"Are you *insane*?"

"I don't think you're in a position to be asking that question," Lennox said softly. The quietness of his voice was worse than any of the yelling he'd done so far. This was a guy who'd seen the sign for *angry* and driven straight past it to *incensed*. "Not when you've done such a good job diggin' your own grave."

"Wait, no," Elliot snapped, because he was guilty of a lot of things but not this. "Are you taking his word for this? Sheridan Pullman is the kind of man who hires *assassins* to intimidate people into doing what he wants. He's not exactly a moral authority in this situation. He sent Lehrer after people before and now he's doing it again—"

"He isn't."

Elliot paused, his momentum derailed. "What?"

"Jonathan Lehrer is in Russia. St. Petersburg, to be precise. Oliver texted and let me know."

Well, that was a missing cog in the clockwork of Elliot's hypothesis, but he could handle that. "He might be gone, but there's no surety that Pullman didn't hire someone else to do his dirty work."

"Because there are a lot of left-handed, gun-wielding hitmen for hire in the area."

Elliot's eyes narrowed. "What do you mean, 'gun-wielding hitmen'?"

Lennox shook his head. "Don't worry about that—get back to the issue at hand. Did you steal from him?"

"No."

Lennox pushed off the wall and walked toward Elliot, every step slow and controlled. It wasn't a walk, it was a *stalk*, and Elliot couldn't move. "Did you steal from him?"

"No."

"This man threatened me. He threatened my *daughter*." Lennox was within an arm's length now, close enough to touch. He stopped, but neither of them reached out. "He had plenty of things to say about you, and none of them were nice, and I'm pretty sure some of them were true." Lennox's eyes pinned Elliot in place, the hypnotic gaze of a cobra right before it struck. "I'm going to ask you one more time, and I want the truth. Otherwise I will walk out that door and you can handle this on your own."

Elliot hadn't realized just how badly the idea of facing this weekend's maelstrom without Lennox's backup would distress him: his throat tightened so fast he almost choked. His eyes roved over Lennox's face, looking for any hint of sympathy, but there was nothing. Nothing of his lover, his friend.

"Did you," Lennox asked slowly, "steal the data for a project called Singularity from Sheridan Pullman?"

"No," Elliot whispered. His eyes were watering, and he wanted to blink but didn't dare. "Lennox, no, I swear."

Lennox stared at him for a long moment, then finally nodded. "Then you'd better explain why he thinks you did."

"Can I sit down to do it?" Elliot smiled shakily. "I think my knees are about to give out."

"Of course you can sit."

Elliot flopped into the beanbag chair with a loud sigh. Lennox sat across from him. "Holy shit, you frightened me."

Lennox made a face. "I wasn't going to hurt you."

"You looked like you were going to rip my heart straight out of my chest if I lied to you."

Lennox shook his head. "I might have wanted to if you'd lied, but I wouldn't have laid a finger on you. I swear. I would have just . . ." He shrugged. "Left."

And left behind a gaping, bleeding wound in Elliot's psyche, but he didn't want to think about that right now, and he certainly didn't want to share. "How are you so sure that I'm not lying? Not that I am!" Elliot added, sitting up straighter to accentuate the point. "But how do you know that?"

"Call it a gut feeling. So. Explain why Pullman thinks you're a thief."

Now things got complicated. Elliot tried to keep his thoughts clear. As long as he didn't stray from exactly the truth as he knew it, he should be fine. "When Pullman was first arrested, all of his hard copy files were being stored onsite at Redback Industries. The police, and I think the FBI at one point, issued a massive search warrant for Redback's files, phone records, visitor logs, payroll records, the works.

Sheridan was paranoid about his research, but too egotistical to hide any of it. He kept a meticulous inventory of everything, backups of everything digital, multiple copies of hard files. After he was sentenced and his company was being broken up and sold off, all of his personal copies of the files were moved from headquarters to his home. Apparently Singularity is missing from the pile."

"Why point the finger at you?"

"Because I was free by then, and he thinks I'm motivated by revenge. As his attorney, I had access to the company intranet. He must assume I copied the files during the chaos. Which I didn't," Elliot emphasized. "I have no use for something like Project Singularity, believe me."

"What is it?"

"I don't actually know much about it. From what I understand, it has to do with a method for manufacturing designer viruses and infecting specific targets with them. Basically, it's finding a way to kill someone with a personal plague rather than a gun." Elliot shuddered. "I'd rather not think about it either, to be honest."

Lennox looked troubled. "And he thinks you're selling this at your Black Box meeting?"

"I guess so. That's all I was told."

The troubled expression changed to annoyance. "When were you told this?"

"On the phone, before he wrecked my car. Which I did tell you about!" Elliot added defensively. "I told you he made some threats!"

"You didn't say they were about returning something that you didn't even steal. It would have been nice to know that before I went and met with the guy this afternoon."

Elliot scoffed. "Well, I didn't know you were going to lose your mind and do that."

"It was logical to try and get a handle on him."

"He's a mafioso-style bully with an overdeveloped sense of vengeance! What is there to try and handle?"

Lennox tilted his head. "Did you just quote *The Princess Bride* at me?"

Elliot thought about it. "Maybe? But the vengeance line is a good one; it's *topical*. Does it matter if I stole it from a movie?"

There it was, finally: a smile, which was as good as a laugh from Lennox and meant that Elliot had been forgiven, at least for this. "You're ridiculous."

Elliot shook his head. "No, and don't take this the wrong way, but you're the ridiculous one. How could you go and speak to him like that? He might have had you killed!"

"I don't think so. But," Lennox held up a hand, "he does have a woman on staff who's well armed and not disposed to like strangers. She's left-handed too, which means it could have been her this morning."

Now Elliot was completely lost. "Her where this morning?"

Did Lennox actually look a little sheepish? "Outside your house. I chased someone through the woods. Turns out they were armed. And the shooter was a lefty, so . . . you know. It's topical."

"*Oh my God*, you *idiot*!"

The end of the working week was a frenzy of checking, double-checking, reassurance, and focused effort. Elliot hardly had time to look at Lennox, much less talk to him, which was fine because Lennox seemed similarly disinclined to get into another discussion that could so easily turn into an argument.

Not that the original had been all that much of an argument. Lennox had taken Elliot's rant about being a "stupid, secretive asshole" stoically, and then countered with, "Either you come up with an actual plan for getting out of whatever trap Pullman's set or you're not going to your Black Box meeting." At that point, Serena had banged on the door and reminded them she was perfectly willing to file a noise complaint against the two of them, which made Elliot back down. He was going through all of this to *avoid* calling the police.

The special election for district attorney would be over by Saturday night, and then he could contact the police without worrying for Vanessa. Unfortunately Saturday night was also the Meetup, right when he needed the police's help. But he could use more time to put his side of the story together anyway. He still had the dongle, but would it be enough to put suspicion on Pullman? And, irritating as it was, Lennox had a point: he had to get through both of his meetings without being shot, kidnapped, or otherwise displaced before he could get his point across.

Friday night ended up being spent with Lee. Lennox had sounded reluctant to take her when Gaby had called, the threat from Pullman obviously still weighing on his mind. Gaby had been on the verge of a meltdown, however, so insistent that her declarations of impending doom through Lennox's phone had been loud and clear to the whole office. "—has just had his tonsils out, and Marcus isn't here and his ex is gone for the weekend, and there's no way I can run Lee around to all her appointments, much less get her to that ridiculous party you and Serena insisted on, while I've got to take care of the twins."

Lennox had sighed. "Gaby . . ."

"And don't tell me again that she can't stay at your place, I'm sick of it! You're a grown man and you need to work on these problems, and your daughter needs to be accommodated because she—"

Serena plucked the phone from Lennox's hand. "Are you crazy? She's staying with me tonight! We have to go shopping for the right dress tomorrow, and if she wants to wear toeless shoes, then we're going to need pedicures."

"Why would you let her wear toeless shoes in the middle of February? Have you seen outside lately?"

"We're going to be inside 99.9 percent of the time! What, you think I'm going to make my niece walk through snow drifts in her gorgeous, stylish shoes?" Serena demanded.

Elliot and Lennox shared a bemused look as they let the sisters hash out Lee's schedule. Five minutes of arguing later, Serena finally handed the phone back.

"She wants to go boxing with you tonight, and then you're dropping her off with me. I'll bring her to the Meetup tomorrow, and I'll take her Saturday night too, so Gaby can stay at home with the twins and not worry."

"She always worries," Lennox drawled.

Serena rolled her eyes. "Worry *less*, then. I swear she's going to fret herself into an early grave if she's not careful. It's getting worse the more Marcus is away."

"Am I going to pick Lee up?"

"Yes, she expects you in half an hour. As for you," Serena turned to Elliot, "everything is ready for tomorrow, all the notices have gone out in the forums, and Stuart has called probably a dozen times today asking whether you've got plans for tonight. I'd love to be able to give him a *real* reason that you're not available." She smiled sweetly. "Like that you're out on a date with your boyfriend and his kid."

Elliot's stomach gave a little flutter when she said that, but he carefully kept any sign of it off his face. "Don't rub it in. You know how petulant he can be. A petulant caterer is the last thing we need right before the Meetup."

"I think he could use some stark truth, frankly. Stuart's never going to understand social cues unless there are consequences for getting them wrong," Serena argued, but she let it slide. "Well? Go get your girl!" She shooed them out of the office, and a minute later, Elliot waited patiently for Lennox to check the underside of his vehicle before they slid into the rental.

"Before you ask," Elliot said when Lennox inhaled like he was about to speak, "no, of course I don't mind having Lee along with us tonight. I recognize that I'm the one monopolizing your free time here, and it would be hypocritical of me to get upset when other people want to be with you. Especially your own kid."

Lennox rubbed the back of his neck. "I didn't mean for you to get drawn into my family's drama."

"I wouldn't describe it as drama," Elliot argued as he started the rental. The engine purred like a cougar, but he found he missed the sound of his poor Porsche. "I like spending time with both you and Lee, and she doesn't seem to mind."

"She's crazy about you," Lennox said, and Elliot smiled a little bit. Lee wasn't his niece, but being around her eased the pang in his heart whenever he thought about his sister's kids. "And she's generally a good judge of character, so I guess you must be okay."

"You're being awfully complimentary." Elliot turned onto the highway and headed toward Gaby's subdivision. "Whatever did I do to deserve that?"

"I don't know, maybe I'm getting soft."

"Or maybe you like me."

"Or that," Lennox said. "That could definitely be it."

Elliot didn't reply, but he bet his smile gave him away. Whatever they were doing, it had gone beyond casual fucking and a twisted need to protect and be protected. No matter what they decided about each other in the end, though, it would have to wait until after tomorrow.

And for him to have a plan. Lennox had shot down everything he'd suggested so far as "too dangerous, unworkable, too reliant on chance, and no, we don't have a drone so that one's not gonna work."

Elliot's rambling thoughts cut off abruptly when he turned onto the street that led to Lee's cul-de-sac and saw her standing at the corner, a full backpack over one shoulder and a murderous expression on her face. He came to a quick stop next to her and put on his hazards.

"What the— What's she doing over here?" Lennox opened his door and Lee unslung her backpack.

"Let's go," she announced. "Dad, I can't get into the backseat unless you get out—*move.*"

"Why are you standing on the street corner in the cold?" he asked. "Why didn't you meet us at the house?"

"Because Mom is being a complete *bitch*, and—"

"Ophelia Sky West," Lennox interrupted her. "You do not call your mother by that word. Never. Do you understand me?"

Lee crossed her arms and glared at the ground. "Fine."

"Do you need to go back and apologize to her?"

"No. We just had a fight, that's all." Lee sighed. "And it's probably because she's stressed out since Jerome is crying 'cause his throat hurts, and Khalil is mad because Marcus isn't around, but *she* still started it!"

Lennox looked at his daughter for a long moment, then got out of the car. "In," he said, motioning her to the back. "Give me a minute to call your mom."

"I promise not to drive off without you," Elliot said. Lennox gave him a little smile as Lee clambered into the tight backseat of the Camaro, then shut the door.

"She's going to yell at him," Lee said morosely. "She's been angry all day."

"He'll get over it," Elliot said. He took in Lee's demeanor for a second, then added, "She brought me up, huh?"

Lee's eyes went wide. "How did you know?"

"I'm good at reading people. So?"

Lee sighed. "Ugh, *yes*, it was kind of about you, but not really. Mom says dumb things sometimes when she gets worked up. She goes to therapy for it and everything. And she'll feel bad tomorrow, but tonight she was being mean. She thinks you're a bad influence and Dad shouldn't be exposing me to you, and then she started talking about Aunt Serena and I told her I was going to wait for you outside." She shrugged. "So I did."

"Bummer."

"Yeah," Lee agreed. "It's like Mom can forgive, but she never forgets, you know? And I think she doesn't like the idea of Dad dating anyone, but especially not another person with a 'criminal history.'" Lee added the air quotes with heavy sarcasm. "She never liked Uncle Oliver."

"Huh." There was a lot to parse there, not the least of which being that Lee thought Elliot and her father were dating, but Lennox chose that moment to return to the car. His movements were a little abrupt, his jaw tight, but he sounded fine when he said, "It's cleared up. Are you ready to do some boxing, sweetheart?"

"*Totally* ready," she said, flopping back and rooting around for the seat belt.

"Good. Me too."

The gym had more people in it on a Friday night, but Elliot carved off a section of the stands and settled in like he owned the place and wasn't intimidated by the vigorous activity. Or turned on. At all.

Honestly, he had never been into muscle-heavy men. His longest relationship had been with someone a lot like himself: slim and fit, but not built. No rippling abs or bulging biceps or any other cliché descriptions he could think of for body parts that weren't the penis. Vanessa had asked him once, back when they'd still seen each other every other day, if he didn't find being with Mischa a bit boring. "You're so similar," she'd said over her third glass of Chardonnay. "How does he ever challenge you? How does he make you better?"

Back then he'd been offended, but in retrospect, Mischa clearly hadn't made Elliot better. They'd enabled each other's worst traits while keeping up a pretty public façade, and it had almost been a relief for them to break apart when the fall came. He'd loved Mischa. He wouldn't have stayed otherwise. But Elliot hadn't really *liked* Mischa a lot of the time, and the fact that they hadn't exchanged half a dozen emails since the trial made Elliot very aware of his ambiguous affection. When he wanted something, he went after it like a shark scenting blood, unrelenting even when it meant he made bad decisions.

He had that urge with Lennox. Lennox had struck Elliot like a fist between the eyes from the very first moment. He'd liked looking at him immediately, liked *him* more. And half an hour of watching him hold pads for Lee to punch, while gratifying, was nothing compared to how hard it was to glance away once someone his own size pulled him into the central ring.

Lennox wasn't the best boxer there. His form wasn't as clean as the man he was fighting, a guy with at least a decade on him, and his defense was a little slipshod. His timing when he threw a punch was beautiful, though, hitting with better power and speed than his opponent, if less frequency. He was hard to predict from a spectator's perspective, and Elliot could only imagine how it felt to be in the ring with him, trying to strike without getting tagged back twice as hard.

"Tito's an old Golden Gloves champion," Lee said as she appeared out of nowhere, slumping down next to Elliot on the stands. She was freshly showered and had either stolen or been gifted with one of her father's Army Rangers sweatshirts. It hung down past her hips and hands, but she seemed comfortable in it. "Dad's one of the only people close to his age who can give him a workout."

"He seems like he's doing pretty good."

Lee stared at her father intently. "He says I could be better than he is."

"I'm sure you can, if you work hard enough at it."

"That's such a parentish thing to say," Lee huffed.

"No, it's a very *me* thing to say," Elliot replied. "Hard work always wins out over luck or talent in the long run. I'm only in the position I'm in today because I kept working at it, not because I was fabulously talented or had a lucky charm. That's how most of the people I know became successful, your Aunt Serena included. She'd make a good CEO," he added.

"What does it take to be a CEO?"

"Well, a company starts from an idea. And a CEO is the person who has the vision to understand that idea, and the means to enact it. A CEO makes a plan and gives the orders, and the employees follow his or her orders to the best of their ability. Kind of like a parent with their kids."

"Huh." Lee glanced back at the ring. "In my family, I think it's Mom who's the CEO, not Dad."

"You're probably right about that." Elliot winced as Lennox took an uppercut to his gut that sent him falling back against the ropes. The grizzled guy who owned the place dinged a little bell, and the other fighter took out his mouth guard and went over to make sure Lennox was okay. Lennox chuckled and shrugged the concern off, straightening up with a wince. His body was bright with exertion, his eyes brilliant with energy despite the beating he'd taken at the end.

"Ouch, Dad," Lee said after Lennox had left the ring and joined them. "Ouch."

"I wasn't that bad," he protested.

"Whatever, that was a total TKO." She couldn't keep her grin under wraps, though. "I guess you did *pretty* good. Good enough to take me to dinner."

Lennox rolled his eyes as he began to raise one gloved hand to his mouth. Elliot stopped him. "I'll help you," he said, starting to untie the laces.

"Thanks." Lennox was a little breathless, but seemed pleased. Elliot tried not to enjoy the scent of fresh sweat too much as Lennox turned to his daughter. "Helpful people get taken to dinner. Hecklers get to eat leftover chili."

"You're bluffing," Lee said confidently. "You won't do that to your favorite daughter."

"You're my only daughter."

"That doesn't mean I'm not your favorite too. We can go to a burger place," she added with an air of compromise. "Not sushi, I promise."

Elliot tugged the glove off, then found one of his hands captured by Lennox's. "Sound good to you?" Lennox asked.

Elliot stared at their mingled fingers for a moment, totally bemused, before he remembered to answer. "Yeah, that's fine."

"Great." Lennox squeezed his hand, then let go and took his glove back. "I'll clean up fast."

They ate at a greasy-spoon diner three blocks from the gym. Elliot was happy to let Lee direct the conversation, still distracted by his own worries. He couldn't check out completely, of course. Not when Lee kept asking questions that Lennox couldn't field by himself.

"What's your favorite Harry Potter spell?" she asked Elliot around a mouthful of burger. Lennox unfolded his napkin and held it up in front of her face until she batted it down and stared at him as she dramatically chewed and swallowed. "I bet it's Felix Felicis," she said once she could talk again. "Working hard is good, but having perfect luck would be even better!"

"That's a good one," Elliot agreed. "Although if we're going with potions, I'd want to have a supply of Polyjuice."

"Which is . . . what?" Lennox asked.

"Oh, Dad, it's so cool," Lee interjected, clearly forgetting to mock his ignorance in her haste to explain. "It lets you look like other people! It's perfect for sneaking into places you aren't supposed to be, and fooling people into thinking you're someone else. I'd want to be Aunt Serena. But just for a little while."

"I'd like to be her for a little while too," Elliot said with a chuckle. "But no one would ever believe I was the real thing. I'd fall right off those heels." He glanced over at Lennox, expecting him to be laughing as well.

Instead he looked thoughtful. "Actually . . . That might not be a bad plan."

Had he been hit too hard in the head during his boxing match? "Polyjuice Potion?"

Lennox half smiled. "Close."

CHAPTER FOURTEEN

Partial transcription of most recent appointment with West, Lennox, Staff Sergeant US Army Rangers (R), January 28, 3:29 p.m.:

JS: I'm afraid that's all the time we have for today, Lennox.

LW: Thank God. Not that I don't appreciate what you're trying to do, Doc, but this feels like pulling teeth.

JS: I understand. It means a lot that you keep trying, regardless.

LW: I told my family I'd keep it up. I'm not going to break that promise.

JS: When will you be seeing them next?

LW: Tonight, actually. Gaby's having a barbecue at her place. Good weather for it.

JS: That sounds like fun. Will you be taking anyone with you?

LW: (Patient laughs.) Even if I were dating, I don't think a meal at my ex-wife's house would be the event to break them in on, huh? Besides, it's not like I've got a lot to offer someone.

JS: You never know what people are going to be looking for, Lennox. Keep an open mind. You might be surprised.

The hardest part about the whole plan, Lennox felt, was that he had to wear a suit. Not just a suit, a *tux*, and one that fit. Elliot had a tailor—of course he did—and that woman could work miracles. In less than twenty-four hours she'd modified a tuxedo to fit Lennox like it had been made for him, and tweaked Elliot's own, nearly identical outfit enough to make room for his new accessories without being obvious.

Betty did the final fitting for both of them in Elliot's office. They were the only three people left in the building. Serena had darted in and out between excursions with Lee, but apart from that, the place had been silent but for Betty's pleasant humming. She had platinum-blonde hair, bright-red lips, and worked in a gown that could have come out of one of Gaby's magazines. She was also resolutely cheerful in the face of Lennox's discomfort, which he had to give her props for.

Lennox didn't even get to tie his own tie. "At least tell me—"

"Say nothing, Betty," Elliot said blithely, texting one-handed as he sipped from a paper cup of coffee. He'd barely glanced up from his phone since he'd woken up that morning. "Lennox doesn't understand the concept of gift-giving. He'll only have a heart attack if you let him think about how much his tuxedo costs."

"If you think a tuxedo is the most expensive thing I've ever worn, you've got another thing coming," Lennox retorted.

"Yeah, but every technological wonder you sported while you were a Ranger belonged to the Army. Whereas this," Elliot waved at the midnight-black ensemble that Betty was making the final adjustments to, "belongs solely to you. And it looks fantastic. Betty, you're a genius."

"Oh, your friend is an easy man to dress," Betty said with a smile, finally standing back and giving the shawl collar one last tweak. "The hardest part was making sure it fit your shoulders without compromising your mobility," she added to Lennox. "It wasn't easy to match your silhouettes, but I think we managed, right?"

It was surprisingly comfortable. Better than his dress uniform, for certain, and that was the only other piece of formalwear Lennox had on hand. He rolled his shoulders, then lifted his arms experimentally.

"Do a jumping jack next." Elliot grinned. "Or, ooh, push-ups! Wouldn't you like to see Lennox do some push-ups, Betty?"

"I'd rather see his shirt stay tucked in," Betty said, walking in a slow circle around Lennox. The hairs on his neck prickled as she closed in behind him, but he let her work in his blind spot. *Nerves*, he told himself. He'd get over them once the plan got underway. He always did.

Elliot pouted a little. "You're no fun at all."

Betty glanced over at Elliot. "Aw, don't be fussy because you have to wait awhile to unwrap him." Then she turned her attention back to Lennox, who was doing his best not to blush. "Do you have cuff links?"

"In the pocket of my jacket."

"Wonderful." She smoothed the fabric over his shoulders one last time. "You look very handsome. If you ever want to consider modeling for me, I'd be happy to pay you for your time and would give you a bespoke suit to take home at the end of it."

Elliot's eyes narrowed. "Are you coming on to my date? I can't quite tell."

"You're just jealous she didn't ask you to be her model," Lennox teased.

"Maybe," Elliot allowed, glancing down at his phone again. "But she's got a point. If anyone could make her suits fly off the rack, it's you."

"Yeah, right." It was flattering to be asked, but Lennox would model suits when pigs could fly. "What are you looking at?"

"Special election results." Elliot smiled tightly. "None yet, but I'll keep checking in. Hopefully the news will break fast and we can save her a scandal when we call things in."

"Can I see?"

Elliot shrugged and handed the phone over. "Not much to see, but sure." Betty closed in on him, which gave Lennox the opening he needed to turn away, pull the tiny chip out of his pocket, open up the back of Elliot's phone, and slip the chip in beside the battery.

He looked over in time to see Betty put her hands on her hips and sigh as she turned a final circle around Elliot. "Remember to keep your phone in your overcoat once you're in the public eye, all right? I already had to adjust things to compensate for the new accessories, and anything else will ruin the line."

"I hear and obey," Elliot promised her, plucking the phone from Lennox's hand. "God forbid I appear anything other than perfect in one of your creations. You'll have people knocking your door down wanting your custom couture."

"Oh, I'm not hurting for business, but I like my clients to always be at their best." Betty motioned them to stand closer together. "Pretty impressive," she said after a moment. "Or it will be once you add the hat." She sighed. "A fedora with a tuxedo, honestly." She handed over a new hat, edged in the same fabric as the wide lapels. "This is the one time you could've gotten away with a top hat. It would have been so elegant!"

Elliot tucked the fedora on top of his head and gave her a little bow. "But then it wouldn't have been me. How will people recognize me without my trademark hat? Now," he continued briskly before Betty could say anything else, "do you need a ride to the Meetup, or are you all set?"

Betty picked up her tiny jeweled clutch in one hand and her much larger sewing kit in the other. "I'll take my own car. Thank you for the offer, though."

"My pleasure." Elliot gave her one last smile. "We'll see you there soon."

"Don't forget your cuff links," Betty said before she swept out of the office in a wave of silky fuchsia fabric and orange-blossom perfume.

"Is everyone you know a Charmed Life client?" Lennox asked once he heard the front door shut.

"Only the best people," Elliot replied. "Betty was one of the first, actually. She helped me with my image and branding. Don't listen to her when she impugns the fedora either; it was all her idea. Something to set me apart, she said." He took it off his head and twirled it in his hand, but his face was pensive. "I suppose it does that. Lennox—"

"Don't overthink it," Lennox advised as he headed over to his jacket. He wouldn't be able to wear the beat-up leather tonight, but it was warm enough for February that he probably wouldn't miss it. He groped through the left-hand pocket until his fingers closed on cool metal studs.

"I just— Are you sure you're all right with—"

"It was my idea. I'm fine with it." Lennox rejoined Elliot in the middle of the room and took the hat out of his hands before he bent the brim. He set it down on Elliot's desk. "Better like this than the other way around," he confessed.

Elliot smiled again, but it was a small, uncertain thing. "That's because you're a bit of a freak, honestly. And a masochist."

Guilty as charged. "Yeah, but you love it."

"I might."

That part sounded entirely too serious for Lennox's liking. He needed Elliot to be charming and confident, so that Lennox could focus on the task at hand. Everything was set up, almost all of the players in place. Now the plan just had to fall together how they both thought it would.

"Here, help me with these." Lennox pressed his cuff links into Elliot's hand. Elliot took one look at them and burst out laughing.

"These are *Batman* cuff links! Why in God's name do you have Batman cuff links?" He peered a little closer. "Are these really silver?"

"Sterling," Lennox confirmed. "And they were a gift from Lee the birthday after she saw the first Batman movie with me."

"And you thought they fit the mood tonight?" Elliot sounded put out, but he was grinning. "Batman is a bit casual for the Meetup. I've got a dozen pairs you could have borrowed."

"But then I wouldn't be me. Besides, I doubt anyone will get close enough to inspect my wrists," Lennox said, and Elliot took the hit with a little nod. "And they're tiny: no one will notice. These are better than the other pair I've got at home."

"Oh really?" Elliot still seemed amused, but dutifully pulled Lennox's cuffs together with the help of the Batman logo. "What are the other ones like? Tiny pistols? Crossed daggers beneath a skull?"

"The namaste symbol." Elliot seemed blank. "Namaste. You know, the greeting? 'I bow to you'? It's kind of a swirly . . ." Lennox couldn't explain it well enough, so he turned his hand over in Elliot's grip and drew the symbol on Elliot's palm with his index finger. "Like that."

Elliot stared at his palm like he could actually see the outline. "You got those other cuff links from your mother, didn't you?"

"Solid-gold hippie mysticism," Lennox agreed. "She's got the same symbol tattooed across her lower back."

"Of course she does." Elliot closed his hand slowly. "I'd really like to meet her someday."

"You will," Lennox said, and it felt as good as a promise. "You ready for the Meetup?"

"Oh darling." Elliot replaced his hat on his head, tilting it at a jaunty angle. "I'm always ready for a party."

It was a good thing Serena had reserved a parking place for them, because downtown Denver was packed with people. There were a huge number of events going on the night before the Super Bowl and the Executive Meetup was just one of the offerings, but their particular batch of attendees stood out in the crowd of jersey-wearing, pre-tailgate party tailgaters. They were better dressed, among other things.

The party itself was being held in a private performance hall that could only accommodate a smallish number of guests, if five hundred could be considered a small number. Lennox felt strange in his tux, the formal skin doing a poor job of concealing the informal man beneath it. He had to admit, though, that he didn't look odd once he was in among the Meetup's crowd.

While Elliot entered through a private door in the back—"I've got to preserve some sense of surprise, after all"—Lennox went in through the front, where Serena and Lee were checking IDs and invitations. Serena had opted for a minidress so sparkling that Lennox shielded his eyes as he walked up to her, getting him an eye roll and a gentle smack on the shoulder for his trouble.

"Don't be so dramatic," she chided before turning to the woman behind him. "Miss Hanes! We're so pleased you could make it." Lennox stepped off to the side so Serena could handle the influx behind him, and checked in with Lee, who was very seriously making notes on the tablet she held. She was in a violet dress that stopped just below her knees, which he decidedly approved of. Her hair had been elaborately pinned on top of her head, and a jeweled comb was doing its best to hold the whole thing in place.

"Hey, sweetheart."

"Dad!" Lee beamed a smile at him. "Check out the dress Aunt Serena got for me." She held her arms out to her side, and seemed one halfhearted consideration over maturity away from doing a twirl.

"It's nice."

Lee frowned. "Only nice?" Lennox scrambled to come up with something else, but Lee's frown melted away into a devious grin. "I'm kidding, Dad, don't stress."

"You are *definitely* spending too much time with your aunt."

Lee shrugged. "I feel like I'm learning a lot, though. You look really nice too." Lee checked his sleeves, then smiled. "You're wearing my present!"

"What else would I wear to a fancy party like this?"

"It is pretty fancy, isn't it?" They stood side by side in mutual silence, gazing out at the people surrounding them. The room bustled with guests exchanging greetings, numbers, and plenty of business cards. Too many of the men wore fedoras in a transparent attempt to be more like Elliot, and the air smelled so thickly of perfume and cologne that Lennox struggled not to sneeze. Was it appropriate to use the pocket square to blow your nose? *Probably not.* He'd grab a cocktail napkin as soon as he could, just in case.

"Not our normal crowd," Lennox suggested, and Lee nodded, but there was a stubborn tilt to her mouth that he recognized all too well.

"But it could be."

"I guess it could," Lennox agreed. "If you're into the wine-and-dine set."

"Dad." Lee stared at him like he was slow. "You *are* into that crowd. You're dating Elliot, aren't you?"

Lennox wasn't sure *what* was going on with Elliot, honestly, but he didn't get a chance to say anything either way before they were interrupted.

"Is that so?" A dark-haired woman in a sleek crimson suit stepped up out of nowhere. "This is a new development since I last talked to Mr. McKenzie." The fingers of her right hand twitched, like she was desperate to take notes. "How long have you two been seeing each other?"

"Now now, Clarissa." Serena fluttered over to them like a guardian angel in haute couture. Her smile was bright, but cold. "You're not here to be a reporter, you're here to enjoy the party. So please." She handed over a flute of champagne. "*Go* and enjoy."

The woman smirked as she took the drink. "Your employer would probably be offended if he thought you were running interference for him. Mr. McKenzie is a big boy, he can handle himself."

"And his friend is here to enjoy himself, not endure the third degree from you, so let's call it a wash."

Serena's smile dropped away as soon as the other woman's back was turned. "Why he invited her, honestly . . . but *you*." She eyed Lennox appreciatively for a moment. "You look like a million bucks. Betty does such good work."

"Just call me the ugly duckling," Lennox said, but Serena tutted and shook her head.

"This is more like gilding the lily, I think. Where's your— Ah." The volume in one corner of the room rose dramatically, and Serena smiled. "Elliot's making his entrance now."

While he was deployed, Lennox had been party to several visits from politicians and entertainers who'd come out to "personally thank the troops" for one reason or another. Those people had by and large been masterful at working a crowd, but they had nothing on Elliot. He was like the rising sun, illuminating every person he came into contact with. He was alluring, magnetic, passing out greetings and compliments and remembering everyone's names, fielding thanks and questions with genuine enjoyment. He seemed as deft at getting *out* of conversations as getting into them, and moved from group to group as smoothly as a summer breeze, welcoming and warm. Lennox realized he was smiling just watching Elliot walk, and when he looked away, it was to find Lee grinning smugly at him.

"Knock it off, smarty," Lennox murmured, nudging her with his elbow. She nudged back, then rejoined Serena checking in new arrivals. Lennox slid over to a spot near the bar, as close to out of the way as he could be in such a busy place, then he let his eyes take a soft focus as he stared out over the crowd.

He didn't even know what he was searching for, or what he expected to see. Suspicious behavior? God, that label could apply to any of a dozen people right now, surreptitiously or openly taking photos with their phones to prove "I was there, see me hanging out with the beautiful people!" It could apply to one of the fast-talkers who sidled through the crowd like silk thread, too slick to hold still. It might apply to one of the three people who were badly concealing guns: two men with pocket holsters, and one woman with a purse that was too big for her to be lugging around at a time like this.

A passing waiter stopped and offered Lennox a tiny quiche. He accepted and forced himself to relax a little. Odds were, nothing was going to happen here. Pullman wanted to ruin Elliot at the height of his career, and that was the Black Box meeting. Elliot was so confident in that that they'd designed their entire plan around it. And if something did happen . . . if some*one* happened . . . well, there was always plan B. Neither Elliot nor Lennox were happy about plan B, which was more of a Hail Mary play than a well-considered course of action, but at least it was there.

The noise gradually increased as the alcohol flowed, people wheeling and dealing, cries of pleasure and recognition and a few of discontent. Lennox wasn't here to be security, though, and was pleased when the security company that Elliot had hired to make sure things went smoothly escorted some disgruntled drunks out when they started to get too insistent. Clusters developed around the biggest fish, a few of them people who even Lennox recognized, and theories flew freely about who would be attending the Black Box meeting.

"Were you invited?"

"Have you heard . . ."

"What about . . ."

After another half hour, Lennox frankly would rather be under fire than having to fend off any more tipsy guests asking who he was and, once word had gotten out, how he and Elliot had gotten together. Passing the buck to Serena only worked a few times, and when the ESPN updates that had been playing on the projector screen stopped and Elliot took the stage, it felt like a weight slipped from his shoulders. Elliot smiled brightly in the glare of the spotlight, and people gave him their attention like it would pay their way to Heaven.

"Welcome to the Charmed Life Executive Meetup." Elliot enunciated every capital letter so precisely Lennox could almost hear the trademark fall into place. That was as canned as his speech got, however. Elliot looked down at the podium in front of him for a moment, and when he looked up again, his eyes burned with authenticity.

"I know I can't speak for everyone, but tonight I'm going to try." He took a deep breath. "We're here together, all of us, because we believe in second chances. We're here because we believe the mistakes in our past don't have to define our futures. We're here because we want to meet like-minded people, and give back to the community that exists between us. You people," his gaze raked the crowd, freezing fidgeters and transfixing the people who met his eyes, "you friends, you *visionaries*—you're here because for whatever reason, you've chosen to believe in yourself. You believed enough to come here tonight, to invest in your future and the future of everyone here.

"All of you, each and every one of you, have something to offer the world. You didn't lie down and die when that felt like the only path ahead of you; you didn't curl up in a corner and wait to be forgotten. You fought on: you fought for the right to have a life, success, and the possibility of a future made brighter by your hard-won knowledge. You're tough, and you're savvy, and you're not spectators to your own existence. Take a look around, see the people surrounding you, and recognize now: you're not alone. All of you are a part of Charmed Life, the most important part. You're the part that believes in you and everyone else here. Hold on to that belief."

There were specifics about what Elliot hoped to accomplish by hosting the Meetup, what he wanted people to do for each other, but it all rolled through Lennox's mind without really penetrating. He could only watch as Elliot, this fallible man who was maybe almost as far from perfect as Lennox himself was, assured his guests that, more than ever, they were meant to be there. Meant for the high life, meant for great things, meant to move beyond the bad parts of their lives.

Shit. Maybe Lennox *should* be a member.

After a few more minutes, Lennox tore his attention away from the stage and skirted the edge of the crowd until he made it to the smaller room that had an exit straight out to the street. The catering crew was in there, Stuart directing them like a manic symphony conductor, sending tray after tray of champagne flutes, truffles, and chocolate-dipped strawberries into the crowd.

The same girl who'd given him a quiche saw him and detoured his way before heading out, proffering her tray of berries with a flourish. They were gorgeous, dipped in dark and milk chocolate swirled with white chocolate stripes. Lennox took one despite not feeling hungry for it, and after his first bite he was glad he had. He closed his eyes for a moment, the richness of the treat a serious distraction.

Not so distracting that he didn't notice when Elliot got close, but it was a near thing.

"That good, huh?" Elliot asked quietly as he stopped half a foot away from Lennox, whose stomach clenched, but not from the food. He couldn't remember the last time he'd been so affected by another person.

"Amazing," he said. Elliot was calm now, calmer than he had been before the Meetup started. He'd obviously found his zone, and it showed in the relaxed way he stood, the confidence in his expression. Lennox was struck with the urge to touch him, and Elliot must have seen it, because he leaned in until their chests brushed.

"Show me," he said, and then his lips were on Lennox's. Elliot didn't taste like chocolate or champagne; he tasted like himself, and it was more intoxicating than anything else. Lennox tilted his head and cupped the back of Elliot's head with his free hand, deepening the kiss. Elliot hummed appreciatively.

When the kiss finally ended, Lennox had to resist the urge to chase Elliot's mouth. "Good?" he managed, not quite needing to clear his throat to speak.

Elliot nodded. "I think you said it best. Amazing." He traced a line down the buttons on Lennox's shirt. "Do you—"

Lennox's phone began to softly beep, and he'd never hated the fucking thing worse, but they'd agreed. "Time to go," he murmured.

"For both of us. Stuart should be prepping the van now." Elliot slowly took his hat off, then set it on Lennox's head. When he stepped back, he was all business. "Good luck. Don't do anything I wouldn't!" he said cheerfully.

"Thanks," Lennox said dryly. He headed for the door leading to the street, hoping it was dark enough, hoping the timing was right, hoping everything worked out the way they wanted it to. Needed it to.

It was definitely dark, and the Camaro was parked away from the streetlamps, so he wasn't too worried about being made. Still, he moved briskly, unlocking and starting the car remotely so that as soon as he slid behind the wheel and buckled up, he could go.

He paused to take the spectrum analyzer he'd borrowed from Kevin—"on pain of death if you scratch that thing, dude; it costs more than three of your cars"—out from under the passenger seat. He flipped up the lid and turned it on, then extended the directional antenna and pointed it down toward the undercarriage of the Camaro. A familiar oscillating line hummed across the screen. Bingo. That was a signal from a tracking device.

Lennox shut off the analyzer, pulled into traffic, which was still heavy with Super Bowl pre-partiers, and slowly wound through downtown Denver until he got on the highway that led back to Golden. Then he called up Kevin and put his phone on speaker. "Is everything ready?"

"Yeah, absolutely! The cameras are rolling, and I left the back door unlocked for you and . . . whoever else shows. And I loaded my P90, for backup!"

"You realize this could take some time, right?" Lennox clarified as he turned onto Highway 93. "And that the last thing we want to do is shoot someone?" It made his brain hurt that he needed to explicitly state this to Kevin. It was like talking with the shotgun-grabby hick again.

"I know, I totally know. But, I mean, we *could*, that's what I'm saying. I'm ready, just in case."

Ready, set, and overeager. Lennox would definitely be making him put that P90 back in his room before anyone else showed up. "Thanks, Kevin." He ended the call and turned onto Castillion Place. There were no headlights behind him now, but he knew they could expect company.

He pulled into the store lot, got out his phone, and texted Elliot: *Found a tracking device. Expecting company soon enough.*

Holy shit, really?

Lennox rolled his eyes. *Part of the plan, remember?*

I still hoped it wouldn't happen. After a long pause, a new text came through. *You don't have to do this. You can leave my car on the side of the road and run.*

That was sweet. Way too late, but sweet. *I'll be fine. Worry about yourself.*

Can't help it. You're too important for me to ignore. There was another pause, possibly Elliot waiting to see if Lennox would reply in kind. He wasn't about to make any important declarations via text, though. It would keep until they were together again. *Going dark here. Call you by midnight.*

He'd better. *Good luck.*

Same to you, babe.

Lennox put the phone away, locked the car, and headed into Castillion's back room. Kevin was waiting for him, grinning, a bag of chips in one hand and a tablet in the other. His beard had crumbs in it. "So, what about Make My Day?" he asked the second Lennox shut the door. "Because I live here, so technically speaking that makes it a domicile, right? So the law would protect us against prosecution if we shot someone breaking and entering here."

"If you're so keen to shoot people, join the Army." Lennox took off Elliot's hat and set it on the counter, then picked up the P90 that Kevin had left out. He inspected it and resisted the urge to sigh. "This is the military model, Kevin. Ownership of these is restricted. If you get caught with this—I don't care if it is in self-defense—you're going to have a hard time justifying using a submachine gun on a person."

"But it's only a *little* submachine gun," Kevin whined. "Come on, Lennox! Why are you ruining all my fun?"

His urge to sigh was rapidly turning into an urge to slap some sense into Kevin, but that would probably take all night. "This isn't about fun. It's about catching someone who's trying to kill Elliot. You can either help me out, or I can banish you to the control room and you can monitor the phone banks, like you're supposed to anyway."

"I'll hear it ring if someone calls," Kevin insisted, but his voice was weak. "Oh, fine." He took the gun back into his room.

"Nothing with an extended magazine either," Lennox called as he checked the time. Almost ten.

"But they're legal to own, just not to buy!"

"Kevin."

"Fine, *God*. What are you, my dad?"

"We're both lucky I'm not," Lennox said under his breath as he heard Kevin reopen his gun safe.

Thirty minutes passed slowly, with Kevin in a huff and Lennox disinclined to make conversation, but eventually Kevin's tablet beeped. "Motion detector," he said. "Let me pull up the camera feed." Lennox joined him and watched a gray video image come to life. It was infrared, not the best quality, but he could make out the outline of the sedan as it stopped right outside the gate leading into the front lot. The car's headlights weren't on, and the brief flare of the overhead lights lasted just long enough to silhouette a figure holding something short and slender in one hand.

Kevin peered at the video. "Is that a gun?" he asked as the person began to move. He switched to the camera in front of the store. After a minute the figure appeared again, making careful progress around the building. "Or a knife?"

"It's a phone," Lennox said after a second. "They're probably using it to identify the car. Leave the tablet, hit the lights, and get behind the table."

"Okay!"

"And try to be quiet," Lennox added as Kevin rammed the nearest chair with his hip in his haste to fall back.

"*Oh-kay*," he whispered, then turned the overhead lights off.

Lennox stayed where he was, leaning against the wall closest to the door and watching the video feed. He held his breath as the person drew up behind the door, laying the phone flush to the metal for a moment. Apparently whatever they were monitoring was acceptable, because the next thing they did was try the doorknob.

It turned. The person opened the door a crack, the faint light doing nothing to illuminate the room inside. Lennox held his position, one hand on the gun at the small of his back. Gradually the door opened further, and after a few seconds' more hesitation, the person stepped over the threshold.

The next few moments almost gave Lennox a heart attack. Just as he turned on the light, Kevin popped up from behind the far table, pistol in hand, and screamed, "*Freeze, motherfucker!*" The person in the black bodysuit and mask responded by pulling a stun gun out of one pocket almost faster than Lennox could track and firing it at Kevin. The prongs got him in the shoulder and sent him quivering to the ground, which was enough of a distraction for Lennox to close the distance. He grabbed the forearm and shoulder of the firing hand and levered them down hard, bending the attacker over at the waist.

The person dropped both their phone and their stun gun, fighting to free themselves from Lennox's grasp. He blocked the vicious uppercut aimed at his groin, then stomped the back of the person's leg, bringing them down onto one knee with a gasp. A high, *feminine* gasp.

"I figured it was gonna be you," Lennox muttered, pulling off the mask. Only it wasn't red hair and a square, stern face that greeted him. It was a black pixie cut and an expression that could have given a viper a run for its money on venomous.

"Get your hands off me!" she snapped. Her voice clued him in: it was the reporter, Clarissa-something from the party.

"Why, so you can try to take me out again? No, thanks." Lennox looked over to where Kevin had fallen. "Kevin? You okay?"

"Hmm-ghnn . . ."

"I need to hear you say yes, Kevin." Lennox wanted to go over and check him out personally, but he didn't have any handcuffs on him and he wasn't about to trust this woman on her own.

"Yuh . . . yeah. Yes. Ow, shit." Kevin's head slowly appeared over the edge of the table. "The fuck did you hit me with?" he demanded in a wobbly voice.

"Kevin, I need you to go and call the police, okay? Go to the phone room and call the cops and stay on with them until they get here. Tell them we've had a break-in but it's under control." The woman tried to surge up at that, to tear herself away, but Lennox just stretched her out until her body was flush to the floor, then set a knee in the small of her back.

"I can . . . No, I can stay and help."

"Calling the cops is the best way to help now, Kevin," Lennox assured him calmly. "Go on. I'll be fine."

"Um . . . okay." Kevin tottered away into the phone room.

Lennox smiled down at the woman spitting curses against the dirty beige carpet. "Alone at last," he said. "Honestly, you weren't who I was expecting."

"I'm glad you're calling the cops," she ground out. "I'm going to sue you for all you've got. Assaulting a woman? They'll eat you alive."

"Subduing a trespasser on private property, who stalked me across town? Who attacked my colleague and tried to attack me?"

"He pulled a gun on me first!"

Lennox shook his head. "That's not what the cameras will show. Those stop on the outside of the building. And it doesn't matter:

he lives here. He could have shot you with impunity as soon as you stepped over the threshold. That's the law." It wasn't exactly what he'd told Kevin, but he hadn't needed the encouragement. "Not to mention, I bet if we take a peek inside your phone, we'll find all sorts of things that aren't supposed to be there. We kept the dongle, you know." She flinched. "Do you still have the software that you used to control Elliot's car on your phone? How do you think the cops are gonna like that?"

"That wasn't my idea."

Lennox hadn't figured it was. "Pullman's, then?"

"Let me up and I'll tell you," she gritted out. "This position is killing me."

"It's pretty comfortable from where I'm sitting," Lennox said, but . . . well. Maybe his knees were creaking a little. "Fine. Sit up slowly, keep your hands over your head, and if you go for another weapon? I won't hesitate to shoot you."

She pressed her lips tight together, but nodded. Lennox made sure her stun gun and phone were both out of reach, patted her down briefly, then let go of her and stood up. He drew his gun and kept it trained on her as she pushed up to her hands and knees with a wince. "Back against the wall."

She went, shuffling on her butt and keeping her hands above her head the whole time. "I'm a reporter, all right? I write for *Shockwave* magazine. We specialize in business and technology. You don't know what Elliot McKenzie is really doing; I'm after the biggest story of my career here!"

"I know what you think is happening at the Black Box meeting," Lennox told her. "You're wrong."

"No, *you're* wrong. I'm on the verge of uncovering one of the most massive acts of corporate malfeasance in history! This could result in saving hundreds of thousands of lives across the globe, not that I'd expect someone like *you* to care about that." The disdain in her voice was so thick it was surprising she could speak through it.

"You work for Pullman, then?"

"Sheridan has nothing to do with this," she insisted. "I got a tip, I ran with it. If I could have exposed both Elliot and his buyers, I would have gotten a Pulitzer for my work and done the world a huge favor at the same time. That's it."

Sheridan, huh? "I don't believe you." Lennox crouched down across from her, his pistol lowered but ready. "I don't think the cops will believe you either. The software you've been using is expensive, not to mention probably illegal; how does a reporter manage that? If your call records are investigated, will they show absolutely no contact with Pullman? That you acted completely on your own without any material support from him? Really? Because I wouldn't bet on it."

"What does it matter?" Clarissa demanded. "The point is, McKenzie is off selling secrets he has no legal claim on to some of the most dangerous people in the underworld! Do you have any idea the kind of damage that could be done with a programmable virus? The people who could be assassinated without anyone the wiser? He's selling the deaths of countless individuals to the highest bidder."

Lennox shook his head. "He's not the thief. You've got the wrong guy."

"History tells a different story."

"History shows that you're on a first-name basis with a man who's willing to hire murderers to get what he wants, so I wouldn't place too much stock in the trustworthiness of the past if I were you," Lennox said. He could hear sirens in the distance. "Here come the cops. I suggest you be honest with them. Don't try to protect Pullman or his bodyguard from their share of the blame."

Clarissa rolled her eyes. "Martine's not his bodyguard, she's his *nurse*, you idiot." Apparently she'd decided to exchange ignorance for insults. "Her whole job is keeping him alive long enough for him to see his rightful property returned."

Lennox's eyebrows rose. "He's dying?"

"He has stage-four colon cancer. He won't live another six months."

Lennox considered that for a moment as he stared at Clarissa, taking in the planes of her face, her sharp and familiar, golden-brown eyes. He didn't trust his instincts very often these days, but this time he knew he was right. "It's hard to say no to family, isn't it?

Especially when what they want you to do comes with a big pile of money attached to it."

Clarissa drew back tight against the wall, biting her lip. When she finally spoke, she wouldn't meet his eyes. "It isn't about the money. It never has been."

"Easy to say."

"It's true," she snapped. "And I'm not saying any more about it to you, the cops, or anyone else without a lawyer present."

"That's probably for the best," Lennox agreed. He might not have all the answers, but he had enough that he was almost limp with relief. "At least now I know why Martine was such a bad shot."

Clarissa frowned. "What are you talking about?"

"Yesterday morning, in the woods outside Elliot's house." Her face didn't change. "When I was shot at by someone creeping around outside," he continued, waiting for her to understand, to confirm his suspicion.

"Martine stays with Sheridan twenty-four seven," Clarissa said instead. "She wouldn't leave him to go randomly shoot at *you*. And if she did, I doubt she'd miss."

A cold feeling started to grow in the pit of Lennox's stomach. "And the photographs? The snake?"

"What snake?"

If she didn't know . . . and Pullman hadn't known either . . .

"Shit."

Lennox needed to find Elliot, *now*.

CHAPTER FIFTEEN

Excerpt from *Shockwave*'s article:

I confess, I came into this interview skeptical of Charmed Life. Startups like this are rarely lasting phenomena; they flare into existence, capture attention for a while, then ultimately die a shady little death with few people the wiser. I didn't understand how the concept could really work. There are already communities for people with less-than-perfect records, plenty of them online, many more available in person. What could Charmed Life possibly offer to make people not only stick around, but pay for the privilege?

Having met Elliot McKenzie, and listened to his passion for his project, I have to admit there's definitely something to what he says about scope. Charmed Life doesn't just want you to find a job flipping burgers once you get out from prison; it wants you to own the franchise. This company endeavors to connect people on a larger scale, and with bigger dreams, than many of them probably ever dared to have before. Charmed Life is selling hope, folks, and the promise of camaraderie. And the hell of it is?

It's delivering. So far, that is. Let's see how long he can keep it up.

I t turned out that intense anxiety could make you pretty damn impressive under the right circumstances. At least, that was what it had done for Elliot tonight.

He'd had two hours of face time inside the Black Box. *Two hours* of making connections, two hours of handshaking and brainstorming and bringing people with great ideas, *unique* ideas, together. Two hours of fine food created, but not carried in, by a reserved Stuart in the kitchen of the private home Elliot had rented for the night.

It was a little ways outside of Denver, close enough to see the city lights but far enough to grant people a bit of perspective. Atmosphere was important, after all.

It had been a short meeting, which worked out well when the pressure was part of the allure: privacy, prestige, and brevity meant people had to be decisive. These two hours were going to pay so many dividends for him down the road, and would do the same for his guests, hopefully. Elliot was reassured that he wasn't steering his guests wrong, and the buy-in for his new ideas had been gratifying. There was still plenty of work to do—was there ever—but now he was sure that he could get there. With this much fresh investment? He could get a hell of a lot of places. The only thing he needed to complete his night now was a call from Lennox telling him that everything was all right.

It had helped, Elliot had to confess, to have that edge of fear in the back of his mind, sharpening his reflexes and honing his attention to a point. He couldn't let it control them, couldn't let the people here know that he was ready to go crazy with worry over what might have happened to Lennox tonight. He still didn't know if Vanessa had won the election, and he didn't know what had happened with Lennox and Pullman's fixer. He almost excused himself to swipe his phone out of his overcoat a dozen times, just to check on them. Eventually he had Stuart lock it in the back of the van so he'd no longer be tempted.

Elliot's focus had paid off, but he didn't want to drag things out any longer. He was ready to go home. He was ready to text Vanessa, hopefully to congratulate her. He was ready for Lennox, safe and whole in his arms.

Stuart had the van mostly loaded by the time Elliot had finished bidding his guests goodnight. As the last car drove away, he unwound enough to chafe his hands over his arms. *Fuck*, but it got cold at night here. The view almost made up for it, though: thousands of stars glittered overhead, gloriously sharp without competition from Denver's pervasive, dull-orange glow.

"We're ready to head out," Stuart said as he finished locking up the back of the van.

"Great." Elliot followed him to the doors and got into the front seat, which was already preheated, and started to relax. He couldn't let go completely until he knew that Lennox had come through everything okay, though. Elliot patted his pockets as Stuart got them rolling, then swore. "I left my overcoat in the back; it's got my phone in it," he explained when Stuart looked at him quizzically.

"It's a little late to be calling Serena, don't you think?"

"It's not her."

"Can't it wait until I get you home?" he snapped. When Elliot started, Stuart sighed. "Don't tell me you're not going to let me give you a ride there. Besides, I've never seen your place before." He sounded a little hurt now. "After all we've done together, you still don't trust me even that far?"

"It's not about trust," Elliot said instantly, although it really was. He'd actually been going to call Lennox to come and get him, but he might be busy. *He might be dead*, Elliot's overactive, asshole imagination supplied, and he swallowed hard. He needed to know what was going on, he needed *Lennox*, but that wasn't a conversation that Elliot wanted to have in front of Stuart. Besides, the man did have a point.

"But yes, I'd love it if you could give me a ride home," Elliot said, almost hearing Serena's groan of disbelief. "Thank you for everything you did tonight, Stuart, it was above and beyond the call of duty."

Stuart shook his head sharply. "I didn't think of it as a duty. I mean, we're *friends*, aren't we? Friends should help each other out."

"Stuart . . ." Elliot sighed. Time to give the speech about boundaries. Again. Stuart beat him to the punch with a non sequitur, though.

"Is Lennox West a friend of yours?" Stuart turned to Elliot, his eyes surprisingly shiny in the dark of the van. "Because I thought he worked for Castillion. So he's a client, isn't he? Like me?"

They were getting into sticky territory. Elliot didn't want to lie, but he didn't want to tell Stuart the whole truth either. He didn't owe him that. "He and I met away from work first," Elliot said, which was . . . well, partially true. Close enough. "The professional relationship came after the personal one."

"So you are having a personal relationship with him, then?" Stuart's voice rose with every word. "I mean, I assumed as much after what I saw at the Meetup before he left, but . . . is it serious?"

"I couldn't say. We haven't known each other for very long."

"Then he's not going to stick around for you? You two aren't . . . on that level together?"

Elliot had a lot of patience, but even he could tolerate only so much prevaricating. "Stuart, what are you getting at?"

"I just want to know what it takes!" he exclaimed, turning the wheel a bit too hard to the right as they headed toward Golden. "What are your criteria for friendship versus maintaining professional boundaries? What has he done that I haven't? Because I've been trying to be close to you for *years* and it seems like he's jumped up to right-hand status in a week."

"That would mean supplanting Serena, and no one does that," Elliot said. He startled when Stuart slammed his hand against the steering wheel.

"Damn it, I'm *serious*, Elliot! Is it because you're having sex with him?" His mouth twisted in distaste. "Is that what it takes to make it to the next level with you? To actually be *invited* to your home instead of getting there because of convenience?"

"Absolutely not." They weren't going to have that discussion. "No, listen. Stuart, you and I met professionally. That aspect of our relationship is always going to come first, as it *should*, because we're both getting a lot out of collaborating like that. That's true for everyone I know through Charmed Life, up to and including Serena. I wouldn't have started anything with Lennox if I hadn't met him before he was a client." Was that true, though? He was, after all, Lennox's client. That hadn't stopped him from going there with the man. It was immaterial, though. "You're a great person and a talented businessman and it's a pleasure to work with you, but I don't have any interest in you that way."

"I don't have any interest in *you* that way," Stuart snapped. "But I don't see why we can't do more together that isn't sexual, or just *be* more to each other. You let me help you tonight, didn't you? I was the only person you trusted to be with you at the Black Box meeting."

"That's true," Elliot acknowledged. "Like I said, we collaborate well on a professional level. But that's as far as I'm comfortable taking things."

"But it might not *always* be," Stuart said pleadingly. "You keep saying that we're supposed to dream big, right? Hope for a better tomorrow and then work to make it happen. That's what I'm doing, Elliot! I've been working *so hard*, just hoping that you'll see that I can be that person for you. Your cornerstone, your backup, your best friend. Nobody knows you like I do, not even *Lennox*." He spat the name like it dirtied his mouth. "I want to know that I have a chance. I'm aware that I can be awkward and pushy, Serena went on and on about it the other day. But I can change! I *will* change, for you. You only have to *let* me. Let me in, and I know I can make your life better, like you've done for me."

He laughed nervously. "God, my heart is racing. This is the most important pitch of my life, so . . ." Stuart turned his glossy gaze on Elliot again. "How did I do, coach?"

"Stuart . . . this . . ." Elliot took a steadying breath and folded his shaking hands together. This moment ranked just behind being shot as the most uncomfortable experience he'd ever been subjected to, and that included running into a mountain. "I think you need to leave Charmed Life."

There was dead silence in the car. Elliot wasn't even sure Stuart's heart was beating for a moment before he gasped, "*What?*" like Elliot's words had opened a wound inside of him.

It hurt to sever him like this, but it was the right thing to do. "I think you've lost sight of the real goal of Charmed Life," Elliot said as gently as he could. "It's about using our community in support of personal and professional goals, not . . . not this. Not transference of emotion, of—of responsibility. I'm honored that you think so highly of me, I really am, but I can't be the person you want me to be, Stuart. I'm not good enough to idolize and I'm not selfless enough to be a messiah. I can't be that best friend for you, I just can't."

"But—but I—"

"I'm sorry."

"But . . . why do I have to leave?" Stuart's hands trembled on the wheel, and the van jerked from side to side. Elliot almost wanted to make Stuart stop to let him out, but they were close to his home, and there was no guarantee he'd get his jacket back if he left now. "I've been a member of Charmed Life since you first began it, it's where I've met most of my clients, I— You can't take all of that from me!"

"You've made so many connections through the program, I'm sure you'll keep them even if you're not actively a part of the community." Elliot breathed a little sigh of relief as Stuart slowed down for the junction leading to Elliot's road. "There's more to you than Charmed Life, Stuart. You don't need it to be a success. You don't need me."

"Clearly you don't need me." His voice was choked, and he wouldn't look at Elliot. "If you can throw me away like this."

"Don't think of it like that."

"What else am I supposed to think?" Stuart sniffed. He pulled the van to a stop in front of Elliot's house, turned it off abruptly, then scrubbed the palms of his hands over his eyes. "It's useless to ask again, isn't it? You're not going to change your mind." He sighed, just once, before his breathing went strangely calm.

Speaking of strange . . . Elliot frowned as he stared at his door. "How did you know how to get here? I didn't give you my address."

"I've known where you live for a long time." When Elliot looked at Stuart, the man had the keys in his right hand, and in his left . . .

It was a gun. Smaller than Lennox's little pistol, and it was pointed at Elliot's chest. Elliot's heart smacked into his rib cage so hard he could almost feel it bruise. His mind was racing even faster than his heart.

"You've been here before."

Stuart smiled sadly. "Many times. Get out of the car, Elliot. I want to go inside."

I don't want you inside there, you'll ruin it. "We can say everything we need to say to each other out here."

"You don't want to die outside in the cold. I know how you like to be warm."

Die. Oh, holy fuck. "You don't mean that."

Stuart shook his head. "You don't know me as well as you think you do. Let's go inside now."

"Stuart . . ."

"Inside, or I'll shoot you in the face right here and leave you in the snow."

Elliot shivered. His hands fumbled to undo his seat belt and the door, and he barely managed to climb out without collapsing. He thought, only for a moment, of running for the woods, but he didn't want to get shot in the back. His best option was to keep Stuart going, keep him talking. The longer he talked, the longer Elliot had to work on him.

Stuart came around the van and motioned at Elliot with the gun. "Go."

Elliot stumbled up the stairs to his front porch, then remembered— "My keys are in my jacket." Along with his phone, oh god, if he could get his hands on his phone—

"Use the spare under the flowerpot," Stuart said coolly. "And don't try anything fancy with the alarm system. Just turn it off."

He knows where I keep my spare. Had Stuart let himself in before? "All right."

Elliot bent down and shifted one of the flowerpots over, its skeletal petunias long since succumbed to frost, so that he could reach his spare key. It had been a long time since Elliot had had to use it; he'd almost forgotten it was there. He brushed the dirt off, then slid the key into the lock. *Click.* With nausea roiling in his stomach, Elliot led his stalker into his house.

"Now the alarm."

Elliot turned it off, trying not to focus on the gun in Stuart's hand. The door shut, and for a moment everything was perfectly still.

"It's nice here," Stuart said quietly as he looked around. "Really nice. It smells like you. Nothing like *him*, although I've seen him in here with you." He smiled a small, one-sided smile. "I didn't hit him on purpose the other day, because I knew you wouldn't want that. Even if he deserves to die more than you do."

Oh God. "Thank you," Elliot managed. "For not hurting him."

"You're welcome."

"Stuart, please, you don't have to do this."

Stuart sighed. "Yes, I do. I wish it hadn't gotten this far, Elliot." He shook his head. "I tried to teach you! But you refused to learn!"

Puzzle pieces clicked into place in Elliot's brain. "You left me the notes."

"And the shoes, which," Stuart said with a frown, "you haven't bothered to use, have you?"

"You put the snake on the porch."

"A warning. You were starting to go down a dangerous path with that *Lennox*. I had to try and correct you before you went too far."

A lump swelled up in Elliot's throat. "You tried to kill Holly."

"She's a crutch you don't need." Stuart stared at Elliot like he was trying to memorize him. "I could have been what you needed, if you'd just let me. Or *almost* everything. But I would have let you keep seeing Lennox, just for sex, if you'd given everything else to me. Now it's too late."

That seemed terribly final. "Wait! The car, tell me how you did the car!" Elliot begged, searching for something else to prolong this with.

Stuart shook his head. "I didn't have anything to do with your car accident."

No, of course he hadn't. Because he wasn't working for Sheridan Pullman; because there were two forces at work here, like Lennox had thought.

"Does someone else want to hurt you?" Stuart said wonderingly. Headlights flickered on the road outside, but Elliot only had eyes for the man in front of him. Stuart held the gun steady, so steady. "Have you strung someone else along like you did me?" His eyes shone like lanterns in the hall light. "But they don't get this part of you. This part, this last part? It's for me." He grinned, and the sight of it filled Elliot with dread. "Just for me."

The only thing Elliot could hear now was the rush of his own blood in his ears. The only thing he saw was the muzzle of the gun. "Stuar—"

Bang.

The bullet struck in the center of his chest, right over his breastbone. The impact of it knocked Elliot flat onto his back, the area rug doing little to cushion his brutal fall. He stared at the ceiling, wheezing: his chest was on *fire*, and he couldn't breathe—his lungs didn't want to inhale. Last time he'd been shot, the second bullet had come so quickly, he hadn't had time to dread it. This time—

Another loud noise ripped through the air, and Elliot's heart stopped beating for a moment. Someone was screaming now, and he wasn't sure if it was himself for a moment. The noise cut off abruptly, punctuated by a thud on the floor close by. Elliot tried to look toward it, but before he could do more than shift his eyes in that direction, someone crouched down beside him.

"*Elliot.*" A warm hand cradled his head as fingers tore at his suit. Elliot blinked as Lennox came into focus above him, his handsome face harsh and lined. "C'mon, no, *fuck.*" Hands ripped Elliot's shirt apart, revealing the vest beneath it, the cause of so much of Betty's dismay when it came to matching their silhouettes. There was a brief, sharp pain as Lennox pressed his hand against Elliot's chest, but it came up clean a moment later.

"It didn't go through." Lennox bent over and kissed Elliot's forehead. It wasn't a romantic kiss, it was a reassuring one, and somehow that meant more than any passionate embrace could have at the moment. "I bet it feels like you got kicked in the chest at close range, but the bullet didn't go through. You're gonna be okay, Elliot."

That didn't seem likely, but as Elliot finally took a decent breath, the fog of fear and adrenaline cleared a bit. "You found me," he gasped.

"Yeah." Lennox stroked the side of his face. "I did."

Elliot wanted to ask him how, what was happening, where was *Stuart*, what had gone on after they parted ways, but now?

Right now it was enough that he was still alive, and Lennox was here with him.

"I'm glad."

CHAPTER SIXTEEN

Partial transcription of most recent appointment with West, Lennox, Staff Sergeant US Army Rangers (R), January 28, 3:40 p.m.:

Progress note: Lennox demonstrated more willingness to engage in meaningful discussion, despite the clear difficulty he experienced doing so. His loyalty to his troops as a commanding officer and his dedication to his family are important personal touchstones to consider in subsequent appointments.

Lennox appears to be approaching a tipping point. I have high hopes that as he learns to forgive himself, he'll be better prepared to form new and healthy relationships.

The rest of the night was a mess of police, explanations, near-arrests for the two of them and one very definite arrest for Stuart Reynolds. He'd gone down like a falling tree when Lennox tackled him, knocked his head on the edge of the first step, and only came to as the police got there. He'd been screaming as the cops took him out to the ambulance that had arrived shortly after they had, yelling over and over, "I just wanted to be your friend! Your only friend, Elliot! *Your best friend!*"

Lennox had already given the cops a workout when they had shown up at Castillion to grab Clarissa Hanes, who had been taken away in stony silence. That they had plenty of evidence to send her to prison, Lennox didn't doubt; whether or not she would give up Pullman to escape herself, he didn't know yet. Right after Stuart had been taken away, Lennox had explained to Elliot how he'd found him and Stuart, via a tracking device in Elliot's phone.

"I was being paranoid. I didn't actually think it would be useful," Lennox had said quietly as he sat down beside Elliot on the couch, pressing their shoulders together. "But I didn't want you to tell me no, because you were worried about the security of your Black Box location, so I . . . didn't tell you." He grimaced. "I'm sorry."

"No, it was a good call," Elliot said weakly. He'd taken his phone back long enough to check whether his sister had won her election. The late results indicated a very close race, but that she was almost certain to come in ahead of her opponent. Lennox had half thought Elliot would call her right then and there, but instead he'd just shut the phone off and tossed it onto the coffee table in front of them.

The paramedics had looked Elliot over and recommended an X-ray, just to make sure his ribs were only bruised, but he passed on it. By the time he finished meeting with his lawyer and made plans to go into the local precinct later that day and give his official statements, Elliot was dead on his feet. Despite that, he resisted when Lennox suggested going upstairs to bed.

"I don't think I can sleep here," he said flatly. "It's—"

"We can go to my place," Lennox offered before he had a chance to talk himself out of it. It was the first time he'd extended an invitation to anyone other than Lee since he'd moved in.

Elliot's expression perked right up. "Really?"

"Sure, as long as you don't mind little rooms, poor heating, and bare brick for walls."

"I like bare anything," Elliot assured him, before slowly climbing the stairs and putting together a go bag.

An hour later they were ensconced in Lennox's much smaller bed under a pile of comforters, Lennox holding on tight as Elliot shook to pieces in his arms. There was nothing Lennox could say that would make it better, he knew that. He couldn't take away the horror of being shot in your own home, by someone you trusted. He couldn't erase the complete terror that hit when you couldn't avoid a bullet, even if you were wearing a backup plan. He didn't try. Talking had never been his strong suit, but he could be there, pull him in close, and promise, with his body if not his words, not to judge, and not to leave.

Seven hours later Lennox woke to the sound of Elliot's phone going off. Elliot was lying flat on his back, his head turned toward

Lennox, one hand wrapped around his own forearm as he slept on. Lennox didn't want to risk waking him, so he carefully slid out of bed, wincing as his feet hit the chilly, scuffed wooden floor, and grabbed the phone. He rejected the call without checking who it was and looked at Elliot, wondering if letting him sleep through the afternoon would be the best thing for him.

The phone rang again. Lennox frowned and glanced down. *Vanessa*, the caller ID read. Shit, Elliot would probably want to talk to her . . . but he was fast asleep, and still seemed tired despite that. Lennox ended the call, then shot her a quick text: *He's sleeping. He'll call you soon.*

Who is this? came through a moment later.

A friend.

A friend named Lennox West?

Lennox stared at the phone for a moment. Before he could decide how to reply, another text came through. *Pick up.* The phone went off yet again. After a second of weighing his options, he took the least terrible of them, walked out into the living room, and answered. "Hello?"

"Mr. West? This is Vanessa Travers. I'm Elliot's sister."

"I know. Congratulations on winning your election."

"Ah . . . thank you." She paused, then said, "I've been hearing an awful lot about my brother today, and none of it's good."

"None of it was his fault," Lennox said automatically. "I don't know what kind of story that reporter is spinning, but—"

"Ms. Hanes isn't the one doing the talking."

"Stuart Reynolds is even worse. He's obsessed with Elliot."

"So it seems." She cleared her throat. "I understand Elliot was shot."

"He was, but the vest caught it."

"The vest provided by Castillion. By *you*."

Lennox knew when he was being fished. He wasn't going to give up anything he didn't have to. "Yep."

"And your association with him consists of . . . what, exactly?"

"You can ask him when he's awake."

"I'm asking you, Mr. West."

"And I'm not answering because I don't want to talk to you." He went on before she had a chance to do more than draw a single offended breath. "Your brother was so afraid of doing something that might impact your election that he decided, against everyone else's better judgment, not to tell the police that he was being stalked. He didn't speak up when the woman you've got in custody almost got him killed, he didn't say a word when his dog was poisoned, and he didn't even want *me* contacting the police until he knew you were the new DA. *That's* how scared he is of losing another chance with you."

He shook his head. "I think it's fucked up, frankly, but you're not my sister. You're nothing to me. *Elliot's* important to me, though, so when he wakes up I'll tell him you want to talk. And you'll answer when he calls and talk to him directly, right?"

"Of course," she said, her voice a little faint.

"Good." Lennox ended the call with a vicious stab of his thumb, then tossed the phone onto the couch. His stomach growled, reminding him he hadn't eaten more than a few overpriced, psycho-made canapés last night. He checked in his fridge. Okaaay . . . an omelet. He could do that. Lee wasn't here, so it didn't matter that he didn't have vegetables on hand for it. If Elliot woke up, he wouldn't mind.

Elliot didn't wake up for the omelet, but he did wander into the living room wrapped in one of the comforters once the coffee was going. He didn't say anything as he located a mug in the cupboard, plunked in a few of Lennox's probably dusty sugar cubes, and then filled it to the brim with cheap brew. He sipped, added another sugar cube, then finally came over and sat next to Lennox on the couch.

"There's food if you want it," Lennox offered, trying to keep it light but also hoping to get some sort of facial expression out of Elliot. Seeing him walk around like a blank slate was disturbing. "Half a ham and cheese omelet."

"Maybe later."

"Sure." The silence might have been uncomfortable if it weren't for the way Elliot took his hand. It wasn't a desperate grip like the hold he'd had during the night, but it wasn't limp or ashamed either. It was steady and secure, and for now that was enough for Lennox.

"What did Vanessa have to say?"

Lennox frowned. "You heard that?"

"I heard you rip her a new one." Elliot smiled faintly. "It was kind of nice."

Lennox shrugged. "I was trying to be tactful."

"You failed, but that's okay." He looked at Lennox expectantly.

"She said she wanted to talk to you, that's it. Wouldn't say about what specifically, but she knows at least some of what went on yesterday."

"Did she seem angry?" He shook his head. "Never mind, don't answer that. I'll call her later, but at the moment . . ." He set his mug on the coffee table and tilted his head back against the back of the couch. "I can't bring myself to care." His free hand rubbed tiny circles over his sternum, where the bullet had hit. "I'm supposed to, I know . . . I would have before last night."

"You're worn out," Lennox said gently. "You'll perk up soon, be more like your old self. And she can stand to wait a while, after all the waiting she's made you do." When Elliot didn't argue with him, Lennox changed the subject. "How's your chest doing? You need another couple Tylenol?"

"It hurts, but not as badly as I think it should." Elliot stared incredulously down at his chest. "I thought I was going to die. I actually thought I *was* dying. And then I didn't, and I don't know how I feel about that."

"I'd try 'relieved,' maybe 'happy,'" Lennox suggested, but Elliot frowned at him.

"You know that's not what I mean. I'm glad I'm alive, obviously, but it's not because I figured it all out myself. I wasn't smart enough to see what was going on with this situation. I assumed everything was Pullman's fault, when it turns out that the person who went the farthest was someone I worked with. Someone I trusted, Lennox. I didn't like Stuart on a personal level, but he was useful, and I . . . well, I used him. And vice versa, I guess, but I didn't see what I'd become to him." He sighed heavily. "Which kind of makes this whole thing my fault."

"Not even close," Lennox said immediately. "No, really," he persisted when Elliot wouldn't meet his eyes. "You are absolutely not responsible for Reynolds attacking you like he did. It doesn't matter if you promised him the fucking moon, you hear me? Charmed Life might be all about endless possibility and bright futures and whatever, but that's not a fucking contract between you and every person who subscribes to your site. Fuck Reynolds if he couldn't tell the difference between fantasy and reality."

Elliot still wouldn't look at him, and he was starting to shake again, so Lennox did the only thing he could think of: he pulled Elliot into his arms, leaned back against the arm of the couch, and held him close.

"You don't owe anyone your life," Lennox murmured. "You don't owe them your safety, or your privacy. I know what it feels like to need to atone, but you can't give everything up. Otherwise you've got nothing left for yourself, and before long there's no you left at all."

"Atonement, huh?" Elliot said after a moment. He was still shaking, but his voice sounded almost normal. "You think that's what I'm trying to do?"

"Not with everyone, and not all the time," Lennox said. "But enough that it got you into trouble this time around." His phone buzzed. "Speaking of trouble . . ." He glanced at the clock on the wall and groaned. "Shit. Gaby's hosting a Super Bowl party today, and she expected me to show up five minutes ago."

"She's got you timed down to the minute, huh?"

"Yeah." Lennox shut his eyes for a moment. He loved his extended family, he did, but he honestly wanted nothing more than to stay right here with Elliot for the rest of the day. Possibly the rest of the week.

Elliot stretched his arm far enough to snag his own phone. "How about I text Serena and let her know we're in no state to go out, she can make your excuses to Gaby, and you can play hooky and watch the game here with me? Unless you really want to go, in which case," he smiled, but it was a small thing. "I'll stay here on my lonesome and wait for you to get back."

"I don't want to leave you alone," Lennox said. "You could come with me."

Elliot shook his head. "I'm ready and willing to do almost anything for you, but hanging out with your ex-wife and her family after yesterday? I'm just not that strong." He tucked his feet up onto the end of the couch and snuggled in a little closer. After a second, Lennox turned his phone off.

"Why are all of our dates so weird?" Lennox muttered.

Elliot looked up at him with wide eyes. "You think we're dating?"

Lennox's heart clenched a little. "If we're not, I've got some explaining to do to Lee."

"Hey, *I* never said we weren't dating."

"So we are, then."

"If you want to be."

"I never said I didn't want to be." Lennox paused a second to deconstruct what he'd just said, then rolled his eyes at himself. "Jesus Christ, this is why I'm divorced. I'm shit at communicating anything other than orders. Elliot, I want to date you. I'd like for this to be one more weird date in a hopefully long line of weird dates with you. I'll call Gaby myself. You order us a pizza, and then we'll watch the Super Bowl on my shitty couch in my hovel. Sound good?"

Elliot's smile was big and genuine this time, the lines of tension in his face smoothing. "That would be great."

It was, actually. What had happened to Elliot couldn't be erased in a single afternoon, and there was probably still a lot of fallout to come. Lennox felt hopeful, though, genuinely optimistic for the first time in what seemed like forever. Elliot wasn't heading into whatever came next alone. Lennox would be there with him, and he'd have Elliot in turn.

It sounded like a pretty decent beginning, for a second chance.

EPILOGUE

Excerpt from news blog *Crime and Punishment*:

There's been new drama in the tech sector today for all the wrong reasons as Sheridan Pullman, the former CEO of Redback Industries, goes back to court to deal with a multitude of charges, among them the attempted murder of a former business associate, Elliot McKenzie. Pullman is expected to plead guilty as part of a deal that will give his sister, Shockwave *reporter Clarissa Hanes, immunity from prosecution for her role in the crimes. What that role was, exactly, has yet to be disclosed to the public.*

"**S**he's going to get off scot-free." Elliot almost had to smile at the disgust coloring Lennox's voice. "How? How can they just ignore the evidence like that?"

"Clarissa is a small fish compared to her brother," Elliot said with a shrug. "Somebody's looking to make their name off this case, and pinning Pullman with another murder charge is a good way to do it. Even if he dies before they can get him back to prison."

"But then she doesn't have to face any consequences for what she did."

Elliot turned from the cutting board and wrapped his arms around Lennox's neck, careful to keep his wet hands away from Lennox's warm skin. "Do you think she needs to suffer some more?" he purred. "Would watching her walk barefoot across hot coals make you happy?" He nuzzled the tip of his nose against Lennox's cheek. "My sweet, bloodthirsty darling. Aren't you supposed to be working on letting this sort of thing go?"

"She could have killed you." Lennox was trying hard to hold on to his disgruntlement, Elliot could tell, but after four months he knew the best methods for breaking him out of a dark mood. Overt affection was at the top of the list. Lennox was a surprising sucker for cuddles. "That's a hard thing to just let go."

"If it makes you feel any better, she's probably not going to get to inherit her brother's millions at this point," Elliot said. "And who'll hire her? Her professional credibility has been blown to shreds. Besides now that Mischa's been implicated in the Singularity theft, she's got no reason to bother with me anymore."

That had been an unexpected windfall courtesy of Oliver, who'd called them up a month ago to pass on that he'd tipped off Interpol to Mischa's attempt to sell Pullman's pet project in Russia. *"Selling guns is one thing,"* Oliver had said, *"but customizing killer viruses? That buys you a whole new level of Hell."*

Elliot turned his nuzzle into a kiss on Lennox's cheek. "The best revenge is happiness and success, and I've got plenty of both. My company is thriving, all the press has been positive on my behalf, and my personal life is better than ever. It's official: I win at everything."

Well . . . maybe not everything. The situation between him and Vanessa was still strained: they spoke to each other once a week on the phone, and had met once in person for drinks. It had been the most uncomfortable half an hour Elliot had ever spent in a bar. He'd been torn between wanting to throw himself at her feet and beg that she take him back, and wanting to throw his glass of water in her face. But dignity had won out, barely, and the channels of communication between them were gradually opening back up. Elliot had high hopes that he'd finally get to visit his niece and nephew over the summer, which had officially started last week.

Lennox's low laughter took Elliot's mind off his family. "I hope you still feel that way after the barbecue this afternoon," he said. Was that . . . schadenfreude in his voice?

Elliot pulled back to look his boyfriend in the eyes. "You promised you'd protect me from Gaby."

"I'll do my best."

"Not good enough. I want an ironclad contract guaranteeing I'll make it out of meeting your ex-wife and her family without suffering grievous bodily injury or significant mental distress."

"Did you make Serena sign one as well?" Lennox asked.

"Of course I did. I'm not going into this without backup. Lee's already offered me her room as a hideout if I get desperate."

Lennox grinned, and Elliot was done with resisting temptation. He grabbed the back of Lennox's shirt and reeled him into a kiss. Not a polite, about-to-go-to-a-family-barbecue kiss either. This was a wet, filthy battle of a kiss, a kiss that promised Lennox all sorts of fantastic things in the near future.

"Dad! Dad, where's the laundry soap, I need to wash my shirt before boxing tonight! Dad— God, ew, *really?*"

Lennox pulled away from Elliot with a quiet groan, and they both turned to look at Lee, who stood in the hallway of Lennox's apartment, staring at them with an expression somewhere between disgusted and amused.

"I'm only going to be living with you guys two days of the week. You can't keep it in the bedroom for two days?"

Lennox seemed to be flushing now—it was hard to tell, he was so tan, but that was his normal response to being embarrassed by Lee. For his part, Elliot just smiled broadly and pressed his cheek to Lennox's shoulder. "I can't help it, your dad is irresistible. Blame him."

"I totally do."

Lennox pointed a finger at his daughter. "You know what? You're thirteen, you can handle seeing two adults being affectionate, and you." He turned his glare on Elliot. "You started it. If anyone should be blamed, it's you."

"Hmmm, no," Elliot said after a moment of mock consideration. "But nice try!"

"But not that nice," Lee added.

"You guys are a riot. Not."

"Maybe not, but now you have avocado bits all over the back of your shirt." Lee looked smug. "*That's* kind of funny. Are we really out of laundry soap?"

Lennox glared at Elliot.

"I . . . forgot my hands were dirty," Elliot said, glancing over his shoulder at the partially assembled salad on the counter. "Sorry."

Lennox rolled his eyes, but when Elliot tried to back away Lennox just reeled him in again. "I already moved the detergent over to the other house. We can wash your shirt at your mom's. Five more minutes and then we're leaving, got it?"

"Got it." Lee took off down the hall, and Lennox turned back to Elliot.

"Where were we?" Elliot murmured, but Lennox shook his head.

"You can't get out of this that easily, babe." Lennox pressed a kiss to his temple, then finally let him go. "I need to change—thanks for that—and you need to finish the salad. We have to be extra charming if we're going to convince Marcus to help us move the rest of my stuff over tomorrow."

"Honestly, I could live without your couch," Elliot said. "But I can't live without watching you lift those weights, so yes. I promise to be as charming as I always am. But not overly so," he added, because Serena had warned him about coming off as trying to play people. The advice hadn't really helped. Elliot didn't know how to get Gaby Rodriguez on his side if she was going to distrust him from the start, but he was pretty sure he'd have time to figure it out. After all, they were going to be seeing a lot more of each other from here on out. "Should I expect a dirty look as our housewarming gift?"

"It's possible," Lennox said, and god, Elliot loved seeing him so easy about what was a big step for both of them, but an undeniably bigger one for Lennox. Getting to the point where he felt comfortable letting Lee stay over in his apartment again had been huge. Giving up his independence, though? Agreeing to constant company with no easy avenue of retreat when he felt stressed or had a bad night? Elliot was still a little surprised that Lennox had said yes when Elliot had asked him to move in. Elliot had had to try, though: they'd been spending five nights out of seven together already, and he'd been tired of Lennox's icy floors—even in June, they were freezing—and lack of cable. And then Lennox had said yes, and Elliot had wondered if he deserved to be this happy.

"But I bet the dirty look will come with a whisk," Lennox continued.

"A whisk." Elliot looked at Lennox blankly. "What the hell do people use whisks for? Isn't that the manual version of the attachment you get with a mixing machine?"

"I'll show you when we get home."

Elliot couldn't resist. He leaned in and kissed Lennox lightly on the lips, with just enough pressure to hint at the warmth that spread through his body every time he remembered that he wasn't alone anymore. "I can't wait."

Dear Reader,

Thank you for reading Cari Z's *Friendly Fire*!

We know your time is precious and you have many, many entertainment options, so it means a lot that you've chosen to spend your time reading. We really hope you enjoyed it.

We'd be honored if you'd consider posting a review—good or bad—on sites like **Amazon, Barnes & Noble, Kobo, Goodreads, Twitter, Facebook, Tumblr,** and your blog or website. We'd also be honored if you told your friends and family about this book. Word of mouth is a book's lifeblood!

For more information on upcoming releases, author interviews, blog tours, contests, giveaways, and more, please sign up for our weekly, spam-free newsletter and visit us around the web:

> **Newsletter**: tinyurl.com/RiptideSignup
> **Twitter**: twitter.com/RiptideBooks
> **Facebook**: facebook.com/RiptidePublishing
> **Goodreads**: tinyurl.com/RiptideOnGoodreads
> **Tumblr**: riptidepublishing.tumblr.com

Thank you so much for Reading the Rainbow!

RiptidePublishing.com

ACKNOWLEDGMENTS

It takes a village to finish a book. Many, many thanks to Tiffany and Caz for making this one possible.

ALSO BY CARI Z

Panopolis
Where There's Smoke
Where There's Fire
Where There's a Will

House Rules (in the *Rules to Live By* anthology)
Tempest
Shadows & Light
Changing Worlds
Cambion: Dark Around the Edges
A Blinded Mind
Surviving the Change
Camellia and Camellia: Spring Blossom with Caitlin Ricci
Perilous

ABOUT THE AUTHOR

Cari Z is a Colorado girl who loves snow and sunshine. She likes edged weapons, prefers books to television shows, and goes weak at the knees for interesting men and exciting explosions (but not at exactly the same time—that would be so messy).

You can find her at carizerotica.blogspot.com, follow her on Facebook at facebook.com/people/Cari-Zee, or on Twitter as @author_cariz.

Enjoy more stories like
Friendly Fire
at RiptidePublishing.com!

The Secret of Hunter's Bog
ISBN: 978-1-62649-374-2

Home the Hard Way
ISBN: 978-1-62649-146-5